"This is a hypnotic and downright spooky story. Maxine O'Callaghan not only takes us into the extremes of evil and innocence, but into that gray area in between where most of us live. O'Callaghan sets her traps cleverly. Reading *The Bogeyman* made me feel like a bug in a spider's web."

—T. Jefferson Parker,
Author of *Laguna Heat*

MAXINE O'CALLAGHAN

The BOGEYMAN

TOR
HORROR

A TOM DOHERTY ASSOCIATES BOOK

THE BOGEYMAN

Copyright © 1986 by Maxine O'Callaghan

All rights reserved, including the right to reproduce this book or portions thereof in any form.

First printing: November 1986

A TOR Book

Published by Tom Doherty Associates, Inc.
49 West 24 Street
New York, N.Y. 10010

Cover art by Jill Bauman

ISBN: 0-812-52350-4
CAN. ED.: 0-812-52351-2

Printed in the United States of America

0 9 8 7 6 5 4 3 2 1

For my two biggest fans: my son, John, who gets to read all the good stuff first; and my daughter and best friend, Laura, who's always there when I need her.

And a special thanks to a unique group of talented people, the Fictionaires, who praise, nitpick, quibble, support and always keep me humble.

Prologue

The Bogeyman is:

    a.   Kind to his dog; sends flowers and candy to his mom on Mother's Day.
    b.   A sociopath, hiding behind a facade of normalcy.
    c.   An ancient malevolent force; evil incarnate.
    d.   All of the above.

His name is Moloch, Goebbels, Speck, Idi Amin, Blackbeard, Manson, Eichmann, Beelzebub, Starkweather, Caligula, Bundy, Himmler, Beria, Herod, Mengele, Gacy, Hitler.

Grown-ups acknowledge him only for long, breath-stopping seconds while a door rattles or a floor creaks. Then they laugh nervously and forget until they read about him in the *Times* or see him on *Eyewitness News*. Small children know that he hides under beds and in dark closets, that he masquerades as tree limbs, shadows, wind laughter, well-loved teddy bears, clown dolls, kindly strangers, baby-sitters, young boys, old men, grandmas, grandpas, mommies and daddies. They are told that unless they are good he will chew them up and spit out their bones. They are good and he eats them anyway.

Because it doesn't matter if you're good or bad; it doesn't matter if you believe in him.

The Bogeyman believes in you.

1
FIRST MEETINGS IN STRANGE PLACES

Joanna spent such a hectic morning she forgot all about the Bogeyman. The flight left at 11:30 and she had allowed plenty of time, but Lizzie kept running to the window every five minutes.

"Daddy *said* he was coming. He said he would try real hard."

Fat chance, Joanna thought grimly, but she couldn't tell a five-year-old that her father was a no-good lying bastard.

"Something probably came up at the last minute, darling." And wasn't *that* a nasty little double entendre? She might—someday—forgive Walt for Tawny and Crystal, maybe even Sherri. But she would never, ever, forgive him for the look in Lizzie's eyes as she stared out the window. Propelled by rage, she finished packing and got Lizzie ready in plenty of time, despite a last-minute panic because Lizzie couldn't find Leon, her stuffed lion. But the taxi was late and traffic on the LAX entrance road, snarled by a CalTrans crew digging up the pavement, moved like some great, lumbering beast. Still they got through check-in and out to the gate a good half hour before departure time.

The packed waiting area buzzed with voices. A crowd had already gathered impatiently around the roped-off entrance to the Jetway. Through the windowed side of the building, Joanna could see the big DC-10, gleaming white in the sunlight. The terminal's air-conditioning system struggled inadequately, so the air felt sluggishly warm and smelled of clashing perfumes and tobacco smoke. Boarding would begin shortly, but Joanna wanted to sit down, even if it was only for a few minutes. Tired. Of course she was tired. Up early, all the rushing around. No, this was more than fatigue. It was a bone-deep, spirit-numbing weariness that permeated every cell.

She found a couple of empty chairs at the end of a row next to a group of Japanese tourists, their excited conversation like the twittering of exotic birds. Across the aisle a grandmotherly woman in pale blue polyester read Erma Bombeck's latest book without cracking a smile.

A mistake, Joanna thought as she settled against the slick plastic. I may never get up again.

The sleepless nights and endless arguments . . . Walt couldn't have done a better job if he'd grown vampire fangs and drained out all her blood. She should have taken Lizzie and left without a word. How come she was always the one with the decent impulses?

But it's almost over, she told herself.

She'd get on the plane as quickly as possible, maybe

during the preboarding. Parents with infants and small children, they always announced. Was Lizzie young enough to qualify? She wouldn't ask; she'd just do it. Then they'd fly away, and tonight she and Lizzie would be on the other side of the continent, sleeping in the house she'd grown up in—*home*—the solid walls and heavy slate roof like a massive fortress. And when Mom and Dad left for their rambling trip through Canada, she and Lizzie would have all summer to explore the woods and discover all the treasures of Joanna's childhood: silvery minnows in leaf-shadowed water, silky milk pods, birds' nests and rabbits' burrows. Lizzie would grow brown and scratched and naughty.

The image was so vivid it was a shock when she looked down at Lizzie. The little girl clutched Leon tightly, chin buried in the tawny mane. Her face was white and pinched against the bright orange chair, the gray eyes huge, oddly opaque.

That Look. She had it when she pleaded hysterically to have the lights on at night. And she had it after the bad dreams and the screaming spells. But—Sweet Jesus—not here, not *now* . . .

"Lizzie?" Joanna cupped the pointed chin and tried to tip her face upward, but her head was too rigid. "*Lizzie.* What's the matter?"

"That place, Mommy. That dark place." She stared past Joanna with a peculiarly fixed gaze.

Joanna turned to look. It took her a moment to realize that Lizzie was staring at the Jetway leading to their plane. She thought, That's silly. It can't be dark. There's always a light on.

But it *was* dark, cavelike, and for just an instant she

11

thought it was full of the darkness that houses bats, and she knew something else lurked there. Something with sharp yellow teeth and foul breath and—

The lights blinked on. Over the loudspeaker a voice announced that flight 54 for Boston was ready for pre-boarding.

Joanna drew a shaky breath. "Lizzie, you stop being so damned *silly*."

(It *was* dark and in the darkness . . .)

"That's—well, it's kind of a bridge—a special bridge we use to get on the airplane."

(. . . something feral and rotten . . .)

"It goes to *our* plane? We have to go in *there*?"

"Yes, baby. It's just a great big sidewalk." A man in a wheelchair went through. A young woman with a baby in a Carri-Cradle. Safe. *Of course they were safe*. "Come on, Lizzie. It's time to go."

"But *he's* in there, Mommy," Lizzie wailed. "He's hiding— "

"Lizzie—"

"—and waiting and—"

The woman across the aisle watched with a little shake of her head as she gathered her belongings. Bad mothers make bad children, her eyes said. Indulgent, permissive mothers.

Joanna grabbed Lizzie's shoulders. "Elizabeth Kerso, you stop it this instant! I'm not going to put up with any more of your nonsense, understand?"

Lizzie shrank away, looking totally betrayed and aban-doned. Pain stabbed at Joanna's temples like a needle-sharp splinter driven deep into the back of her eyes. She willed herself to be calm. "Sweetheart, it's okay, really.

See the other people getting on the plane? They're not afraid. We have to leave now, so we can go to Grandma's. Don't you want to go to Grandma's?''

"Yes, but—let's go outside and get a ladder and climb up, Mommy. We can do it. I saw it on TV."

"No, we can't," Joanna said firmly. "The plane's too big. Listen, darling, I'm right here and I won't let anything hurt you. You know that. And you have Leon. Remember what Daddy said?''

("He'll always be here to guard you, Lizzie, and bite the mean ole Bogeyman, and I'll always be here, too." Lying bastard.)

Lizzie nodded slowly, but when Joanna stood up and shouldered her carry-on bag and reached for Lizzie's hand, the child screamed, "Noooo!" and clung, leechlike, to the chair.

"Last call for preboarding—flight 54 to Boston—"

Oh, God, Joanna thought. We're not going to make it.

Everybody would board and the plane would take off and leave her, and Walt *would* show up and there would be another fight and dammit to hell, she couldn't *stand* it.

She dropped her things and seized Lizzie, began trying to pry the tiny fingers loose. "Let go, Lizzie. You hear me? Let go!"

"Got a problem?" A tall man in a blue uniform, one of the flight crew, had stopped beside them.

"She's just—" How do you tell somebody your kid thinks a monster lurks around every corner? "She's just a little upset and—Lizzie, see? This nice man is worried about you, darling, so please—"

"No!" Lizzie screamed. "*He's* in there and he's gonna eat me up and *I want my daddy!*"

13

"What is it she's afraid of?" the man asked quietly.

He was in his late thirties, Joanna guessed. Kind eyes and a sensitive mouth softened a long, bony face.

"The Jetway," she said, too tired to pretend. "She's got this thing about the Bogeyman and—"

He nodded, asked the little girl's name, then dropped down so he was at the child's eye level.

"Lizzie, I'm Officer Blanchard and I'm copilot of your flight. That means I'm the boss, okay? And I definitely do not allow any Bogeymen on my airplane. Now, then—"
She had relaxed slightly. Before she realized what he was going to do, he picked her up and said, "Just hang on tight."

Joanna hurried after him as he strode toward the big plane with Lizzie in his arms. The Jetway was brightly lighted and softly carpeted with nothing at all lurking inside. Only a faint, damp odor—quickly gone, easily forgotten—and it was a long time before Joanna knew it was the scent of an open grave.

2

After two miniature bottles of gin mixed with a minimum of tonic, Joanna shook off the crazy feeling she'd had in the terminal. She'd been so damned pooped. Maybe she'd even dozed for a minute. Whatever—Lizzie's anxieties, transmitted over that powerful mother/child link, had found her in a highly susceptible state. Now even Lizzie seemed to have forgotten the incident. She'd released her choke hold on Leon and accepted a Coke and a Jr. Pilot kit from the flight attendant. Better still, the big plane whined eastward, piling up mileage at a marvelous clip. Joanna felt as though she'd sprouted wings and was doing it herself.

So much for you, Mr. Bogeyman.

Another drink and then lunch. Chicken for her—can anybody really eat airline beef?—a hamburger and french fries for Lizzie, who ate it morsel by morsel. The attendant took Joanna's tray, and while she debated about brandy, a familiar blue-uniformed figure walked down the aisle.

He leaned on the empty seat next to Joanna and smiled. "Hello again. Everything okay? How's your hamburger, Lizzie?"

"It's very nice but not as good as McDonald's."

"Well, of course not. Nobody's is. Enjoying the flight?" he asked Joanna, but his eyes said: How are you really doing?

"Everything's fine." Unusual to see the flight crew in the cabin these days because of hijackings. "Thanks again, Mr.—" She had to sneak a quick look at the plastic name tag pinned above his jacket pocket. *Thomas P. Blanchard.*

"Make it Tom," he said. "Okay if I—?" He indicated the empty seat.

"Of course. Please." He must have come back especially to see her—and Lizzie, of course. "I'm Joanna Kerso. I really meant what I said. I don't know how to thank you. I'm afraid I wasn't handling things very well back there. But you seemed to know just what to do. You must have a kid of your own."

"No, not—no."

For an instant his eyes looked as haunted as Lizzie's. God, now what had she said? "Well, maybe it's just a natural gift. Anyway, it was a good thing you came along. If I'd missed the plane with my poor mom and dad sitting in Logan—"

"We're going to see Gramma and Grampa," Lizzie said, "but it's just a visit. We live in California. My daddy lives there, too."

"Actually, it's an extended vacation." Like forever.

16

"I see." He did, too, she could tell. Those kind brown eyes didn't miss much.

She was suddenly very conscious of how narrow the seats were, how little space separated them, how close his hand was to her thigh. She wondered if it really was possible to have sex in airplane lavatories. My God, where had *that* come from? For months now the only thing she'd wanted to do with male genitalia was to take a swipe at them with a good sharp butcher knife. Afraid he'd read her thoughts, she turned away, began dabbing at the ketchup stains on Lizzie's mouth.

"Is Boston your home?" he asked. "Originally, I mean."

"No—Vermont."

Maybe it was a good sign, this spark—lust, call it what it is, for God's sake. And was that so bad? He was certainly attractive, lean and fit, with thick dark hair cut short, the kind that would be curly if allowed to grow. Did he work out? Ski? Not a health nut, she decided. He probably jogged, knowing he needed to rather than training for the Boston Marathon.

"I have a cottage near Brattleboro," he said. "Up near Mount Snow."

So close. Feeling a momentary sexual itch was one thing, but did she really want . . . "We're just over in Maple Grove," she said hesitantly.

"No kidding. I haven't been coming up very often . . ." That haunted look again, moving like a shadow behind his eyes. "But if I do, I mean, if you wouldn't mind—"

She told him that she and Lizzie might take some day trips, but if he wanted to take a chance her parents were listed in the phone book. He said he wasn't sure, of course, but maybe. Mutual attraction. Mutual ambiva-

17

lence. She was relieved when he stood up and said he'd better go back to work.

"Good-bye, Lizzie." That sad/sweet look in his eyes again. "I'm glad you're having a good time. Just remember what I told you: No Bogeymen are allowed on this flight, so you're perfectly safe."

"I know." Lizzie dragged her last french fry through the ketchup, leaving a blood-red trail.

Well, hallelujah, Joanna thought, and Tom Blanchard gave her a thumbs-up signal before he headed forward.

Joanna smiled down at Lizzie. "Isn't that wonderful, baby? We just flew off and left that ole Bogeyman behind."

"No, we didn't," Lizzie said. "He doesn't have to fly."

It started to rain during the ride home from Logan International. As they drove through Massachusetts, lightning bolts sizzled through early darkness. Joanna expected Lizzie to be terrified, since full-blown thunderstorms were rare in California. Instead the little girl watched with wide-eyed fascination while her grandfather explained how to tell how far away the bolts were, and they chanted, "One one thousand, two one thousand—"

It was going to be all right. It really *was*. Joanna had known it from the moment she saw her parents standing there waiting, her father's comfortable bulk and her mother's love shining on her face. Joanna realized with a pang that they always looked slightly diminished every time she saw them after a long absence. Were they really smaller or was reality gradually whittling away at her larger-than-life memories? It didn't matter. Once their arms closed around her, she knew that Matthew and Ruth Hart were the solid, immutable core of her life.

Dad had carried Lizzie, and Mom had insisted on shouldering the carry-on bag, leaving Joanna to walk between them, suddenly free, light-headed with freedom. Now, watching Lizzie hang over the front seat to count down the thunder with Dad, she felt snug and safe, cocooned against the night. Her thoughts drifted, wandering back to Tom Blanchard. She hadn't seen him again after the plane landed. Maybe she never would. Just as well. Because it would be crazy to get involved with somebody right now. Still . . .

She started guiltily; Mom was telling some involved story about Uncle Wallace and Aunt Mimi. She tried to listen, but she still seemed to hear the roar of the jets and she ached with fatigue.

By the time they finally arrived home, Lizzie was drooping like a flower and went to bed in Joanna's old room without a peep. Dad carried in the suitcases while Mom went to make tea and sandwiches. Joanna wasn't hungry, but she managed to eat a little. Their eyes asked questions, but they didn't press. Maybe they could see that she was incapable of stringing two coherent thoughts together. She did worry briefly about the sleeping arrangements. The walls in the old house were thick.

"I hope I can hear Lizzie if she wakes up. She . . . well, being in a strange place . . ." She was too exhausted to tell them about Lizzie's nightmares, to answer questions, defend herself—from Mom and Dad?

"I put you right next to Lizzie," Mom assured her, "and you can leave the doors open. I'll listen, too, just in case. Oh, Jo, I'm so *glad* you're here."

Her mother tucked her in bed as though Joanna were a child again, and it was wonderful. There was a clean smell of freshly laundered sheets. A huge bouquet of lavender stocks and white daisies on the nightstand. The sound of rain dripping from the eaves . . .

Birds chirped her awake the next morning at six o'clock. The first night in months she had slept straight through without being awakened by Lizzie's screams. She wanted to snuggle back under the covers, but she needed to go to the bathroom. Night-chilled air raised goose bumps on her body as she crawled out of bed. The hallway was shadowy and smelled of lemon wax and yesterday's heat. As she opened the bathroom door, she noticed a quilt mounded in a corner next to the stairwell. Lizzie—asleep in a patchwork huddle, clutching Leon.

Poor baby, Joanna thought. She was probably looking for me. Maybe she did have a nightmare and I never heard.

Lizzie stirred as Joanna scooped her up and carried her back to her room. Damp curls stuck to her forehead. The ridges and swirls of a crazy-quilt imprinted one rosy cheek.

"Mommy?" she said sleepily.

"Silly ole Lizzie bee." Joanna tucked her into bed and kissed her. "What were you doing in the hall?"

"Hiding," Lizzie said.

"Oh, baby, you don't have to do that. This is the safest place in the world. I promise."

Through sleep-tangled lashes, Lizzie watched her mother leave the room. Mommy and Daddy always said that she was safe, that she didn't have to worry. But it was a lie. Not the same kind of lie ole Buddy Duffy told when he spilled the fingerpaints and then pointed straight at Lizzie

20

as soon as Miss Garcey asked who did it. He *knew* it was a lie. He *meant* it to be. But Mommy and Daddy only said things they really wanted to be true. They didn't seem to know the difference.

So they lied and lied.

You are safe, Lizzie.

I'll always be here to protect you, Lizzie.

But Daddy *wasn't* there to protect her. He went to live with somebody Mommy called "that ho-er" and he always broke his promises. "Sorry, honey, it's business, but tomorrow . . ." He even forgot to come and say goodbye. And now he was a long way off. There was nobody to protect her, not even Grampa because Mommy said that he and Gramma were going on a long trip and leaving them all alone. There was only Mommy and Leon, and she had an awful, crawly feeling that Daddy had lied about Leon, too. That nothing could keep *him* away.

When Mommy told her they were coming here, Lizzie had hoped so hard that *he* would stay behind. That maybe he only lived in their house in her room, hiding in the dark until she was alone. But he'd been in the airport and now she knew. She had to be careful, had to hide, to fool him.

He was coming soon.

3

When the alarm went off at six o'clock, Amos Fowler was already awake. He seemed to wake up earlier and earlier while Hattie slept like the dead, gargling and blowing. He nudged her with his elbow and yelled, "Time, woman."

She gave him a dazed, pleading look as if hoping just this once he'd change his mind, but he glared at her and she jumped out of bed like an arthritic rabbit and began fumbling with her bathrobe.

Jesus God, had her way, they'd be laying in bed till all hours. Oh, she'd brought it up once right after he retired, humming and hawing, and talking all kiss-ass about the years he'd spent getting up at the crack of dawn and going out all hours of the night, and how he deserved a little *rest*. Like he was some broken-down old mule put out to pasture, for God's sake. Well, he straightened her out damn quick. He might not be the chief of police anymore, but by *God* he wasn't going to turn into one of those pussy-whipped old geezers in checked pants and alligator shirts following their wives around in the shopping mall. And, badge or not, he still had work to do.

After she stumbled off downstairs, he peed and shaved and showered. Then he put on brown chino pants and a brown short-sleeved shirt, military-pressed. Even after five years he felt naked without his gun and visored hat. At times he got a nagging suspicion that the loss of these tangible symbols of authority somehow gave Miles Angstrom a slight edge in their daily confrontation. He was dead wrong if he thought so, because Fowler was as good a cop as ever.

Hattie had breakfast waiting. Three fried eggs, bacon, rye toast. She poured his coffee and sat slumped over her own cup. He noticed she didn't drink any. It fed a suspicion that had been growing for some time now. He was beginning to think as soon as he left the house she went back to bed. Didn't want caffeine to keep her awake. One of these mornings he'd double back, catch her at it and kick her skinny butt good.

But not today. It was going to be a scorcher and he wanted to get started because he was feeling the heat a bit more than he used to. He smoked a Roi-Tan with his last cup of coffee, then went upstairs. Brushed his teeth—his own, by God—and had a bowel movement. By then it was 8:45, and he headed through the woods at the back of his lot until he picked up the path that cut through the old Jones property. It was wooded most of the way. Shady, thank God. He walked steadily, ignoring a gritty feeling in

24

his left hip. Seventy years old, by God, and still a better man than that four-eyed turd, Morton Lankersheim, the township hired to replace him. Wasn't in six months before he had to have two more men, another squad car and now—the latest—a goddamn *computer*.

Jesus, it was hot. Sweat dripped into his eyes and he felt like he could spit cotton. He paused under a sweet gum tree and mopped his head. His heart thumped, and for a second he pictured himself flopping like a landed trout, gasping for air, with nobody around to help. Stupid thought. He was sound as a dollar. It was just too damn hot. Got to take it easy in this kind of heat.

He slowed down, and it was fifteen minutes later than usual before he left the wooded path and angled through an open field to the junction of Old Mill Road and County 15. A roadside produce stand occupied the northwest corner, neatly built of weathered wood and asphalt shingles, set back a ways with a broad sweep of gravel for parking. Letters burned into a slice of maple read: "Angstrom's Acres." A couple of people picked through tilted bins that held early peas, strawberries, lettuce, radishes, carrots, mushrooms—all grown on Angstrom's carefully tended land. Tomatoes, celery, squash, onions, cabbage—anything that wasn't in season—Angstrom bought in the produce market in Brattleboro on early morning forays. Timmy Lafferty helped after school and during summer vacation. Now there was just Angstrom himself, walking up and down the colorful rows, carrying a hose with a trigger spray attached, washing off the vegetables.

Fowler approached the spare, hard-muscled man, thinking, Maybe today's the day. Heat did peculiar things to people. He'd blink in the wrong place, say one false word . . .

Maud Delsey muttered, "Chief," and sidled out of his way. He could smell the peppermint that she chewed to cover her boozy breath. He picked up a paper sack and put in a sheaf of carrots, a glossy bell pepper. The fruity scent of ripe strawberries hung in the still air.

Angstrom looked up from his spraying. Forty-four, five-eleven, 165 pounds. Pale brown hair and gray-blue eyes. Fowler had the physical details as pat as a rap sheet. It was the things hidden away within the narrow skull that he wanted to dig into.

"Amos," Angstrom said. "Going to be a hot one."

"Ayuh." Fowler added spring-green lettuce to his sack. "Good time to go up to the mountains. Do a little fishing. Maybe even a little prospecting. Gettin' to be the thing to do, I hear."

"That so." Angstrom lined up a row of tomatoes, picked out a soft cucumber and dropped it into a trash barrel at the end of the counter.

"What I hear. What d'you think, Angstrom? Any buried treasure in these hills?"

Angstrom smiled but his eyes gleamed, icicle-hard. "I think you'd be wasting your time."

"Could be." Fowler handed him the vegetables. "But then, you never know."

"Sixty-five cents."

Fowler handed him a crumpled dollar bill. Angstrom put it in a metal money box and gave him change. Fowler saw a flicker of pulse beating in the blue veins of Angstrom's right temple. He looked straight into Angstrom's eyes and told him silently, *I know you, you murdering bastard. I know you.* Then he turned deliberately, walked over and threw the sack of garden-fresh vegetables into the garbage.

4

Lady chased the rabbit—her very first rabbit—with the long-legged exuberance of overgrown puppyhood. She was a mixture of red-boned hound and stockpot mutt with all of the tracking instincts but none of the training or common sense.

Which was understandable, since she was only six months old, and had spent most of her life behind fences and doors, passed around from ''good home'' to ''good home'' as soon as people discovered she peed when she got excited, chewed hard surfaces such as door frames and antique table legs and was going to grow up to fit her huge, lion-sized paws. Finally, a week ago, her latest owner brought her to the boy. He complained only a little when he had to clean up her puddles, sneaked her up to his room every night and took her for long glorious walks through fields full of wonderful smells.

Today one scent, freshly laid, filled her head with drumming wildness. Head down, she followed, forgetting the boy, forgetting everything but the hot quivering odor. Almost in front of her nose a rabbit sprang up and leaped away.

She galloped after it through meadow grass and Queen Anne's lace, the blood song drowning out the boy's cries of "Lay-dee. Lay-deee." The rabbit right-cornered. Clods of dirt flew as Lady skidded and turned. Desperately the rabbit darted back and forth, trying to work his way back to his hole, but Lady was too quick, too persistent. The rabbit bolted for the woods.

Lady plunged after him, jumping deadfalls and dodging slapping low-hanging branches of small shrubs. Startled birds fluttered up and cried in alarm. The boy's voice faded completely.

Lady lost the rabbit, found it, then—suddenly—the rabbit was gone. She quartered the area, nose to the ground, the rabbit's scent overlaid by other, darker smells. She was in a small clearing edged by tall hemlock trees, and the odor was all around—old blood and marrow combined with a mixture of loam and leaf mold. She tracked up and down, stopped where the smell was most powerful and began to dig.

"Lady, you bad, *bad* dog!" The boy stormed into the clearing and seized her collar, dragging her away. "Can't trust you at all, you shit-headed mutt. Now, come on. Come *on*."

She whimpered and licked his hand as he clipped a leash

to her collar. Ears and tail drooping, she followed him home.

It would be long weeks before the boy trusted her again to freely roam the fields. All she could do was dream—whimpering, foot-twitching dreams—of chasing rabbits and digging for long, white, worm-picked bones buried in the dark earth.

5

COUNTING DOWN
THE THUNDER

At six o'clock Ruth Hart gave up trying to sleep and slipped quietly downstairs. Most of her life she had considered herself a morning person. She and Matt always went to bed at 10:00 and got up at 5:30. Then, after Matt retired, he began reading late into the night, indulging his love of history, and she rediscovered her fascination for old movies on television, using a pair of lightweight earphones so he could enjoy his heavy reading undisturbed. After a brief bout of Calvinistic guilt, she found herself reveling in the luxury of staying in bed long after the sun rose, and she slept better than she had for years.

Or at least she had until Joanna came home. The past five nights had been fragmented by worry.

"Well, what did you expect?" was Matt's comment when she tried to talk to him about it.

Sometimes she thought Matt had more rapport with people who lived two hundred years ago than he did with his own family. Of course Joanna was going through a miserable ordeal and she expected her daughter to be depressed, wounded, even scarred. But obviously there was something more, something—well, *worse* . . .

She hesitated at the foot of the stairs. Early morning sunlight streamed into the front hall through a panel of old, handmade glass blocks, warming the pegged oak floor and . . . Lizzie, lying beneath an antique table.

Ruth caught her breath as she stumbled the remaining few steps and dropped to her knees. If Lizzie had fallen down the stairs . . .

Lizzie lay snuggled in a nest of pillows, cuddling her stuffed lion, sound asleep. Ruth drew a shaky breath and remembered night before last when she had heard a noise in the hall and gone out to check, and there was Joanna coming from the guest room with Lizzie in her arms.

"She must have used the bathroom and then got turned around," Joanna had said.

Now here Lizzie was out of her bed again. The nagging worry planted by the other incident turned into a full-blown alarm. Something *was* wrong.

The stairs creaked and Ruth looked up to see Joanna hurrying down. She wore an oversize Garfield T-shirt that emphasized her thin arms and legs. All that sun in California—how could she be so pale?

"So there she is." Joanna avoided Ruth's eyes as she knelt and eased Lizzie from under the table. "Little scamp. I'll take her up, Mom, and we can all go back to bed."

"I'm wide awake," Ruth said, "and I'm worried. I want to talk to you."

"It's awfully early and—"

"Joanna." She hated using that old "no nonsense, young lady" tone, but it worked.

"Okay," Joanna said wearily. "Could you please make some coffee?"

Over steaming cups Joanna still avoided her eyes. She had put on a blue terry robe and sat with one foot tucked under her, hands wrapped around a bright yellow mug. Light brown hair that had once been as blond as Lizzie's framed a face filled with planes and angles Ruth had never known were there. She had been such a happy little girl, constantly in motion, falling out of trees, requiring Band-Aids and kisses, tears quickly turning to smiles, and now . . .

Walt Kerso, you son of a bitch, Ruth thought, surprised by the savagery of her feelings. What have you done to my child?

"Jo," she said. "Please, darling, can't you talk to me?"

"I will. Soon. But—right now—I don't mean to shut you out, Mom, but I want—I need—just to rest and not have to think about it."

"All right. When you're ready—"

"I know." Joanna reached out to squeeze her hand.

"But," Ruth said, "this thing with Lizzie is a different matter."

"Mom, please."

"No, Jo. This can't wait. Something's wrong. Lizzie's too quiet and she's scared of everything. And this business of her wandering around at night. It's happened twice now and—" She looked at Joanna sharply. "It's been more than twice, hasn't it?"

"You have to understand." Joanna stared down at the

mug, lashes hiding her eyes. "To Lizzie this is a strange house. She's having a little trouble adjusting."

"Are you sure she's not sleepwalking? My God, what if she'd fallen down the stairs?"

"She's never walked in her sleep and I'm sure she's not doing it now. She just wakes up and—gets confused—I don't know. Maybe she's playing a game. I'm not worried, Mom, really. She's so much better—" Joanna broke off, jumped up. "Are there any more of those Sara Lee pecan rolls? I'm kind of—"

"Better?" Ruth said. "What do you mean, better? She *is* sick, isn't she?"

"Mom, relax. She just had some bad dreams. You know how kids are."

"I certainly do. Now, will you quit beating around the bush—what kind of bad dreams?"

"Mother, for God's sake. She's five years old and her whole world is falling apart. It's no wonder—" She sat down and reached out to cover Ruth's hands with both of hers. "Look, I won't lie to you. It was awful. She'd wake up screaming and—" Ruth felt her shiver. "But don't you see? Since we've been here, she hasn't had a single nightmare. I knew it would be that way, that she'd be all right once she felt safe and secure. She just needs a little more time."

"Still," Ruth said, "I don't like the sound of it and I'd feel a lot better if I'm here to take care of both of you. I'm going to talk to your father."

"Mom, no. Daddy's planned this trip for so long—"

"Graveyards and old battlefields won't disappear."

"Look," Joanna said, "it's bad enough that my life is so messed up. Do you know how terrible I'd feel if you canceled your plans because of me? Mom, *please*. Tell you what. If it'll make you feel better, I'll take her in to see Dr. Henderson, okay? I'll make an appointment as soon as his office opens this morning.''

"Well," Ruth said. *Does it ever get easier to know when you're smothering your child or helping her?* "Let's see what Bob has to say.''

Bob Henderson's nurse scheduled Lizzie's checkup for the following Monday morning. Ruth and Matt were planning to leave on July 5 in order to avoid the holiday traffic. "So that means we'll be here for a week after Lizzie's examination," Ruth said. "If Bob has to do tests—" She stared helplessly at Joanna.

Don't think about what kind of tests.

"—well, if he does, then I'm certainly not going off to Canada.''

"At least don't tell Dad. It's nothing, Mom. You'll see. No sense worrying him for nothing.''

Her mother agreed reluctantly, worry shadowing her eyes.

Good show, Joanna. Now this silly nonsense might spoil Mom and Dad's trip. And it *was* nonsense. A little girl's nightmare . . . and Lizzie wasn't even having them anymore. Why had she brought it up? There was just this business of not staying in her own bed at night . . . *hiding* . . . What the hell do you do to get rid of the Bogeyman? Silver bullets? A stake through his heart?

I'm the one who should be seeing Bob Henderson, Joanna thought. *Tell me what to do, Doc. Tell me how to put my life back together and then maybe Lizzie will be okay, too.*

But of course nobody could do that. It was something

she had to do herself. Starting right now. Movement—that was good. And a little positive thinking couldn't hurt.

She gave her mother a big hug. "Everything's going to be just fine. I promise you." Then outside, quick, before Ruth could come up with any more "yes, buts."

Overhead the sky was the blue of a baby blanket, afloat with cotton-ball puffs of cloud. She leaned on the wooden railing of the back porch and took a deep breath. The air was so different from California she might as well be on another planet. Denser. Greener. Soothing in the lungs. Dad had cut the lawn earlier. Tire tracks from the riding lawn mower looped down the sloping yard to a broad field of wild grasses, circled pussy willow and lilac, then cut a swath along the honeysuckle hedge back to a huge old sugar maple. The tree had always been there, ancient when Joanna was Lizzie's age. She'd spent long hours climbing the knobby trunk, playing in the swing Dad had hung from a strong, gnarled limb.

There had been a play-set for Lizzie in California, a flimsy thing of aluminum tubing that Walt had never gotten around to securing to the ground. Nothing like that swing in the old maple . . . oh, Lizzie would love it.

Lizzie was enchanted by the idea, and Matt was easily persuaded to leave the cleaning of the Winnebago long enough to fasten long strands of rope and cut a board for a seat. Holding Lizzie in her lap for the first ride, Joanna pushed the swing into higher and higher arcs while Lizzie crowed with delight.

The two of them came in pink-cheeked and laughing for lunch. See, Mom, no problems. For the first time since their arrival, Lizzie finished her food and while the table was being cleared asked what they were having for dinner.

"Fried chicken," Ruth said. "Unless you don't like that."

"I *love* fried chicken. And biscuits, Gramma. Can we have biscuits?"

"I know what I want." Joanna took placemats to the sink and shook off the crumbs. "Fresh vegetables. Does Miles Angstrom still run his produce stand?"

Lizzie seldom napped anymore and was definitely too keyed up for one today so Joanna took her along. Ruth's five-year-old Chevy wagon felt clumsy and slow on winding Route 15. Joanna longed for the zippy surefootedness of her Celica. She'd have to go back for it. And everything else. Furniture, clothing—anything that hadn't fit into the three suitcases she'd brought. Just the thought of dividing up their belongings with Walt brought back the horrible weariness seeping into her bones. Walt never gave up anything without a fight, even something he didn't want anymore. And when it came to Lizzie . . . she had a sudden sick image of the two of them each holding one of Lizzie's arms, pulling, shouting . . . and the little girl ripping in half like a paper doll.

"Are we almost there, Mommy?" In the constraining hold of the seat belt Lizzie tried to look out the window.

"Almost." Joanna gripped the steering wheel and concentrated on driving down the shadow-dappled road. How could divorce possibly be any worse for her daughter than the past two years? "See, there's the sign, Lizzie."

A board propped on an old wagon bed said: "Angstrom's Acres, ¼ mile. Nature's Finest Bounty."

Woods gave way to the cultivated fields of Angstrom's farm. Ahead, Joanna could see the two huge walnuts at the junction of Old Mill Road that shaded the produce stand. Along the road, honeyed sunlight gilded rows of emerald corn. Knee-high by the Fourth of July—wasn't that the growing rule? Well, it would certainly be that tall. Some kind of fat-leafed vine grew in another patch, full of trumpet-shaped blossoms.

"Look, Lizzie. Those flowers are going to be pumpkins. We'll come and buy one for Halloween. Won't that be fun?"

"But Daddy always takes me out to Irvine for a pumpkin." Unless he forgets. Unless he's too busy. "Daddy says they've got the best pumpkins in the whole world."

She had to tell Lizzie soon. Say the word and get it over with. Divorce. Ugly and final. Why hadn't she said it before? Was there some small flicker of hope that Walt would come to his senses, beg her to forgive him, that they would live happily ever after?

I'm as bad as Lizzie, Joanna thought as she slowed and turned into the graveled parking lot in front of the farm stand. She remembered years ago when old Mr. Angstrom simply put out a table under the two big trees during the summer. Now there was permanency in the U-shaped counters, tilted bins, a shingled awning that provided shade until the sun moved into the west.

Three other cars and a pickup sat in the small lot. Joanna started to roll up the car windows, stopped and chided herself. This wasn't L.A. Locked cars were unnecessary. She probably knew most of the people here. As if to prove the point, a tall woman in a yellow sundress walked to her car, called a greeting. Margaret Loman.

"Joanna! Ruth said you were here for a visit. Be sure to come by the club."

Joanna said she would, waved good-bye as she went around to help Lizzie from the car. The little girl got out reluctantly. From outgoing and sunny to this fearful timidness in less than a year.

Mom was right, as usual. Why had she waited so long to admit that Lizzie had a problem?

"Come on, sweetie. Look at all the wonderful stuff." She was turning into a babbler, trying to drown Lizzie's apprehension in a torrent of positive brightness.

"I'd rather go to a regular store, Mommy. Don't they got a Ralph's here?"

"Oh, Lizzie." Joanna smiled and nodded to more familiar faces.

There was no breeze now and the dense shade from the dark old trees seemed to concentrate the heat, intensifying the smells. Earthy odor of potatoes and mushrooms, the tang of onion and, overriding everything, a ripe strawberry sweetness.

On the other side of the U-shaped counter a gangling teenaged boy replenished the green beans; at the end, an older man counted change from a cash box and handed a woman her paper bag of produce.

Joanna recognized Miles, of course, although somehow in the years she'd been away, she'd expected him to become a plump, gray-haired version of his father. Silly. He wasn't that old. Mid-forties? Yes, that was about right. And he looked younger, lean and trim in faded blue jeans and a navy T-shirt. He glanced over in Joanna's direction and then stood very still, staring.

Trying to place her, that was understandable. She had seen him a few times in passing during visits home, but it was a long time ago that she had baby-sat with little Sarah

Ann so he and Bonnie could take in a movie. A long time since his wife and small daughter had vanished.

"Mr. Angstrom." That sounded stiff, formal. "Miles. Hello." Holding Lizzie's hand, she walked toward him.

As she approached, his gaze shifted and she realized that he had been staring at Lizzie, five-year-old Lizzie with her elfin face and tangled corn-silk hair.

"You be good, Sarah, and let Joanna brush your hair before you go to bed." Fine blond hair around a solemn pointed face.

"I will, Daddy."

"Okay. A big hug, then. We'll be home soon."

Joanna's heart turned over as she remembered how much Lizzie looked like that lost little girl. Pain flickered in Miles's pale blue eyes, then they were quickly opaque, like louvers closing.

"Miles, it's so nice to see you again. I'm Joanna Kerso—well, it used to be Joanna Hart."

"Of course. Joanna. How are you?" His gaze slipped back to Lizzie.

"Fine. I don't think you've met my daughter. This is Lizzie."

"Lizzie . . . hello."

Lizzie turned away, gripping Joanna's leg. "Lizzie, can't you say hello? Sorry, she never used to be so shy, but lately . . ."

"That's all right." Miles came around the counter. "I have just the thing for shy little girls."

He led the way to the strawberry table. Smaller berries than the ones in California, their fragrance heady as wine. Miles knelt by the table and reached beneath it to pull out a cardboard box. Inside, a big white cat nursed a half-dozen kittens of varying shades of gray and white.

"Oh, Mommy, it's kitties!" Lizzie leaned over the box, her shyness forgotten.

"Only three days old." Miles picked one up, the tiny white body curled in his hand.

"Can I hold him? *Please*. I'll be really, really careful," Lizzie promised.

"If you sit right here and just for a minute." An anxious meow from the box. "Oh, it's all right, Mamma. Lizzie won't hurt your baby." Miles smiled at Joanna. "I'll watch her. You go ahead and pick out what you need."

Miles put the kitten in Lizzie's lap, and the little girl ran one finger over the tiny head, along the ears, crooning, "So soft, such a sweet little kittie." Her wispy hair shone in the darkly shaded space below the strawberry table.

Miles felt his heart expand, as though a giant fist had been clutching it tightly all these years and suddenly released its hold. For a few brief seconds, he could believe that Sarah Ann had come back to him.

6

"Oh, Mom, I'd forgotten what wonderful stuff Miles has. Strawberries. And fresh peas!" Joanna popped one in her mouth, pod and all, and closed her eyes as she chewed.

"Oh, yuck!" Lizzie said.

"They won't be yucky when we cook them. Want to help? Look." Ruth cracked one and slid her thumb down the inside ridge of the pod, letting the shiny green peas fall into Lizzie's hand.

"Have fun." Joanna grabbed a carrot and headed for the door. "I'm going to help Dad with the Winnebago."

Bouncy. Bright. Ruth didn't believe it for a minute.

She and Lizzie sat in the big glider on the back porch to shell the peas. Matt had added a parking area along the side of the garage for the RV. They could watch him and Joanna working. Lizzie snuggled close. Damp ringlets

43

fringed her face. She smelled sweaty, a child's clean, salty odor.

"Know what, Gramma? Mr. Angstrom has this cat who had kittens in a box right under the strawberry table. He let me pet them and they were sooo soft. He said I could have one but I told him they make Daddy sneeze."

"Honey," Ruth said gently, "your daddy doesn't live with you anymore."

"But maybe he will. If I'm real good, maybe he'll stop loving that ole Sherri and come back and love us and the Bogeyman will stay away and not hurt us."

Ruth almost dropped the saucepan. "Who is this—" Careful. "—this person who's going to hurt you?"

"The Bogeyman. He—" Lizzie looked up and suddenly her eyes grew veiled, cautious. "He's not real, Gramma. Daddy says he's a pigment of my imagination."

"Well, your daddy's right, pumpkin." She put the peas on the porch and held Lizzie close, setting the glider in motion. "Everybody gets scared. When I was little, I was so afraid of the dark my mom had to leave a light on every night. If you get scared again, maybe that would help."

"Mommy did that," Lizzie said, "but then I could just see him better."

"It was just the nightmare, Mom." After all her hedging, her mother had found out about that bloody dream anyway. Joanna had come inside for some Windex, and Ruth followed her into the kitchen.

"But she even has a name for this—this thing. Where did she pick that up? Are you sure somebody wasn't scaring her? I hate to say it, but maybe Walt—"

"No, Mom. I can't blame Walt for that. The first

couple of times Lizzie had the nightmare we were out and the airhead who was baby-sitting explained all about the Bogeyman.'' And when I told her exactly what I thought about her insensitivity, when I told her I never wanted her near my child again, first she got screaming mad and then she took a great deal of delight in telling me about the little bonus Walt had been giving her when he drove her home.

''When you take Lizzie in for her checkup, I think you should tell Bob about it,'' Ruth said. ''And if he thinks she needs professional help—''

The telephone rang. While her mother answered it, Joanna grabbed the Windex and headed for the door. Talk about being saved by the bell.

''Joanna.'' Ruth covered the mouthpiece. ''It's Walt. He says it's important.''

Reluctantly Joanna took the phone and handed Ruth the Windex. She waited until her mother went outside, then took a deep breath before she said hello.

''Jo-Jo,'' Walt said, ''how was the trip? I thought you promised to call when you got there.''

''I thought you promised to come and say good-bye to Lizzie.''

''I did my best.'' But he had a client he simply couldn't reschedule. Have to hustle to stay on top of the real estate game these days, you know how it is.

She knew, all right, and Walt was always on top—of everything and everybody. She pictured him, only four years removed from Boston, transmuted into the quint-essential California male in his low-slung Calvins, Olivera Street *huaraches*, shirt unbuttoned to show black hair curling on a perfectly bronzed chest.

''Thing is,'' he said, ''the deal I got tied up with the

morning you left—it was Sherri's house. The couple made an offer but they need to move in right away. So I wanted you to know we came back here.''

''Here?''

''Our place. Home,'' he said patiently. ''As long as you're going to stay at your folks' all summer, I didn't think you'd mind.''

My house? She was never going to live there again, but dammit, it hurt anyway, the pain deep and unexpected. ''Do what you like,'' she said. ''Anywhere you like. How about the sheepskin rug in front of the fireplace? I seem to remember it was one of your favorite spots.''

''Christ, Joanna, we'd all be so much better off if you'd get control of yourself. How's Lizzie?''

Are you still making my daughter crazy? He didn't have to say it. They had their own language of inflections and button pushes.

''So nice you finally asked about her,'' Joanna said coldly. ''Now, why don't you just fuck off. And don't call back until you get your priorities straight.''

She slammed down the phone and turned around. Lizzie stood by the kitchen door, solemn and small.

''Was that Daddy?''

''Yes, it was and he said—he said he loved you.'' The smile she pasted on hurt her lips. ''And he sent you a big kiss.''

Lizzie's huge gray eyes filled with a desperate hope. ''Are we going home soon, Mommy?''

Unable to trust herself to speak, Joanna shook her head and watched the hope in Lizzie's eyes turn to despair.

THE BOGEYMAN

* * *

Lizzie lay in her bed and listened to the cool darkness. Old boards shifted, sighing a soft complaint. Somewhere in the walls a mouse made a *scratch-scritch* sound as he ran along electrical insulation and copper pipes.

The room wasn't really dark. An orange-slice moon shone through the restless leaves of the big old maple, creating shifting patterns on the polished oak floors. Pearly light glimmered on the brass pulls of a tall chest, pooled in the mirror of her mother's dressing table.

Lizzie hugged Leon, listening and waiting. She had seen a movie on TV where a soldier stood guard at a secret installation. *Halt! Who goes there?* She remembered his words and the big gun he carried, the way he marched up and down. Lizzie instantly recognized his job as the same thing she was doing. She was only five years old but she was a sentry, too. Lizzie wished she could make her mother understand what she was doing, what she had to do.

A dream, her mother called it. Her daddy did, too. But dreams happened when you were asleep and *he* came when she was wide awake to sit and grin at her and whisper. *I see you, Lizzie.*

Old Buddy Duffy and some of his friends had a club last summer she had been desperate to join. One day they told her that just maybe she could be a member. "If you come and look at something." Buddy's eyes had danced, darkly gleeful. "If you come and look and don't act like a baby."

When she smelled the terrible, sweet odor down in the corner of the park, she tried to run home but they grabbed her arms, thrusting her forward so that she had to look at the possum's bloated body. It quivered like gray pudding with maggots working below the skin and crawling out the eyeless holes in the pointed face . . .

He was like that. A shapeless, runny thing, only she had the awful feeling that he wasn't decaying away like the possum; he was slowly turning to solid flesh, to some-*body*, and if she could only stand to look at him she'd see who he was. Somehow that was the most awful thing of all and she'd shut her eyes tightly so she couldn't see.

Lizzie was only five years old and she'd never heard of paranormal research. She didn't know about ESP or precognition, couldn't theorize that time might bend and loop, that she might see the future, a distorted child's-eye view translated into something she could understand.

She saw the Bogeyman and he was a real thing, grinning and whispering. She *had* realized, finally, that she was the only one who could see him. She was alone, like the soldier, standing watch.

Listening carefully, she decided that Mommy and Gramma and Grampa were asleep. She gathered up Leon and the patchwork quilt and tiptoed quietly out into the hall, staggering a little under the bulky load. Tonight she would go to sleep under the dining room table. *Hiding*. Trying to fool the Bogeyman.

Lizzie was only five years old and there was nothing else she could do.

7

Tom Blanchard stopped in Brattleboro for enough groceries to get him through the weekend. Since he hadn't been to the cottage for four months, he added a broom and a can of Raid. He could stand a few field mice but he couldn't live with cobwebs and bugs.

On the way out of the supermarket he noticed a telephone booth and immediately thought of the woman and the little girl on the L.A. flight—what was the woman's name? You know damn well, he told himself. Joanna Kerso. Visiting her parents, Matthew and Ruth Hart, in Maple Grove.

He still wasn't sure he wanted to call her. The lady had problems, and God knows he didn't need that. He put the groceries in his car and headed north. It had been raining when he left Boston but here whipped-cream clouds clotted the pastel sky.

The Greenes lived on the corner at the turnoff to his cottage. They were year-round residents and Jack kept an eye on the place. Tom had made the mistake only once of offering to pay Jack, an offense that almost ended their friendship. Instead, Tom arranged to have the local garage plow his private road in winter, saying casually that the man might as well clear the Greenes' drive as well.

Painfully thin, bearded and tan, Jack balanced on one crutch while he trimmed bushes down by the road. He'd left a foot in Vietnam and still had problems. He never talked about it, but sometimes you could see the pain in his eyes, and Tom knew he went regularly to Boston for treatment. He waved a greeting as Tom tooted, pulled over and stopped.

"Went up and turned on the refrigerator," Jack said. "Will you be around for a while?"

"Just for the weekend."

"Well, Donna says be sure and come for dinner one night."

Tom promised he would and drove off down the narrow road where trees grew so close you could touch them. Birch, maple, pine—laced together overhead to turn the whole world green. The asphalt strip ended in a clearing beside the cottage. Beyond lay Hickory Pond, dark beneath a gilding of afternoon sunlight. He got out of the car and stood for a moment, breathing in the smell of leaves and earth. Out on the lake, a loon called.

He unpacked the car and went inside. The old refrigerator hummed loudly. Jack had left a six-pack of Becks beer. Tom uncapped one, drank half of it before he put the food away, then sipped the rest while he opened windows.

The cottage had two rooms. The larger combined kitchen

and living areas. The smaller one was a bedroom. A loft added extra sleeping space. The heavy rock-maple furniture dated back to the twenties when his grandfather bought the place from the profit he made on his sole venture into the stock market. Claire had recovered the sofa and platform rocker in a heavy cotton print of warm browns and rusts. She bought a book on upholstering and made a project of it that last summer . . .

"Looks like a pretty big job." He had put down the bolt of material and her tools, the last of the stuff from the station wagon.

"Well, I'll have plenty of time."

An awkward silence that she filled by fussing with the teakettle. So many empty spaces between them lately. He often felt as though he were flying in fog without instruments.

"Everything looks okay but I'll double-check before I start back," he said.

She pulled tea bags from their little paper envelopes, put them into brown stoneware mugs, poured in boiling water. Her hair hung from its side part, a silky chestnut wedge, shadowing her face.

"I'm sorry I can't stay," he said. "But my flight leaves so early—"

"You didn't have to come along. I could've managed."

"I wanted to come. I want to make sure you're all right. I don't like the idea of leaving you out here alone."

"Oh, don't be ridiculous," she said sharply. "I'll be just fine." She poured the freshly brewed tea into the sink, then stood looking down into the empty mugs. Her hands began to tremble and she gripped the edge of the counter.

Tom went to her, putting his hands on her shoulders. "Claire, darling, it's been a terrible couple of years—"

"No." She pulled away. "That's what you can't understand. It's been exhausting—upsetting—sad. But never terrible. I loved Andy."

Andrew Thomas Blanchard, their son, born severely retarded, blind, his heart valve damaged. The doctor had advised immediate institutionalization. Tom, heartbroken, agreed. Claire refused, fiercely adamant, saying, "I won't give my baby to strangers. Not ever, do you hear?"

She structured her life around the little boy, a schedule that soon left her drained and remote. Tom tried to help, but he was sure she had never forgiven him for wanting to put the baby in a foster home. He had found himself looking forward to the out-of-town layovers, then feeling guilty for wanting to be away from Claire and his son.

He leaned against the counter and stared blindly out at the lake. "I loved him, too, you know. Not the way you did, but I loved him." Even though, God help him, he'd felt such relief when Andy died. "We should be together, Claire. To get back . . . where we were, before . . ."

"I can't. Not yet. Please, Tom. Give me this time. I really need to be alone, to sort things out. And it's not as though we won't see each other. You'll come up when you can. And Donna and Jack will be right down the road."

So he had left her there despite his misgivings, hoping time really would heal, that things would be better.

Now Tom went over to an end table and picked up a gold-framed photograph of the two of them sitting on the pier, drenched with sunshine. He'd brought it here two months after Claire disappeared, spinning a fantasy about Claire having amnesia but somehow finding her way to the cottage. She'd see the picture, remember everything, call him . . . It was a pretty good fantasy except it didn't explain the smear of blood on the front seat of Claire's Olds wagon when the police found it in the supermarket parking lot. And then the fantasy had shattered completely when he discovered what Claire had been hiding . . .

He put down the picture, knocking over two more of the collection on the table. So many happy memories, like elusive big game captured and mounted. Claire's parents one Christmas. Tom and Jack displaying a day's catch of trout.

Suddenly the room seemed small, crowded with old dreams, smelling of dust and ashes. He went outside and got into the car. No ghosts tonight. Jack had offered dinner. He'd drive back to town, buy a bottle of wine. Instead, he stopped at the first gas station with a phone booth. The phone book was missing so he dialed information.

"What city, please?"

He took a deep breath and said, "Maple Grove, Vermont."

Joanna sat in the booth across from Tom Blanchard, feeling nervous and awkward. On the drive over they'd covered the weather and the state of the economy. What was left?

"Nice place," she said.

"The food's good, or at least it used to be. I haven't been here for a while."

The old inn sat on the edge of the Connecticut River. Some of the interior was probably faked, but a lot of it was genuine—paneled walls and huge beams shaped by an adz and stained by woodsmoke. Framed copies of shipping posters provided the only decoration. The one above their booth featured the R.M.S. *Titanic*. She hoped it wasn't an omen.

Their drinks arrived. Not a minute too soon, Joanna thought, sipping the cold gin and tonic.

"I feel like I dropped a bombshell on your folks," Tom said. "I take it you didn't tell them about meeting me. Or the problem with Lizzie at the airport?"

Joanna shook her head. "I didn't want to worry them."

"The Bogeyman hasn't shown up again?"

"No." *Not yet.*

She shivered. Maybe Walt was right. Maybe she *was* making Lizzie crazy because she was crazy herself . . . No, dammit. No more guilt trips. Maybe she wouldn't have said yes to Tom if it hadn't been for that call from Walt on top of the scene with her mother, but she was here now and she was determined to enjoy herself.

The food was good as promised. She ate too much and talked too much. What did he think of our foreign policy? Read any good books; seen any good films? Exactly how did one become a copilot on a wide-bodied jet, and was man really meant to fly anyway? By the time they left the restaurant, her piano-wire nerves were tuned about three octaves too high and she was exhausted. In the car she leaned her head against the backrest and stared out into the darkness.

"Do you think this was a mistake?" Tom asked quietly.

"Probably. For you anyway. I can't seem to remember the moves, you know? Did it really used to be so easy?"

"I doubt it. Just less complicated."

"That's the word, all right." She watched him in the glow of the dashboard lights.

"Do you want to talk about it?" he asked.

"No, but I have the feeling if we don't we may have to talk about politics and the weather forever."

She began slowly and it was easier than she thought. Maybe it was the darkness and the fact that she didn't have to look him in the eye. A father confessor, she thought, just what I need.

She told him about Walt's affairs—not about the first one—never about the first one, not to anybody. The expurged version included the stormy scenes and the reconciliations she couldn't explain because she didn't understand them herself. The last months when he moved out and she had sat, immobilized by some strange inertia, unable to end a marriage that had been over for a long time. How her mother had pleaded with her to come home, at least to try to get a different perspective. Then how as soon as she had picked up the phone and made the reservations to Boston, the paralysis lifted.

"So what do you think?" she said brightly as they turned into the driveway. "Is this great soap opera or what?"

Tom stopped the car and shut off the engine. She could hear crickets and the *hoo-hoo-hoo* of an owl. "You're sure it's over?" Tom asked.

"Oh, yes. Or it would be. Except for Lizzie . . ."

There were no sobs, just her face suddenly wet. Maybe he saw the tears shining on her cheeks in the moonlight. He opened his arms, gathered her in and simply held her, his face against her hair. Nothing sexual about it, but for those few seconds she felt closer to him than she ever had to Walt during intercourse.

Then the intimacy turned awkward and she moved away,

feeling dumb and weepy. "You have a talent for knowing the right thing to do. How anybody could let you get away—" My God, what was she saying? He had a cottage in Vermont that he used for weekends, but that didn't mean— "I'm sorry, I guess—because you seem to understand so well—I assumed you'd been through something similar."

"No, not quite. I—lost—my wife about three years ago."

A space opened up between them that had nothing to do with measurable distances. "Oh, Tom, I'm so sorry." She wanted to comfort him the way he comforted her, but she knew she'd never be able to reach him. "I wish I knew something to say—look, would you like to come in?" They might stumble over Lizzie, or Mom might come down, but she'd deal with that if she had to. "How about a nightcap? Or some coffee?"

"Thanks, but I'd better not." He planned to get up early tomorrow, so many things he'd neglected around the cottage, you understand.

She did. She stood on the porch and watched him drive away, sure she'd never see him again, feeling strangely bereft at the thought.

8

When dawn poked long gray fingers into the narrow street, Kevin McDowell rubbed grainy eyes, took a slug of vodka, looked at the half inch left in the bottle, said, "Aw, what the hell," and drained it. Raw fumes stung his throat and the back of his nose, starting a fire in his stomach that spread in small explosions through his bloodstream.

He hefted the empty and stared out the car window at the crumbling brick building. What if he threw the fucker against the wall . . . smash, bang. Might as well. And while he was at it he could shoot off a couple of rounds at that goddamn neon sign on the corner, blinking its Oriental squiggles in his eyes all night. The stakeout was a bust anyway.

Unless the Thu Duc Tien family went to bed before nine o'clock, nobody was home in the fourth-floor-front apartment. He'd dozed off and on, but he'd been awake enough—and sober enough since he'd rationed the vodka—to know that nothing was happening up there. Hell, nothing was happening down here either. Within minutes after he'd shoehorned the Plymouth into the line of tightly parked cars in front of a fire hydrant, activity on the street melted away. His blue jeans and windbreaker hadn't fooled anybody.

Cautious people down here. Little Saigon—his name for it—linked the edges of Chinatown to the Combat Zone. Nothing here in Boston like the boat people ghettos on the West Coast but big enough so he got a chill of recognition when he went to see *Blade Runner*, with its vision of a future glutted by Asians.

A few refugees had managed to bring along enough pure heroin to provide the cash necessary to slip right into the good old American way of life. But before they could make the transition, some began turning up in the harbor with their throats slit, victims of the good old American way of death and Yankee competition.

He squinted at his watch. 4:42. Give it another fifteen minutes. And that brought up another big decision. Should he use the large economy-size Yuban instant jar or go piss in the alley? Since he sure as hell couldn't wait to get back to the station house and he needed to stretch his cramped legs, he tossed the vodka bottle in the back to join layers of Whopper wrappers and *Globe* sports pages, and got out of the car. Yesterday's rain had left the air with a clean washed sharpness that heightened the sense of smell. Great stuff if you happened to be strolling on the Commons sniffing daisies, but in the black cave of the alley it only accentuated the odor of the urine he splashed on the wall and the residual stink of moldy garbage and dog shit.

What the hell am I doing here? he wondered. If anything was coming down with this Thu Duc Tien, the hotshots from narcotics would've pulled ranked by now.

Shivering, he lit a cigarette and headed back to the car. Almost July, but the north wind had a sour tang that reminded you there were still icebergs off Newfoundland.

Headlights flashed as a black-and-white rounded the corner. He climbed over the back bumper, leaned against the Plymouth and waved the patrol car to a stop.

"You packing it in?" The driver, Neary, propped a massive arm on the open window.

He took up so much space his partner, Viggiano, had to lean over and peer around him. "Hey, Mac, how's it going?"

"It's not," McDowell said. "I don't know where you got your information, but nobody's home."

"You been up to see?" Neary said.

"Oh, sure. That's what you do on a stakeout, Neary. You kick in doors, climb in windows. Make sure the whole neighborhood knows who you're after."

Neary's jowls purpled and his throat muscles bulged. The fight was an old one that started a long time ago when McDowell and Neary rode together, both bucking for detectives, McDowell making it and Neary getting left behind. Neary had acted like an asshole ever since. Wrong. Neary was always an asshole; he just moved up a notch to fucking asshole.

"Hey, listen," Viggiano put in quickly, "I don't know why he ain't around but I'm telling you that guy, Duckwhatshisname, and your wheelman on the jewelry heists were real tight, Mac. Solid information. I guarantee it.''

Solid. Drunken whispers four times removed from some junkie snitch looking for a fix.

"You decide to go up there," Neary said, "let us know. We wouldn't want you to do it all by your lonesome.''

Neary stamped on the gas and the patrol car jumped, belching exhaust and bouncing off down the potholed street.

"Bastard," McDowell muttered. He ground out his cigarette, got back into the Plymouth on the passenger side and slid over. But what if that fat fuck was right? Maybe he'd dozed longer than he thought. Maybe . . .

He gripped the steering wheel, and sweat seeped from every pore. Suddenly he could smell himself and it was the acetone stink of a drunk sleeping it off in an alley.

He fumbled his way out of the car, leaned against the cool metal roof and took a deep breath. So he had a little booze to keep warm and get him through the night. That didn't mean . . . he *dozed*, for Chrissake. A few minutes, that's all. Nobody'd been near that apartment.

And what difference did it make if they had? Losing sleep and busting his kidneys just to question some squint-eyed slime who probably didn't speak a word of English or would pretend not to. Might as well call it quits. The whole neighborhood had made him by now anyway. Go back to the station, file the paperwork and forget it. Another dead end. He had a whole file cabinet full of them.

But if the gook *was* up there . . .

Damn Neary!

He headed for the building. The old bricks glowed a soft

rose in the morning light. Typical setup: a small entrance with an inner door flanked by mailboxes. Push buttons next to name slots. Designed for the days of civilized privacy when you rang for somebody to buzz you through. Now there were no nameplates in the slots. Hell, there was no inner door. Ugly gashes marked the frame where the hinges used to be. He went through the splintered doorway and headed for the stairs. Might be daybreak outside but in here it was still night.

He hesitated, unzipped his jacket and touched the butt of the thirty-eight tucked in his waistband. Reflex. Just reflex. Get on with it, for Chrissake. Pain hammered the base of his skull as he went up the steps. One dim light bulb. Strike a match and you'd have more light.

Second floor. A few people up, moving around, the sound muffled behind heavy doors and thick walls. Something cooking—oily, sweetish, alien. Jesus, he hated Oriental food. He wished he had a gallon of hot, strong coffee. He wished he had a drink.

Fourth floor and he hung on to the banister, breathing hard, cherry bombs going off in the back of his head. Forty-two years old and he couldn't climb up three flights without wheezing like an old man.

Used to run every morning, work out at the gym twice a week. One year he rowed on the Charles like that Polack detective on TV—who was it? Banacek. Hot sun, cold rain on his face—he didn't give a shit. Some chick told him he looked like George Peppard. Ten years ago he probably did. Now ole George had joined the A-Team, but McDowell . . .

He drew in a long, steadying breath and walked down the hall. Corner apartment, fourth floor front. He knocked on the door. Nothing. The murky darkness had grown gradually brighter. He could make out a faded pattern in the worn, stained carpet. Suddenly queasy, he leaned against the door frame. Nobody cooking up here but—something—an odor, brassy and familiar. He pounded harder. Nothing.

Fuck Neary. Nobody here, just like he thought. He pressed his clammy forehead against his jacket sleeve and walked toward the stairs. He felt sticky all over. Even his shoes . . .

He stopped and turned slowly. Sunlight streamed through the windows now. Bright enough to see the footprints he'd left on the carpet, leading back to the door, and in front of the door a dark red stain . . .

Back down the hall, crouching, gun in his hand, the door locked but a solid kick and one more splinted door frame and he knew even before the odor hit him, crawling up his nose and filling his head, *blood*.

Blood on the walls, great gouts of blood, arterial spray from the headless woman against the far wall.

Bloody rivers running on the sloped floor (remember the Red River Valley?), blood from three small children and a man propped near the door, throat slashed and eyes gouged out, empty eye sockets staring . . .

Fucking Neary was right. The Thu Duc Tien family had been home all along.

9

Every time the phone rang that weekend Joanna tensed, waiting. She was sure Tom wouldn't call but she waited anyway and parried her mother's questions. Yes, he seemed very nice but no, she doubted she'd see him again. It was just *dinner*, for pete's sake. She'd met him on the plane—a casual conversation—and discovered he had a cottage near Brattleboro.

Caught in your own trap, she told herself.

At first she hadn't wanted to talk about that crazy incident at the L.A. airport, so she didn't mention Tom. Now it was the other way around. If she went into detail about meeting him, it meant worrying her mother even more about Lizzie.

More waiting . . . he didn't call.

* * *

On Monday morning Dr. Henderson greeted Joanna with a hug. "Is she still falling out of trees?" he asked Ruth.

"Not lately," Ruth said.

This big bear of a man had pulled Joanna through mumps, chicken pox and assorted fractures. She felt a surge of relief as he suggested that the examination room might be a bit crowded and asked her mother to wait outside. Had he always been so tactful?

Lizzie looked apprehensively around the small room and clung to Joanna. "Did you bring a urine specimen? Good." Dr. Henderson sat down on a low stool so he was more at the child's eye level. "Now then, Lizzie, Mrs. Stiers is going to find out how much you weigh and how tall you are. She'll bring you right back."

"It's okay," Joanna said.

The nurse took Lizzie's hand and led her out the door, chatting easily.

"Well, now." Dr. Henderson flipped open a manila folder. "Why don't you sit down and tell me about your daughter."

Joanna perched on the edge of a hard chair. She told him that Lizzie was having trouble sleeping. "Mom's afraid she's sleepwalking."

He looked at her thoughtfully. "You and your husband having problems, Joanna?"

"You could say that." She explained they were separated and that Lizzie had gone through a period of terrible nightmares mostly about a recurring monster. "That seems to be over now. No bad dreams since we left California." And that was the truth . . . except for the incident at the airport. It seemed so silly now. The child had been searching for an excuse, any excuse, not to leave without seeing her father. "I'm sure Lizzie's going to be fine as soon as she gets used to being here. Mainly I brought her in to reassure Mom. She's talking about canceling their vacation because she's so worried."

He asked a few more questions. What was Lizzie actually doing when Joanna found her out of bed?

"She was just—" Hiding. From the Bogeyman? Surely she would have told Joanna if she'd been having the dream again. "She was just sleeping." And yes, Lizzie did remember it later.

Mrs. Stiers came back with Lizzie, collected the urine sample and a blood smear and left again. Then Dr. Henderson began his exam, interspersing the routine with the same observations he'd once used on Joanna. "What have we in this ear? Potatoes? Carrots?" Old and corny and wonderfully reassuring. It still worked, too. Lizzie relaxed and let his big gentle hands do their job until he said, "Mommy tells me you don't like to sleep in your bed at Grandma's. Why don't you like it?"

"I don't know." Joanna saw the wariness in Lizzie's eyes. "I just thought it would be nice to sleep in the hall."

"You remember all about it?"

"Oh, sure," Lizzie said. "Do I get a sucker now? I like purple ones best."

He sent her along with Mrs. Stiers, asking the nurse to have Ruth join them in his office. After they were settled around his desk he said, "Lizzie's fine—blood count, urine, everything normal except she's underweight and a bit too pale." He looked at Joanna sternly. "And so are you, young lady. As for the sleepwalking, Ruth, you can relax."

He went on to explain that although somnambulant episodes are triggered by anxiety and Lizzie qualified on that score, she had none of the other classic symptoms. "I'll give you an example. A patient of mine got up one night and did her washing and ironing and never remembered a thing about it next morning. No, I think Joanna's instincts about this are good. Lizzie just needs some time to settle in. Her biological time clock is probably off. Kids can have jet lag, too, you know."

"What about the dreams?" Ruth asked. "The way she talks about this—this thing. Bob, she thinks it's real."

"That's not surprising," he said gently. "Children often confuse dreams with reality. And this is an anxious time for Lizzie. Now, then. Here's my prescription, Ruth. Everybody needs a vacation. I'm going to take one myself as soon as I can. So go on that trip with Matt and enjoy yourself. Joanna, you see to it that Lizzie takes her vitamins, gets regular meals, fresh air, sunshine. Lots of exercise. Tire her out and she'll sleep. I guarantee it."

"Now maybe you'll stop worrying." Joanna squeezed her mother's arm as they came out of the doctor's office. Sunshine sparkled through the leafy branches of maples lining the grassy square of the town green directly across the street.

"I'll try." Ruth dabbed at Lizzie's sticky mouth with a Kleenex. "But I'll feel a lot better when I see some roses in these cheeks."

"How about if we start right now? While you pick up those things Dad wanted, I thought I'd take Lizzie to the playground. How about it, sweetie? Want to go on the swing?"

"Not if it's a baby swing," Lizzie said. "Do they have a teeter-totter, like the one at school?"

"Let's go find out."

Ruth said she'd drive by to pick them up when she finished shopping and went off toward the hardware store.

The doctor's office was in the middle of the block, so the best route to the playground was straight across the green. Joanna took Lizzie's hand and waited between two parked cars for the signal on the corner to change and the light traffic to clear.

"I hope they have a slide at the park." Lizzie bounced up and down with anticipation. "I love slides. Let's go, Mommy."

"Just hold your horses and wait for the light."

"Hold your horses." Lizzie giggled. "Hold your horses."

A pickup with a dog in the back slowed and pulled into a parking place nearby. A man and a boy got out and the dog jumped down. A matched set, Joanna thought. The man had dark red hair, the boy's was a lighter shade and the dog's coat was lighter still.

"Don't you disappear," the man said. "I'll be right back."

"We won't, Dad." He ran off toward the green with the dog at his heels.

Sunlight poured down. The top of Joanna's head felt hot and the bare skin on her arms and shoulders tingled. The light turned green and she started to cross the street, but Lizzie resisted.

"Come on, sweetie," Joanna said.

"I just remembered, Mommy. I got sick on the teeter-totter at school and threw up on Buddy Duffy, and Miss Garcey said I shouldn't go on teeter-totters ever again."

"You did?" Funny, she didn't remember the teacher saying anything about it. Maybe she blocked it out. She'd blocked out a lot of things the past few months. "Then you can just go down the slide and I'll stand right there and catch you."

"Maybe we better go find Gramma. She might forget where the playground is and we'd have to walk all the way home."

Sweat trickled down Joanna's temples and between her breasts. She held a hand against the glare. "Now, stop it, Lizzie. You're just being silly. Come *on*."

She crossed the street with Lizzie dragging in the hot asphalt like an anchor attached to her arm. On the shady green the red-haired boy threw a stick, and the dog bounded after it.

"I wanna go home." Lizzie's voice was thin and frightened. She stopped on the sidewalk, staring, That Look, but there was nothing to see. Just the shady rectangle of the green with the white meeting house at one end and the dog galloping toward the boy with the stick in its mouth.

"Lizzie—"

"I wanna go home, I wanna go *home*."

Joanna knelt beside her and got a child's-eye view of the green. The dog dropped the stick at the boy's feet and came running toward them. Joanna went limp with relief. It was the dog, the damned dog. Lizzie had never been afraid of animals before, but this one—really an overgrown puppy—looked huge as it pranced around them, tail wagging, big pink tongue lolling out and a silly grin on its face, ignoring the boy's shouts.

She put one arm around Lizzie and patted the dog. "Honey, it's okay. She's just being friendly. See?"

Lizzie shivered violently. "Get it away from me, Mommy. Get it away."

The boy ran over yelling, "Sit, Lady, *sit*!" The dog obeyed and he clipped a leash to her collar. "What's the matter with you, you dumb mutt?" Lady looked at him with adoring eyes. "I'm sorry about that," he said to Joanna. "She listens pretty good most of the time. Is your little girl okay?"

"Scared, that's all." Joanna could feel Lizzie quivering. "I'm sure she's a nice dog but if you could just please—"

"Oh, right. I gotta go anyway. My dad's ready to leave."

Joanna picked up Lizzie and carried her over to a bench, holding her tightly until the trembling subsided, murmuring, "It's okay, baby, it's okay." But was it really? Should she take Lizzie back to Dr. Henderson? And then what? All she could tell him was that Lizzie was scared by the dog. It *had* to be the dog . . .

"Lizzie," she said, dread crowding her throat. "Did you—you didn't see the Bogeyman again?"

"No, Mommy." Lizzie's eyes seemed to look into some dark and secret place. "Not this time."

10

On Friday morning before the Fourth of July weekend Joanna drank her second cup of coffee and watched Lizzie devour a stack of pancakes. Lizzie wore a milk mustache and her skin was pink from the sun. Everything had been so normal since Monday and that scare over the dog . . . it *was* the dog that scared her, no sense making more of it than it was . . . and last night she slept through without getting out of bed.

Dr. Henderson was right. Sunshine and fresh air. Exercise. Lizzie had been doing so well it was easy to put off having a talk with her about the divorce. Why upset her now? Later, when both of them were stronger . . . they needed this time.

Joanna had slept well herself after their long afternoon ramble. The shadows under her eyes had diminished and she had the beginnings of a tan. Tom Blanchard, eat your heart out.

Yeah. Sure.

He hadn't called and he wouldn't. She was sure about that.

Lizzie finished her milk. "Can I go swing now?"

"Teeth first."

"Do I have to?"

"Yes, ma'am. All the teeth," she called as Lizzie headed upstairs.

She carried the dishes over to the sink, then took her cup out on the back porch. The boards felt rough and warm beneath her bare feet. The air smelled of honeysuckle and roses, incredibly sweet. A blue sky gleamed through a canopy of maple leaves and she was comfortable in her shorts and tank top. By afternoon it would be hot enough to take Lizzie to the pool at the club. Mom had been urging her to go. She had to stop avoiding people sometime. It would be good for Lizzie and something to fill the long summer afternoons after her parents left.

She could hear them talking inside the big RV parked by the garage, going over her father's careful, endless lists. The camper gleamed inside and out; the engine had been inspected and tuned; supplies bought and stored. Only four days and then—

I wish they wouldn't go.

The thought startled her. Keep at it, she told herself. Maybe you can regress all the way back to a fetal position in a rubber room.

She had drained the rest of her coffee and started back inside when Mom and Dad climbed out of the camper and walked toward the porch. "All set?"

72

"Yes," Mom said firmly.

"Well." Dad wiped his hands on a scrap of terry toweling. "It wouldn't hurt to have another flashlight and maybe some rope. Just for emergencies."

"What kind of emergency are we going to have where we need a rope?"

"Now, Ruth, you know I just like to be prepared. Whoa, there." He grabbed Lizzie as she charged out the door. "What's the rush?"

"I'm gonna go swing. Will you push me, Grampa? Please?"

Joanna and her mother watched them—Dad with his bearlike shamble, and Lizzie, fragile as a butterfly. "She *is* all right, isn't she?" Ruth asked.

"I told you, Mom, she slept through the night and she ate like a little wolf. So stop worrying and start packing."

"You're sure?"

No, I'm not sure. I'm scared and I don't know why and I don't want to be alone. "Absolutely. Now, if Lizzie and I are going to do the shopping for the weekend, we'd better get a list made. The store will be mobbed."

She was getting very good at changing the subject.

Joanna made Angstrom Acres their last stop. It was busier than usual but a peaceful oasis compared to the crowded lines at Safeway. Lizzie ran straight to the strawberry table to check on the kittens, then back to Joanna with shining eyes.

"They're getting sooo big, Mommy. Can I play with them now? Can I?"

"Maybe we'd better ask Mr. Angstrom." She waved to

Miles, who counted out change to a customer and then came over.

"I bet I know why this young lady is here." He ruffled Lizzie's hair and smiled at Joanna.

"Can I play with your kitties today, Mr. Angstrom?" Lizzie asked.

"If you're very careful and their mamma thinks it's okay." He took her hand, leading her over to the table.

Joanna followed. The tautness in his face relaxed as he settled Lizzie with the kittens. He looked younger. Well, he wasn't that old. There was only an age difference of—what?—fifteen or sixteen years between them. Not that much really, but when she was in junior high he was already married with a family and she had automatically lumped him in with her parents' generation. And later—if she thought of him at all—it was as Maple Grove's tragic figure.

My God, how did he stand it? Splitting up with Walt was bad enough, but what if one day he and Lizzie had vanished? She remembered Miles's wife, Bonnie, a tall restless woman, and his little girl. When they disappeared without a trace that summer before Joanna left for college, a kind of doomed anticipation had settled over Maple Grove. So much senseless slaughter in the headlines, it seemed inevitable that Bonnie Angstrom and her six-year-old daughter would be found, bodies butchered and brutalized. Eventually opinion changed. Whispers of gossip rose like oil on slimy water—arguments between Miles and his wife, rumors that Bonnie had a lover and ran away with him.

Joanna shuddered. How do you deal with something like that? Somehow, Miles had. Surely Lizzie reminded him of his daughter, but he seemed completely at ease, his head bent close to the little girl's as he lifted kittens from the box. The mother cat had no objections. She yawned and walked away as if she was losing interest in the whole project.

"Isn't that a picture?" No shadows in his eyes as he stood up and smiled down at Lizzie with her candy-apple sundress, a pink-ribboned ponytail and a tumble of fluffy white and gray kittens in her lap.

"If you don't watch out, she may become a permanent fixture around here." Joanna picked out a handful of zucchini. He opened a paper bag, held it out so she could put the vegetables in.

"Sounds good to me." He had strong, graceful hands, the nails clipped short and gleaming. "Are your folks leaving on their trip soon?"

"Tuesday." She moved on to collect a sheaf of green onions, a bouquet of radishes.

He followed her, easily lifting a full crate of tomatoes and placing it on the counter. "Are you going to the picnic on the Fourth?"

He sounded casual enough, but something about the way he looked at her—just your imagination, she told herself, but she was suddenly aware of the ropy muscles under his light cotton shirt and his clean, soapy scent.

"Yes, we'll all be there."

"Would you like me to save you a table? I have to go early and—" He broke off, staring over her shoulder, his face grown suddenly hard and watchful.

She turned to see what had stopped him, recognizing the familiar figure. Amos Fowler's thinning hair was completely gray and his skin sagged as if time were slowly shrinking the bony substructure, but he still carried himself with military erectness inside the sharply pressed tan chinos.

"Chief Fowler?" She knew he'd retired but it was impossible to think of him without the title.

It took him a second but then he said, "Joanna Hart—no, wait—Kerso. I don't forget much, do I, Angstrom?"

"Nothing at all. Excuse me. I have a customer."

Chief Fowler watched him go with a hint of a smile tugging the corners of his mouth, then turned back to Joanna to ask if her parents were all set for their trip. "Told Ruth I'd keep an eye on you and your little girl, so if anything happens, just give me a call—at home, I mean. I suppose you know we've got a new man in the police department, but he's too busy playing with his computers to be much help in an emergency."

Leave it to Mom to cover all the bases. Joanna promised she'd call if she needed anything and asked to be remembered to his wife. He moved down the rows of vegetables, carefully choosing a bunch of carrots, as she went back to her own shopping. She was picking through a pile of green beans when he took his selection over to be weighed.

"So you're staying in town for the picnic," he said to Miles. She didn't mean to eavesdrop but they were only a few feet away. "Not going to your cabin?"

"No," Miles said shortly. "That'll be seventy-five cents."

"Funny how you keep holding on to that place. Bonnie told me one time you were a man who liked his comforts and it was too rustic for you up there."

It wasn't so much the mention of Bonnie Angstrom's name but the way he said it that made Joanna turn and stare at them. He was looking at Miles the way a stalking cat watches a bird. He held out a dollar bill. "How long's it been now, Angstrom?"

"You know as well as I do." She couldn't see Miles's face but she could hear the stony flatness in his voice. "Eleven years in August."

"Eleven years on August second, to be exact. Like I said, Angstrom, I don't forget much." He accepted his change and then, very deliberately, dropped the bag of fresh vegetables into the trash barrel next to the counter.

Joanna couldn't get the scene between Miles and Chief Fowler out of her mind. After Fowler left, she had watched Miles stand with his body bowed, rigid, wanting to say something to him, but instead she turned away, repelled by the ugly undertones in the conversation. She didn't understand what was going on between the two men. Nasty as it seemed, was Chief Fowler taunting Miles with the old rumors about his wife's affair?

"It's worse than that," her mother said when Joanna told her about the incident. They had tucked Lizzie in bed and gone out on the back porch to sit in the glider in the soft summer twilight, leaving her father to his Auto Club maps. "Amos is a good man and God knows he did a wonderful job all these years, but when it comes to Miles he's completely irrational. He still thinks that Miles—that he . . . did something to Bonnie and little Sarah Ann . . ."

Joanna felt something monstrous creep into a corner of the silky darkness and watch her with red, feral eyes. "But why—was there evidence—something—"

"I don't really know." Her mother sighed. "Amos arrested him but couldn't prove anything. The whole thing was a terrible mess. Amos wouldn't give up. He had most of the farm dug up, looking for the bodies. He wanted to do the same thing at Miles's cabin, but he had no authority up there and he couldn't get a warrant.''

"I can't believe I never knew about this," Joanna said, shaken. "Did you tell me?"

"I'm sure I did. But it was your first year in college and then you had the summer job in Boston. You had other things on your mind, darling."

Joanna shuddered. Somehow it was even more appalling to think that her mother had told her about this horrible thing and she had brushed it aside. "It happened so long ago." *Eleven years on August second, to be exact.* "Why does Chief Fowler keep hounding Miles? Do you think—is there a possibility—"

"Oh, no. Miles could never—he was crazy about his family. Amos—well, it's become an obsession." Ruth added that it was also the reason he was asked to retire. The Town Council would probably have kept him on after he turned sixty-five, if he had dropped his suspicions.

"Can't Miles do anything?"

"I think he probably could. He did get a court order to keep Amos away from his cabin. I sometimes wonder if Miles puts up with this business with Amos because it's a kind of penance, that he still blames himself somehow. Oh, it's all so awful—can't we talk about something else?"

Joanna was glad to drop the subject. She remembered a morning in California, full of pale yellow light and birdsong, when she went out to pick up the paper. The delivery boy had missed the driveway and it lay on the lawn. She never saw the slug, only felt its fat gray body turn to slimy pulp beneath her bare foot. She had that same feeling now. She'd blundered into something repulsive and all she wanted to do was take a long hot bath and forget about it.

11

The morning of the Fourth, Joanna watched the sunrise paint the horizon with crimson streaks. Red skies at morning—how did it go? Not good, she was sure of that.

She'd slept badly, getting up twice to put Lizzie back in bed, but she was determined not to spoil the day. She bounced downstairs, sending the all-clear signal to her mother's questioning eyes, hiding the lie in a frenzy of preparation for the picnic.

She had a bad moment when they arrived at the town green. She'd glossed over the episode with the dog—another lie, might as well admit it. If Lizzie got upset again—but her daughter crossed the street without hesitation and immediately spotted Miles.

"Mr. Angstrom!"

"Lizzie. Joanna." He waved, then went back to turning

hot dogs on a big bricked-in grill, put some in buns and handed them to a noisy group of children.

"Smells great," Joanna said.

"Hungry?"

"I am," Lizzie said. "I'm starving."

"Well, we can't have that." He wore jeans, washed milky blue, and a red tank top that revealed a smooth tanned chest. He had very little body hair at all, Joanna noticed, even on his arms. The sun beat down, fiercely hot, and Joanna could feel sweat trickling down her back, but Miles looked cool and clean. He pointed out the table he'd saved, and Joanna and her parents carried their picnic things over while he prepared a hot dog for Lizzie.

The table sat in a perfect spot, maple-shaded, relatively quiet. On the opposite corner of the green a small carnival lured kids with carousel music and the clank of a minia- ture Ferris wheel.

"Now, if Chief Fowler doesn't come by," Joanna mur- mured to her mother.

"Don't you worry," Ruth said. "I can handle Amos."

As soon as somebody relieved Miles at the grill, he joined them and opened a styrofoam chest filled with bottles of Heineken and cans of pop nestled in crushed ice. Joanna sat on a webbed chaise, gradually relaxing, pleasantly giddy from the beer and the heat, letting her mother field questions from people who stopped to say hello.

Invariably they asked about the trip. And what are your plans, Joanna, after your folks leave? Just call us if you need anything.

I need my mother, Joanna thought.

When the Fowlers came by, Miles and Matt were at the carnival with Lizzie. Why do I worry so much? Joanna wondered. Look how things work out for the best.

Miles waited in line at the refreshment stand watching the merry-go-round begin its slow spin in time to the recorded sound of a calliope. Lizzie was somewhere on the other side with Matt. Miles had wanted to go on the ride but he didn't suggest it. He was spending the whole day with Lizzie. Best not to be greedy.

As the carousel turned, he saw her astride a unicorn on the outer edge. At that distance with the light on her hair . . .

Sarah Ann flying past with Bonnie standing beside her, waving, Daddy, Daddy, look at me . . .

"Mr. Angstrom?"

Startled, he looked up, realizing he'd worked his way to the head of the line.

"Mr. Angstrom, I said, what would you like?"

"Three lemonades," Miles said. "And one cotton candy."

Sarah always loved cotton candy.

Lizzie came back from the carnival sticky and tired, pink from the sun. She curled up with Joanna and fell asleep instantly. Joanna dozed, too, and awakened to find Miles watching, reminding her of the way Tom had looked at them. Why was she surrounded by men with haunted eyes?

Mom saved a surprise until after the fried chicken and potato salad. "Miles and I had a long talk about the kittens, Lizzie. If it's okay with your mom, you can bring one home as soon as it's big enough."

"Oh, can I, Mommy?" For once Lizzie's happiness was uncomplicated by thoughts of her father.

"Of course." Fresh air and sunshine. And a warm little cat to sleep with. Why hadn't she thought of it?

By evening thunderheads boiled in the west, flattened bottoms tinged with purple. Lightning flickered, competing with the fireworks. They sat on blankets to watch skyrockets spangle the darkness. Miles was behind her and when she leaned back, her head touched his shoulder. He cupped her elbows, steadying her, inviting her to stay close.

She wondered if he was drawn to her because of Lizzie. They must be a powerful reminder of what he had lost. What if he wanted to see her again? Well, why not? She wasn't attracted to him the way she was to Tom Blanchard but so what? Chemistry wasn't everything and she had the marital scars to prove it.

It wasn't as though she was planning anything permanent, for pete's sake. With her parents away, it would just be pleasant to have somebody—an adult somebody—around, to talk, to share a meal. And Lizzie liked Miles, which was a plus. If anything else happened . . . well, it happened.

She let her head relax against the bony cradle of his collarbone and felt him shift to mold his body against her. No fireworks except the ones in the sky. It was just—well, *nice* to sit close to him in the velvety blackness, sharing a delight in the brilliant sprays of color that filled the sky.

When the fireworks ended and they were packing up to leave, he said he would call her soon. She told him, truthfully, she would like that. Later, Mom came to say good night and said, "I couldn't help noticing . . . you and Miles. He's quite a bit older, Jo—"

"Oh, Mom. It's nothing like that. Believe me."

"I'm sorry to be a buttinsky. I just worry about you."

She hugged Joanna. "Dad wants to leave about five. You don't have to get up." Joanna clung to her, terrified by the realization they really were going away.

"Take care of yourself," Mom said. "I'll call as often as I can. If anything happens and you need me, darling, just say so and I'll come back. I'll go to the nearest airport and fly home."

"Oh, silly. Lizzie and I are going to have a wonderful summer." Somehow she managed to hold back the tears until she said good night to her father and was back in her room.

During the night it started to rain and the air thickened with the odor of wet, hot earth. Joanna dreamed of damp soil filling her nostrils, a suffocating weight squeezing her lungs. She woke up gasping, heart thumping against her ribs. The dream was so vivid she was afraid to go back to sleep, so she lay there, listening for the muffled sound of her parents slipping out of the house.

She wouldn't get up to say good-bye. She couldn't. If she did, she knew she'd beg them not to leave her alone.

The DC-10 took off from Los Angeles International west over the Pacific. All flights left that way into the prevailing wind, then turned and circled back to head east. From the copilot's seat Tom Blanchard looked down at the coastline where bursts of fireworks rivaled the glittering sweep of the L.A. basin. He'd be home by morning and then he had four days off. He could fill one day with piddling things—a tune-up for the car, some shopping, laundry. Claire's mother had called several times. He really should drive down but he didn't want to go.

He wanted to go to Vermont.

And then what?

Finish cleaning up the cabin. A little fishing with Jack. Oh, sure. Who're you kidding?

He wanted to see Joanna Kerso again.

Kevin McDowell rolled off the girl and lay panting, his skin greasy with sweat. Rain drummed on the hotel's dirty windows, smearing neon reflections into long bloody streaks.

"Don't worry about it, honey," the girl said. "It happens all the time."

"Shut up," he said. "Just shut up."

He got out of bed and put on his clothes, slid his bare feet into his Adidas. What the hell was the matter with him? He couldn't sleep, couldn't fuck—he needed to work, for Chrissake. Take a week off, Galvin had said. Bunch of maniacs running around chopping off heads and they wanted him to take a fucking vacation.

The girl watched as he picked up his revolver, zipped up his windbreaker. She hadn't said a word about the gun. Stupid bitch. He'd seen dozens just like her—shot, knifed, burned, garroted. Bodies turned to hamburger. He'd picked her up in the Combat Zone, shivering in a doorway. Bony, no tits. No wonder he couldn't make it.

A few slugs of vodka remained in the bottle he'd brought with him. He finished it and left, feeling a lot better. Outside the hotel, rain had turned to a fine mist. He couldn't remember where he'd put the car. Didn't really matter because the station was only a few blocks away.

He walked, ducking into doorways, stopping once at a bar to avoid a sudden downpour. When he arrived at the station, it was about two o'clock in the morning. The squad room smelled like wet socks, ancient dirt and cigarette smoke. Phones rang and typewriters clattered, a noise that went on twenty-four hours a day. During the few years he'd spent over in District 13—Area E, city hall called it now—this time of night was so quiet you'd go nuts sitting around waiting. The murderers killed with just as much bloody insanity. They just kept better hours.

Dick Twohy, hunched over a battered Royal at the next desk, looked up from his two-fingered assault. "Hey, Mac. You look like shit, man. What're you doing here?"

Stupid question. All this fucking work. Stacks of folders for current cases. More in the cabinet. Unsolved. Going back five, six years. Even a few from the Thirteenth that he kept hoping—

"Mac, are you crazy?" Twohy stood over him, face like a big white moon. "If the captain sees you—go home, man. You're drunk."

"I'm not drunk. I had a drink but I'm not drunk. Jesus Christ, I just came in to get a little work done."

He fumbled open the cabinet, pulling files at random. Some of the contents spilled on the floor. A picture stared up at him. Two people sat on a sun-drenched pier, water sparkling behind them. He picked it up. "See this? Happened over at the Thirteenth. This woman disappeared. Just went out to buy some Cheerios and poof—gone. Blood in the car. No body, nothing. But she's dead, Twohy. I know it. And this son of a bitch—" He put his finger on the man's smiling face.

"Mac, will you listen to me? That was a hell of a mess you walked into the other night. All that blood—"

Blood.

On his shoes.

Still there. A rusty stain edging the sole.

He stared at the picture in his hands and couldn't remember who it was.

"McDowell!" Captain Galvin stood at the door to his office and yelled across the room. He waited until McDowell stood up and walked over, then went back to his desk. "Shut the door."

McDowell discovered he still had the picture in his hand. He folded it up and shoved it into his pocket.

"What the hell are you doing here?" Galvin was stringy, juiceless. He wore five-hundred-dollar suits that always looked like they came from the bargain basement at Filene's.

"Just catching up on the paperwork, Captain."

"Paperwork, hell. I've had it with you, McDowell. Everybody's had it with you. Do I have to spell it out? Lay off the booze. Get your shit together or you're out on your ass, understand? Now, go on. You got a week's suspension to go with your vacation time. Come back before it's up and I'll give you some more."

He felt numb, and there was a high-pitched buzzing in his head. Everybody in the squad room got busy when he walked out of Galvin's office, except for Twohy, who hovered by the door, muttering, "Well, shit, Mac. I tried to tell you."

McDowell shook his head, afraid if he opened his mouth he would vomit. He stumbled downstairs and went out in the rainy darkness. Kept walking until he found someplace warm and dry where he could get a drink and have a smoke.

He woke up about three o'clock the next afternoon still in the same clothes. His lip was split and his eye puffed up. He had a vague memory of being thrown out of a bar.

As he inched his way to the shower, he found the folded picture in his pocket and smoothed it out.

No problem remembering who the people were today. Claire Blanchard, missing for three years. And Tom Blanchard, grieving husband.

What else are you, Blanchard?

He threw the picture in the wastebasket. Didn't matter. Everybody had forgotten about the case. Except him. And he didn't need the picture to remind him.

12

Lizzie lay in the grass and watched a bumblebee in the honeysuckle hedge. He was fat and black with yellow stripes on his stomach. He lurched around the white flowers, his heavy buzzing the only sound except the *swip swip* of the big shears her mother used to trim the hedge at the other end of the yard.

Lizzie could feel the warm ground beneath the grass. The flowers smelled sweet, sweeter than the overripe strawberries Mr. Angstrom let her help pick out and throw away yesterday.

"I know what I'm gonna name my kitten," she had told him. "Strawberry—'cause that's where he was born. Do you think that's a good name?"

"Well, it might be quite a mouthful. Just like this." He

took two huge red berries and popped one in her mouth, one in his.

She chewed blissfully, dribbling juice down her chin, and leaned over to look in the box where the kittens slept in a fluffy pile. Hers was all white except for a pink nose and a gray spot behind his ears. "Well, then," she had said, "I can always call him Berry for short."

Her pad of paper and Crayolas lay on the grass next to her. She'd tried to draw a picture of Berry, but it was hard to make a white cat. The sun glinted off the paper, so she turned her head and stared down the hedge toward Mommy. The sun gleamed on the shears, too.

Ss-wip ss-wip. It sounded like Mommy was mad at the honeysuckle. She'd been acting like that since Gramma and Grampa left. Sort of angry and sad at the same time. And she worked all the time, polishing Gramma's furniture or cutting the grass. Yesterday Lizzie heard Mr. Angstrom ask if Mommy would like to go to dinner. "Maybe in a few days," Mommy had said. "I've got so much to do."

Last night when Lizzie went to hide from the Bogeyman she heard Mommy crying and this morning her eyes were red and her nose was stuffed up. It made Lizzie sad, too. And she didn't want to be sad. She liked it here at Gramma's and she wasn't so scared anymore. Maybe she had been wrong. Maybe the Bogeyman wasn't going to come, after all.

Sswip sswip, the shears whispered.

So warm. So many smells. Honeysuckle, syrupy sweet. Waxy crayons. The greeny scent of cut leaves.

Sswip sswip. The bumblebee staggered in the white blossoms and—something else there, white and fluffy.

92

"Berry," Lizzie said. "What are you doing here?"

The kitten stood on his hind legs and tried to swat the bee. The bee staggered off and Berry followed it down the hedge toward where Mommy was working.

Ss-WIP Ss-WIP. Blades flashed.

Mommy, Mommy, watch out for my kitty—but it wasn't Mommy using the shears. It was *him*.

I found you, Lizzie.

And the shiny blades.

SWIP SWIP SWIP.

"Ber-rreee!" Lizzie screamed.

The sound sliced Joanna like an icy scalpel. She dropped the garden shears and ran.

Lizzie lay on her stomach, elbows bent as if she were trying to get up. She was chalk white and staring . . . staring at Joanna. No, not *at* her. *Through* her toward some horror that caused that long keening shriek.

"Sweet Jesus. Lizzie?"

Joanna picked her up. The stiff little body shook with tremors. If it was a convulsion . . . keep her from biting her tongue. Force her mouth open. Nothing to use but her fingers and pray God . . . Lizzie drew a rattling breath. The trembling stopped and her eyes focused on Joanna.

"Oh, baby. Are you okay? Are you all right?"

Lizzie's mouth was dirty from Joanna's fingers, but her color was better. "Mommy, Mommy. Berry's dead."

"Who?"

"My kitty." Tears spilled down her cheeks. "First it was you, Mommy, but then it was *him* and—and Berry was all bloody and—"

"Lizzie, darling, your kitty's not here. He's at Mr.

93

Angstrom's, remember? We can't bring him home until next week."

"He's dead," Lizzie sobbed. "He's dead and the Bogeyman killed him. I *saw* him."

Damn it to hell this can't be happening. I did what the doctor said and it can't be *happening*.

"No, Lizzie," she said sharply. "It was a dream. You must have fallen asleep."

"I wasn't s-s-sleeping. I was dr-dr-drawing and—"

Sunlight shimmered on the paper pad. Squiggly black lines formed a round body, a round cat face. In the middle of the body a piece of crayon had melted into a red, runny blob.

"Oh, Lizzie, look." Joanna felt giddy with relief. "You did fall asleep and your mind played a trick on you. You had a nightmare, baby, right in the middle of the day."

"—n-n-not a dream. It was him. I saw him—"

"Shh, hush," Joanna said as she carried Lizzie inside and called Dr. Henderson. She explained about the dream and told him her daughter might have had a convulsion.

"Should I bring her into the office?" Joanna asked. "Or should we go to the emergency room—"

"Now, Joanna, just calm down." After a lot of questions, he said it didn't sound like a convulsion to him. Probably just another nightmare. "These things take time, Joanna. You have to be patient. Watch the child closely the rest of the day and, of course, if she has any more problems, give me a call."

"If you're sure," Joanna said.

"I am," he said firmly. "And remember, your reaction is going to be the thing that influences Lizzie the most."

She knew he was right. She took Lizzie out to the glider

and rocked her, murmuring soothing words. But Lizzie kept repeating, "Berry's dead, Mommy. He's dead," heart-broken and inconsolable.

This has got to stop, Joanna thought. She has to know that nothing happened to that damn cat.

And if something *had* happened, if Lizzie had a—what?—some kind of clairvoyant flash? Crazy—but there was one way to find out. She put Lizzie in the car and drove straight to Angstrom's Acres. Miles looked up, startled, as she walked in with Lizzie in her arms.

"She's worried about her kitten," Joanna explained. "I just wanted her to see that he's all right."

The little white cat was curled up in the box sound asleep. So much for ESP, Joanna thought as Lizzie stroked him. She leaned against the strawberry table, suddenly exhausted. Her shoulders ached from carrying Lizzie, and pain throbbed in her temples.

Lizzie was tired, too, and she didn't protest when her mother said it was time to go home. In the car she leaned against Joanna, limp and sweaty. Joanna was sweaty, too, and green plant juice stained her hands.

"I think we both need a bath," she told Lizzie. "And then a nap." When the little girl's eyes widened in alarm, she added, "You can sleep in my bed with me. I need a nap, too."

After a lilac-perfumed soak, she swallowed aspirin, pulled the blinds and lay beside Lizzie in the cool darkness.

Maybe she shouldn't listen to Dr. Henderson. A professional—say it, a psychiatrist. Was she putting off getting help for Lizzie because she was afraid of what he'd tell her? It's your fault, Mrs. Kerso. You made a bloody mess of things and now your daughter is paying for it.

I have to stop this, she thought. Stop borrowing trouble. Bob Henderson wasn't a specialist but he had doctored a lot of kids, including her. He said it would take some time and a lot of love and she was sure he knew what he was talking about.

She stroked the fine hair curling damply around Lizzie's pointed face. My baby . . . so small. Bones like a bird, skin soft as feathers.

If anybody tried to hurt her—he'd have to kill me first.

The fierce surge of protectiveness didn't surprise her. She'd felt it the moment the doctor placed Lizzie on her stomach seconds after she was born and it was always there, simply a part of her. But knowing exactly what she'd do if the threat came from something made of flesh and bone was one thing. How could she keep Lizzie safe from a monster who existed only in her daughter's mind?

As soon as Lizzie was soundly asleep, Joanna slipped out of bed, pulled on shorts and a T-shirt and went to put away the garden tools. That done, she prowled the house with a dustcloth, polishing surfaces that already gleamed.

You wanted this, she told herself. Time alone, to sort things out, make some decisions. She wasn't going back to California. She'd known that from the moment she phoned Mom that she was coming home. But beyond that—a job, school, actually filing for a divorce . . .

Not now. It was too damn much to handle on top of this thing with Lizzie . . .

Immediate problems were better. Supper. Hamburgers, she supposed. Lizzie might be tempted with that. She was taking patties from the freezer when the phone rang.

"Joanna? It's Tom Blanchard. I'm over at my cottage. How about dinner?"

They sat on benches at tables covered with red-checked plastic cloths. She and Tom shared something called Glutton's Delight, and Lizzie ate a small cheese pizza.

"I think we both needed this," Joanna said. "Thank you."

When Tom had suggested they bring Lizzie along, she didn't think the little girl would be up to it, but the idea of going out for pizza worked a miraculous cure. After all that worrying, here was Lizzie stuffing her face and begging to play Pac Man after dinner.

Joanna agreed to a couple of games in the arcade next door. "A five-year-old video game freak," she said. "Do you believe it?" Tom drove them home and suggested a walk. If Lizzie had any qualms about being in the yard, she didn't show it, but Joanna steered clear of the honeysuckle hedge. While Lizzie chased fireflies in the big field in back of the house, she and Tom sat on a log.

"The other night," he began, then fell silent.

"You don't have to talk about it. Just because I'm a blabbermouth—"

"We're a hell of a pair," he said wryly. "But I would like to see you again." He had to be back in Boston tomorrow but he would have several days off the following week. He promised to call.

They watched a fat yellow moon come up and then started back to the house, Tom carrying a tired Lizzie. He took the child upstairs, laid her on the bed and said quietly, "I think I'd better go. Stay here. I can see myself out."

"She'll be okay." Joanna put Leon in Lizzie's arms and followed him out the door and down the stairs. "You don't have to rush off." Stay here. Hold me. Sleep with me. "I'll make some coffee."

She was on the last step, so she could look directly into his eyes. Not brown at all, she saw, but a dark hazel touched with yellow and green.

He reached out, ran his fingertips down her face and slid his thumb across her lips. She felt as though she were melting inside. "If I stay for coffee, I'll never leave. It seems to me we ought to think about this, Joanna. Neither of us needs any more scars."

Every nerve in her body shrieked with longing but she said, "I guess so, it's just—you will call me?"

"As soon as I get back to Boston. Let's not rush this, Joanna. We've got lots of time."

Lizzie listened sleepily to the voices from downstairs. Mr. Blanchard's made a low rumble. Mommy's was higher, kind of like a song. Lizzie's eyelids felt heavy, but she forced them open and looked carefully around the room.

There was no sign of *him*. Mommy said it had all been a dream, and Berry *was* just fine. But the way he grinned at her with his awful melty face—he looked so real, almost like somebody she knew, and what he said . . . *I found you, Lizzie*.

She shivered and hugged Leon. She wished Mr. Blanchard would stay here. Mommy would like that, too, she could tell. Mommy looked so pretty tonight. She wore a white skirt and a silky pink blouse. Her hair was all fluffy and smelled like flowers. If Mr. Blanchard stayed, they could have pizza every night and take walks together and he could sleep in the extra bedroom next to Lizzie. Unless . . .

What if Mr. Blanchard wanted to sleep with Mommy in her bed? Maybe they would lock the door so they could do that thing that grown-ups did and then the Bogeyman would come and they'd never hear Lizzie, or they would say, Not right now, Lizzie, go back to sleep, or maybe . . .

The bedroom door opened and Mommy came in. Lizzie could hear Mr. Blanchard's car starting up outside.

The words tumbled out before she could stop them. "Mommy, are you going to leave me with Gramma and go live with Mr. Blanchard?"

"Lizzie! What a silly question." Mommy sat down on the bed. Her cheeks looked pink and her lipstick was smeary. "Mr. Blanchard and I are just friends and anyway, I'm never going to leave you, don't you know that?"

"Daddy did."

"Well, I won't. Not ever." She cupped Lizzie's face and kissed her nose. "Now, let's get you ready for bed, young lady. We've got a big day tomorrow."

"What are we going to do?" Lizzie held up her arms for the pj top.

"We'll go to the mall down in Springfield and buy tons of stuff. Maybe we could get some things for the kitten. A litter box and food, of course. How about a squeaky mouse?"

Lizzie could see the big shears and Berry's bloody fur. "I don't want the kitty anymore. I'm gonna give him back."

"Sweetie, what are you talking about? I thought you loved him."

The place behind Lizzie's eyes filled with big, hot tears

99

and her chest hurt. "I can't bring him here. The Bogeyman is going to do something awful. Please, Mommy, I don't want him here."

"Oh, Lizzie, what am I going to do with you? Don't cry, darling. If you don't want the cat, I'm not going to force you, but—let's talk about it tomorrow, okay?"

She wiped Lizzie's face with a Kleenex and said, "Now, blow," then kissed her good night. Lizzie lay in the darkness, hugging Leon. Berry would be safe and she ought to feel better, but she felt all empty inside. What if Mommy was right? If seeing the Bogeyman hurt Berry had really been just a dream . . .

I found you, Lizzie.

She pulled the covers over her head and squeezed Leon tight. Mommy was wrong and now it wouldn't do any good to get out of bed and hide.

The Bogeyman knew where she was.

13

I SEE YOU, LIZZIE

Nothing Joanna said could change Lizzie's mind about the cat. When Joanna took her to Angstrom's, Lizzie held the kitten, stroking its fur—grieving, Joanna saw, pain twisting in her own heart at the bleakness on Lizzie's face.

"She had a nightmare," Joanna told Miles. "And now she's convinced something will happen to the cat if she brings it home. Maybe I shouldn't pay any attention to it but—" How could she explain without opening that whole can of ugly, unexplainable worms?

"Tell you what, Lizzie." Miles balanced on his heels next to the little girl. "Berry can still be your kitten but he can live with me and you can visit him whenever you like. Then if you ever want to take him home, there'll be no problem."

Lizzie's face filled with relief and joy. "Oh, can I? Oh, thank you, Mr. Angstrom."

"Miles, you're a lifesaver." Joanna watched Lizzie chase after two of the kittens who had escaped the box.

"Glad to help." He was dressed, as usual, in jeans and a light cotton shirt, everything immaculately clean. Plain brown hair lay neatly against his narrow skull, faintly marked by comb tracks. "How about that dinner date you promised me?"

"Well—" She'd already put him off once, and there was no reason not to accept his invitation, but after her evening with Tom—

"Lizzie can come along, too, of course," Miles added.

Lizzie heard her name and hurried over. "Me, too, what?"

He swung her up on a counter. "I asked your mom if the two of you would like to go to dinner."

"Oh, boy," Lizzie said. "Can we get pizza like we did when Mr. Blanchard took us out?"

"We'll think about it," Joanna said, trying to avoid Miles's eyes.

"Guess you're not quite as lonely as I thought," he said, toneless. "Sorry, Joanna, I didn't know you were dating somebody."

"He's just a friend," she said defensively.

"Mr. Blanchard flies airplanes," Lizzie said. "He's real nice."

"I'm sure he is." A bitter smile thinned Miles's lips.

"Oh, for pete's sake," Joanna said. "Just because Tom— listen, Miles, we'd love to have dinner with you. Give me a call, okay?"

*　　*　　*

Now, why in the world did I say that? she wondered on the way home. And why should she feel guilty about seeing Tom? Dammit, it was none of Miles's business. She had been friendly to the man, that's all. If he wanted to read something into it, that was his problem.

On the seat next to her, Lizzie kept up a stream of questions. "Are we really going for pizza with Mr. Angstrom, Mommy? Are we going tonight? Can I play Pac Man? Could we bring Berry?"

"Lizzie, *please*. Mr. Angstrom's very busy so let's just cool it, okay?"

"But you said—"

"I said I'd think about it."

A few beats of silence, then, "Don't you like Mr. Angstrom, Mommy?"

"Well, of course I do."

I just don't want to have dinner with him. Simple enough. When he calls, I'll say no. I mean, I'm so *good* at it.

Look at how long it took her to say no to Walt. No, I will not stand for your screwing around. No, I will not be a doormat just for Lizzie's sake.

Oh, to hell with it. Tom would be back in a few days and she simply was not going to spoil the anticipation by worrying about Miles.

She stayed away from Angstrom's, trying to distract Lizzie with long walks in the mornings, games and books in the afternoon. The day they went to the mall in Springfield she had bought new pillows for the glider—a thick pad for the wooden seat, some squashy throws—all done in leafy greens and blues. She made pitchers of icy lemonade and they sat there in the dense shade, rocking, while she read to Lizzie—"Winnie the Pooh" and "The Wind in the Willows." Around them the long afternoons flowed past with a peculiar underwater quality.

She surfaced only when the phone rang, walking into the kitchen slowly, relieved when it wasn't Miles. She just wasn't up to making excuses. Except for Mom checking in, the calls were unimportant. Salesmen, friends who didn't know the Harts were away. For once Joanna could truthfully report to her mother that things were normal. Lizzie finally seemed adjusted to sleeping in her own bed.

Of course since she hadn't told Mom about the nightmare that day in the backyard, she had to add another lie about bringing the cat home. Lizzie had sneezed while holding the animal. An allergy maybe, like her father. If lying really did make noses grow, she'd have Pinocchio beat all to hell.

On Thursday Tom called from Los Angeles, the satellite connection varying from next-door clarity to tin-can echoes. His schedule has been changed. He would arrive in Boston late tomorrow with only two days off. Then he had to deadhead back to Los Angeles because he'd been assigned the L.A.–Honolulu flight.

"You mean I'm not going to see you?" Wild schemes for driving into Boston percolated in her head. Could she find a baby-sitter? Did she have enough nerve to suggest it?

"Oh, I'll be up," he reassured her. "But only for the day." He'd come on Saturday. Whatever she and Lizzie wanted to plan was fine with him.

"Let's not plan anything," she said. "I'll make dinner and then—later—we can just . . . talk."

God, she thought after she hung up, did that sound as suggestive as I think it did?

Friday passed in a happy blur. She shopped in town—steaks and all the ingredients for a salad at the supermarket—brushing aside Lizzie's plaintive request to go see Berry. She felt sure she emitted a pre-foreplay glow that Miles would pick up.

He called Saturday morning to ask them to dinner while she was toweling her hair. "Oh. Sorry, Miles, but—" Lizzie came down with typhoid? I broke both my legs? "Well, I've made other plans."

"I see." Pleasant enough, but she was sure he knew exactly what her plans were. "Is it all right if I call you again next week?"

"Sure," she said. "Of course."

Good show, Joanna. Saying no is the best thing you do.

Joanna dried her hair in the sun, the liquid warmth seeping into her bones and staying there while she dressed. Over her sheerest bra and panties she wore a gauzy blouse that matched the peachy tones in an India-print wrap-around skirt bordered by elephants.

They had been up early, and by late afternoon Lizzie was heavy-eyed and cranky, but Joanna didn't push for a nap. Maybe if Lizzie was tired enough, she'd go to bed early.

Tom arrived in plenty of time for a leisurely drink before starting charcoal to grill the steaks. Lizzie scarcely left them alone for a minute, but the child's presence seemed to encode everything Tom and Joanna said with double meanings.

"Lovely twilights this time of year." *Lizzie can't stay up forever. And then . . .*

"The moon will be out later." *. . . and then we'll watch it together.*

Visions of the night ahead swam in Joanna's mind, luminous with possibilities. With Lizzie watching, she tried not to touch Tom, but she seemed to be constantly brushing against him—fingertips, breasts, thighs. The windows in the dining room were open. A warm breeze ruffled her hair, drenched her in the sweetness of honeysuckle and roses as she took away the dinner plates and served melon for Tom and herself, chocolate ice cream for Lizzie.

The little girl propped her cheek on one hand, stirred her dessert to an icy mush.

"All done?" Joanna asked, reaching for the dish.

"No, I want it." She ate tiny dabs while they had coffee.

"You've had a long day, sweetie," Joanna said, her nerves stretched to the breaking point. "I think you'd better say good night now."

Lizzie's eyes were full of ancient knowing. "I'm not sleepy. I wanta go for a walk. I wanta catch lightning bugs."

"Not tonight," Joanna said firmly. *I love you, baby, but I have to have this time—I need it.* "I'll be down in a minute," she said to Tom. "Why don't we have brandy on the back porch?"

He waited for her in the glider. Through the branches of the sugar maple, the sky faded from mauve to plum, the soft darkness touched with gold from the moon that was still below the horizon.

He hadn't bothered with the brandy and there was no need for words. The softness of the new pillows, her clothes sliding away so easily—Good Lord, she thought, delighted. I must have planned the whole thing.

Sleep hummed in Lizzie's head, even though she fought it. For the longest time she couldn't hear Mommy and Mr. Blanchard talking. She knew they were on the back porch because her room was just above it, and she could hear the creaky sound of the glider swinging back and forth. Then they started whispering and laughing, and she hated them both because they made her stay up here all alone.

" 'S not fair, Leon," she mumbled, burying her face in his mane.

She slept and then she was wide awake. Her ear pressed against Leon and she could hear her heart pounding. Something had awakened her but she didn't know what it was. Mommy and Mr. Blanchard were swinging again, their voices very soft. Maybe the moonlight woke her up. It was so bright coming through the window that it made shadows on her wall.

She lay there, listening, a bubble of fear forming in her stomach, rising to her throat. She could feel all the little hairs on her arm standing up. Moonlight spilled on the wood floor, making a golden path to the window. She pushed back the sheet, sat up, swung her legs over the edge of the bed. Moonlight felt warm on her feet as she walked over to the window.

Maple leaves were black and lacy, the tree trunk heavy and black, moving—not the tree but something beside it. A black paper doll. *Him.*

The moonlight felt like ice now, like cold water pouring

over her. If he looked up, saw her, if he knew she was all by herself . . . but after a while she knew she was safe for tonight. He didn't see her because he was busy watching Mommy and Mr. Blanchard.

14

Just before dawn, cool breezes and mosquitoes drove them indoors, but only as far as the couch. The house was dark. Starshine through an open window illuminated Joanna's satiny skin.

"Not here." She pulled away, tilting her head to listen. "Lizzie might come down. I've got a perfectly good bed upstairs."

"I have to go anyway." He kissed her lips, a good-bye touch. "It's after three."

"Now? Why? Lord, I'm freezing. Stay right there while I get a robe."

She came back, wrapped in a blue terry-cloth robe, and sat on the couch, one foot tucked beneath her, watching him dress. Her slender body looked fuller, lush. Happiness softened the taut face.

"Why do I feel like we've played this scene before?" she asked.

"You mean last week?" He reached for his shirt and wound up smoothing her tangled hair. "That was quite a speech I gave. Something about scars."

"Ah, yes, scars." She gave him a wicked grin. "Appendectomy, wasn't it?"

Her fingers touched a spot just below his belt, tracing the path her lips had made earlier. He felt himself harden in response, and a part of his mind calculated how tired he would be, if he'd even have the energy to leave. Gently he took her wrist, pulled her hand away.

"Sorry, love, but I have to go. You wouldn't want to start a lot of gossip, would you?"

"No, you're right. Especially not now. I'd just as soon not give Walt any kind of ammunition—for the divorce wars, you know. And then there's Lizzie . . ." She was silent for a moment. "It scares her, Tom. You and me. Everything. My poor baby. I wish there was time to tell you . . ."

"What?"

"It'll keep—till you come back. You will come back?"

He held her tightly, kissed her, memorizing the feel of her body, the taste of her mouth. He was halfway back to Boston before he realized that he had never answered her question.

You will come back?

That was easy enough. He doubted he could stay away. *Why* he'd return—that wasn't so simple. Sex was the obvious answer. There'd been damn little of it the past three years. A few hasty, unsatisfying encounters—shut a door, turn a corner, boom, forgotten. Nothing like last night. So—it was good sex. For Joanna, too. What was wrong with that?

Not the time to think about it, not now with no sleep and his stomach rumbling with hunger. He stopped at Howard Johnson's for a huge breakfast, then finished the drive home in record time. Early Sunday morning only a few churchgoers and fishermen were out. The streets were eerily deserted.

Yesterday he'd stopped at the apartment briefly to shower and change and pack an overnight bag. The place was a mess. Dust, discarded clothing, a week's worth of mail sorted quickly into bills, sales pitches and one letter—from Claire's mother. He tapped it against his palm. The hell with it. He'd read it later after he had a few hours' sleep and could think straight.

A red light on the Record-a-Call indicated a message, but there was only a hiss on the tape, no sound of a dial tone that meant somebody had called and then hung up. It had happened before, an intermittent malfunction that left the service department scratching its collective head. Should he check in with the dispatcher? Hell with that, too.

Too tired to get undressed, he slipped off his shoes and went to lie on the bed in the apartment's one small bedroom. The mattress was hard and unyielding. It came from the guest room in their house in Brookline, the double-bed proportions too small for him, but he'd picked what would fit in the apartment and stored the rest, winding up with bits and pieces of his life that never quite added up to a whole.

Just as he drifted off to sleep, the telephone rang. Let the answering machine get it, but it might not be working, and if it was the dispatcher . . .

It was Claire's mother. "Tom, we haven't heard from you in such a long time. Did you get my letter?"

"I don't know, Emily. I just got in and haven't had time to go through the mail."

You're the world's worst liar, Claire used to say. Good thing her mother couldn't see his face.

"Oh, I see. Well, Everett and I—we wondered if you'd decided about finding a new detective agency."

"Emily—"

"I know it's expensive," she went on quickly. "But we thought—Everett has this small insurance policy we can cash in. We want to do it, Tom. We can't just—give up."

"It's been three years." And during that time Everett Whittiger had changed from a vigorous man to an anxious, embittered recluse with one mild coronary as a warning. "We're going to have to face it sooner or later . . . she's gone, Emily."

"How can you say that? You hear stories all the time— Claire might've lost her memory, be out there sick, wandering around—or some maniac may have her. Did you read about that woman in California? A man kept her chained up in a box for years—" Her voice thickened. He knew she was crying. "How can you just forget her?"

"I haven't forgotten." But he had, last night, for a little while.

"Then why are you doing this? You've never forgiven me, have you? What I did—you're holding it against me."

"That's not true." His head throbbed with a sudden vicious pain centered behind his right eye.

"She's my child. She came to me and I helped her. What else could I do? And now I can't stop thinking—

what if—maybe that's the cause—maybe her mind snapped and—''

"Stop it, Emily, for God's sake." He massaged his temple; sparkles of light danced on his retinas. "You're upset and I'm dead tired." He explained about the L.A.–Honolulu assignment and promised to come up to the Cape when he got back.

"And you'll think about another detective agency—please, Tom."

"I'll think about it."

He went to the bathroom, swallowed two Percodan and came back to lie with his arm across his eyes to shut out the light. Poor Emily. She carried as big a load of guilt as he did. If she'd said something right away . . . but he didn't blame her. She was wrong about that. The only person he couldn't forgive was himself.

"Are you sure you know where we're going?" Ruth peered out at another nameless lake, sparkled by afternoon sunlight.

"North," Matt said comfortably.

"That helps a lot." She thought about dense woods giving way to muskeg and tundra. "I suppose there are telephones."

"Ruth, don't you think it's about time you stopped worrying about Joanna? She's a grown woman."

"I know. It's just—" How could she explain the bone-deep fear that wouldn't go away? Especially to somebody as rational as Matt.

"Comes a time, mother hen," Matt said, "when the chicks have to scratch for themselves."

"Maybe I am being silly—but she hides things from me, Matt."

"Well, sure she does. She gets it from her mother."

"Matt, what a thing to say." But it was bluster and she knew it. Because she did keep secrets—mostly small and unimportant, but necessary because a long time ago she had slipped into the role of a one-woman road crew, surreptitiously filling potholes and smoothing asphalt over the surface of everybody's life. And Matt knew it.

It was the reason he could say vaguely, "Oh, you take care of it, Ruth," and bury himself happily in his business or his books.

Although she was satisfied most of the time, occasionally she wanted to scream at him for his myopic view of things. But after thirty-five years of marriage she was stuck with the situation.

"Okay," she said. "I'll try to stop worrying about her as long as I can check in every couple of days."

"Deal," Matt said, slowing down and turning off a rutted side road toward the lake. "Now, what do you say to some blue fin for lunch?"

After church, Amos Fowler drove out of Maple Grove on County 15 and headed for Angstrom's Acres. He'd parked the car in the shade during the service, but it was still hot inside. When he retired, the Town Council let him buy the Dodge Charger and he liked the car's full-throated hum, but it gulped gasoline especially when the air conditioner was on. Next to him, Hattie, thinning hair pinned up in a bun, sweated in her dark Sunday dress, looking as though she were sucking a persimmon.

She hated going to Angstrom's, but she'd given up her

114

feeble protests of "It's the Lord's day, Amos, and it just doesn't seem—well—right somehow," after he thundered back, "Right? You think it's right for a murderer to go free? You think the Lord likes that?"

Of course that wasn't what really bothered her and he knew it. She was worried about what people would think, what they might say. But she'd soon learned to keep her mouth shut.

There were quite a few cars in the shady parking area next to Angstrom's, including a light blue patrol car with Mort Lankersheim leaning on the hood. Fowler pulled in beside it. Hattie slumped down as though she wanted to hide under the dashboard. Fowler ignored her, loosening his tie and taking off his jacket as he got out, then tossing them into the back seat and closing the door.

Sunlight filtering through the overhead leaves glinted off Lankersheim's glasses. He was a weasly man with a sagging butt and narrow shoulders. Jesus God, Fowler thought, disgusted. Maple Grove better pray this guy never had to catch a real criminal.

"Lankersheim." He nodded curtly.

"Amos. I thought you'd be stopping by."

"Ayuh. Real good detective work. Musta used your computer."

A slight flush colored Lankersheim's sallow face. "It might be better if we had this discussion in my office," Lankersheim said.

Old man Fitzhugh idled past, eyes bright with curiosity.

"This official?" When Lankersheim shook his head, Fowler added, "Then say what you got to say and let me get on with my business."

"All right." Lankersheim took out a folded handkerchief and mopped his receding forehead where the skin was mottled with red.

Serves the damn fool right for not wearing his hat, Fowler thought.

"What you're doing here comes close to harassment," Lankersheim went on, "and a lot of people don't like it."

"Has Angstrom complained?"

"No, but—"

"Then you got no business here."

"Not now, maybe. But one of these days Miles is going to put a stop to this and then it will be my business."

Fowler clenched his hands, blood throbbing in his head, and watched Lankersheim walk back to the car. Little shit-for-brains, what did he know? What did any of them know? A goddamn murderer walking around in their midst and he was the only one who had sense enough to recognize him. The only one, he thought grimly as he walked toward the tables of brightly colored vegetables, who could do anything about it.

15

Lizzie slept late, so Joanna was able to sleep in, too. She awakened feeling more rested than she had in weeks. Didn't they say sex was better than Seconal? Lizzie only wanted cereal for breakfast. Barefoot and still in her night-shirt, Joanna carried her second cup of coffee out to the glider and sat there to sip it, staring dreamily at the green sweep of yard and field.

"Mommy?" Lizzie stood in the kitchen doorway. "I finished my Fruity Pebbles. Can I go swing now?"

"Sure, baby."

Lizzie had dressed herself this morning. Orange shorts and a purple Care Bear T-shirt. Not the greatest color coordination but a wonderful sign. She had been a very independent little girl until the past six months, when she'd regressed to the clinging insecurity of a toddler.

Joanna watched her running across the yard, skinny little legs working. Maybe Lizzie was over the worst of it. Please, God, let it be true.

"Come push me, Mommy," Lizzie called.

The grass was cool and damp beneath Joanna's feet. She wore nothing under the nightshirt. It covered her fanny, but just barely. Plenty of trees and enough distance between the houses guaranteed privacy, but what if somebody dropped by? Don't be a prude, Joanna. So you'll sit in the swing and hold Lizzie on your lap.

She told Lizzie to hang on tight and sent the swing flying. After a couple of good pushes she stepped back. "Pump, Lizzie. Remember how I showed you? Use your knees." She put a hand on the tree trunk, leaning, the feel of the rough bark like touching an old friend. Up there was the branch that had been lookout, headquarters, refuge. And where was the heart she and Mikey Matusak had carved when they were twelve years old?

She moved a few steps, looking at the back of the tree. Big yellow-white patches scarred the bark, freshly made, the living core chipped and gouged. Sap trickled like blood from a wound.

"Damn it." Sick fury rose in her throat as she stared at the maimed trunk. Somebody had used—a hatchet? A knife? Whatever, the heart was gone, that preteen love as real as anything she'd ever felt, erased, hacked away.

"What is it, Mommy?" Lizzie had left the swing to stand beside her.

"Somebody—kids—sick little monsters—look what they did. If I get my hands on them—"

"It wasn't kids, Mommy," Lizzie said. "*He* did it."

"Oh, for God's sake—" The Bogeyman again. Always

and forever the goddamn Bogeyman. She grabbed Lizzie and pulled the child in front of her, cupped the small face and held it so Lizzie had to stare at the maimed tree trunk. "Look at that. That was done by a real live person, not somebody from one of your dreams."

"But I saw him, Mommy—I saw him. Standing right there last night, watching you and Mr. Blanchard."

Joanna felt her skin crawl. Was it possible? Was Lizzie having another one of her nightmares or had she really seen somebody down here last night? Watching while she and Tom made love in the glider . . .

"Let's go inside, Lizzie." She tugged at the nightshirt, suddenly aware of how short the damn thing was and how her nipples were plainly visible through the thin fabric.

"But, Mommy—"

"Don't argue."

In the kitchen she locked the screen, the first time she could ever remember doing that in her life.

"It's all right, Mommy," Lizzie said quietly. "He's not out there now."

"Oh, Lizzie." Hysteria bubbled in the back of her throat. She could feel that high-wire demarcation between rationality and gibbering lunacy. "I want you to stop this crazy nonsense, you hear me?"

"But I *saw* him—"

"No, you didn't. You might've seen a person, a real person—" She could hear her voice rising, could see Lizzie cringing away, knew she was shouting and couldn't stop herself. "You might've seen a kid or a nasty old Peeping Tom, but you didn't—*you did not see the Bogeyman!*"

Lizzie burst into tears. She sat down on the floor as though her legs had folded up and she wept.

"Oh, Lizzie, baby—" Joanna sat beside the little girl, gathering her up. "I'm sorry. I didn't mean to yell. Don't cry, honey. Please."

She rocked Lizzie, feeling the flood of tears and mucus soaking through her thin nightshirt. She talked softly, explaining that she'd yelled because she was a little bit scared, that grown-ups get scared, too, that it was scary to think about somebody creeping around the house. "I want to call the police about it, so I need to know for sure if you saw anything. Do you understand, Lizzie?"

"Yuh—yuh—yes."

"Then tell Mommy exactly what happened."

"I wo-woked up and I was afraid."

"Of what? Did you have a bad dream?"

"N-no. I was just—afraid—and I went over to the window and I saw h-him—by the tree."

Further questions made it clear that the child had only seen a dim shape in the shadows, nothing else. Maybe she hadn't seen anything at all. Still, the tree had been vandalized and it couldn't hurt to report it to the police.

Lizzie's T-shirt was a mess, too, so Joanna sent the child up to wash her face and change while she made the call. The man who answered identified himself as Officer Stimson, sounding young and trying hard to be briskly official. He listened politely to Joanna's report, asked her to wait and put her on hold. To her surprise, a few seconds later the call was picked up by a man who said he was the chief of police, Morton Lankersheim.

"Stimson tells me you may have some trouble out there, Mrs. Kerso. A prowler, you think?"

"I'm not sure." She described the damage to the tree and told him Lizzie might've seen somebody.

"So this guy was just standing there?"

Watching you and Mr. Blanchard . . .

. . . naked in the pillow-banked glider, her legs wrapped around Tom, her hips rising to meet his thrusts . . . and every thrust duplicated by a knife plunging into the maple's pulpy bark . . .

"Mrs. Kerso? I said was he doing anything suspicious?"

"I don't—no, no, I'm sure he wasn't." She licked dry lips. *I was screwing around in the porch swing and this creep was probably watching.* No, even if she could bring herself to say the words, she wouldn't have that admission in a police report. Not if there was a remote chance of Walt finding out.

"Lizzie's only five, so she's not the most reliable witness. I just wondered if you've had any other reports like this."

"No, ma'am, nothing. It was probably just kids, horsing around, you know, but I'll be glad to come out and take a look. Maybe if I talk to your little girl—"

"No." Joanna could just imagine what Lizzie would tell him. "I mean, thank you but it's really not necessary. I'm sure you're right—about it being kids. If you could just have the patrol car come by once in a while. I'm a little jumpy with my folks away."

"Of course. And if you hear or see anything, anything at all, you call and we'll be right over."

After she broke the connection, she held the receiver for a second, wanting to call back and blurt out everything. And what good would that do? Even if Lizzie had seen somebody last night, Chief Lankersheim wasn't going to post a twenty-four-hour guard because some sicko might've been getting his jollies watching her and Tom. More than likely, the vandal was just what the chief said, a kid acting out his teenage rebellion with a little destruction of private property.

Anyway, no free show tonight, so if he came back, he wouldn't hang around. If he came back . . . *and if he does . . . do watchers only watch?*

Dammit, she'd been feeling so good and it was such a beautiful day. She decided she'd be careful but not paranoid. After lunch she took Lizzie into town for a Muppets matinee and an ice-cream cone. That night she locked all the doors and windows. Long past midnight she was wide awake, and several times she went to the window to look down into the shadowy yard. She never saw a thing except a lone rabbit, peacefully eating clover in the middle of the lawn.

The combination of Percodan and fatigue knocked Tom out for eight soggy hours. By then it was too late for an early evening flight to L.A., so he caught the red-eye, settling into an empty seat in the first-class section. His sleep schedule was hopelessly out of sync now. If only he could nap a little . . .

He closed his eyes and relaxed in the comfortable seat. Packing and getting ready to leave had kept him busy enough, so he didn't think about his conversation with Emily. Now it all came back.

Was Emily right? Had he given up too soon? Another detective agency . . . how could he go through that again? The hoping, the waiting and the crushing sense of loss when all they reported were the same, frustrating dead ends. He'd have to go up to Cape Cod and talk to Emily, to make her see how useless it all was. To tell her . . . how about the truth? How about letting the poor woman off the hook? She'd kept her daughter's secret for a whole year before she told Tom, haunted by the possibility that it might have made a difference to the investigation. He'd reassured her, never mentioning his own culpability. *I knew the secret, too, Emily, and I kept my mouth shut. Not to honor Claire's confidence but because I was scared, so damn scared.*

Claire had been gone for three weeks when he found out what Emily already knew. By then the intense police activity had dwindled, too many other muggings, riots and murders taking precedence. He was frantic with worry. He took his vacation time, spent every waking hour driving around Boston. Slums, the waterfront, streets where his blood ran cold when he thought of Claire behind one of those filthy, graffitied doors.

One day he'd wake up convinced she was dead; the next day he was just as sure Claire had left him. He couldn't tell what the police thought, except for the one detective, Sergeant Kevin McDowell. His questions and that flat cynicism in his eyes . . .

You slept for twelve hours on your layover in L.A., Mr. Blanchard? And you didn't talk to anybody the day you were there? Uh-huh. Explain to me again about the fight you had with your wife just before you left.

The man suspected—Christ, *believed*—that Tom had slipped back and forth to L.A., that he'd come home and—Tom fought to keep from smashing his fist into the man's cold skeptical face. "You stupid son of a bitch,"

Tom said, "stop wasting time questioning me and find my wife."

McDowell told him they were doing everything they could, watching him all the while, especially when he mentioned Tom's fight with Claire.

There had been a fight. The neighbors heard it. They always seemed to be arguing. He couldn't even remember what this one was about. God, maybe she had run away and it was his fault.

She'd returned from her stay at the cottage tanned, rested—and more remote than ever. She had the flu, then a touch of food poisoning, and was listless for weeks. Her time alone hadn't narrowed the distance between them. Things were getting worse. Things were going to hell and he had never known why.

He found out one cold November night after scouring South Boston. Chilled and damp, he was going through the mail and there it was, just a bill mixed in with Allstate Insurance and AT&T. He flipped past it but the return address caught his eye: Family Services, Inc. Addressed to Mrs. Claire Blanchard. He ripped it open and read the itemized listing. Blood workup, anesthetic, intravenous glucose, abortion procedure . . .

He'd been kicked in the stomach once playing football at Michigan State, a solid blow that paralyzed his diaphragm and shut down his breathing for several long agonizing moments. He felt that way as he looked at the impersonal computer printout. The total amount less cash payment received left a fifteen-dollar balance. Somebody had been sloppy with the math or otherwise he might never have known.

Claire's long bout with the flu, the food poisoning, her continuing withdrawal.

Abortion procedure . . .

He was at the clinic when it opened the next morning. The cheerful receptionist—"Hi, I'm Cindy," her plastic I.D. badge said—looked up the records and told him that Dr. Vernon was Claire's physician, that Dr. Vernon would be in surgery all morning. Would he like to make an appointment?

Tom said he'd wait, all day if necessary. He went and sat on a comfortable sofa. The room was done in warm shades of brown and ecru with plenty of plants and lots of bright, flower-filled pictures. By ten o'clock it was full of people. Couples of all ages, sometimes two women together. All of them giving their information to Cheery Cindy in low murmurs, then sitting down and not saying another word. A woman in a pretty pink uniform came out regularly to call a name and carry on a companionable, one-sided conversation as she took the silent patient away.

Surely Claire wouldn't have come here alone. Had *he* come along, sat with her, waited as she was led off through that wide, birchwood door?

Claire's lover.

Bile rose in Tom's throat. Christ, how could he have been so blind? No wonder she'd wanted him to stay away from the cottage. Had she brought the son of a bitch there, slept with him in their bed?

Cindy kept glancing at Tom, her smile beginning to slip. At 11:25 Cindy announced with relief that Dr. Vernon could see him for a few minutes. The lady in pink came to collect him, chatting about the weather. As he followed her, he saw a room with women sitting around in sunny yellow hospital gowns and paper booties. Silent women. He recognized them as ones who'd left the waiting room earlier.

Dr. Vernon wore scrub greens and a pained expression. He stood by his desk, smoking and drinking coffee, and he didn't invite Tom to sit down. "I don't have much time, Mr. Blanchard. They said you insisted on seeing me." He picked up a manila folder with a red tab, flipped it open. "The procedure was normal and Claire's post-op was fine. What's the problem?"

"The problem is I never knew Claire was pregnant until I got your bill." The bitterness in his voice supplied the rest.

"I see." Vernon closed the folder. "I'm afraid I can't discuss this with you. If you want to know anything, you'll have to ask your wife."

"I'd like to, Doctor, but my wife vanished three weeks ago."

"Christ." Vernon stubbed out his cigarette and shook another from the pack. "What can I say? I'm sorry. That's got to be damned rough. Still, your wife's medical records are privileged information and—"

"Listen, please. I'm not upset—no, dammit, that's not true. I feel sick and betrayed, but none of that matters right now. Claire's gone. Maybe she just went off with her—with him. But if she didn't, I need to know all the other possibilities. Could she have hemorrhaged? Was she suicidal?" And was any of it my fault?

Dr. Vernon stared down at his nicotine-stained fingers. "You've wasted your time, Mr. Blanchard. I never spoke to your wife. A nurse-practitioner does the workup and the post-op. I only saw Claire when I performed the—the procedure, and she was sedated. I never saw her again.''

Vernon told the staff to answer Tom's questions. None of them had more than a vague memory of Claire. Was anybody with her? A complete blank there except for the pink-uniformed nurse, who thought, maybe, it was another woman.

During the drive home, Tom ran through the list of her friends and discarded them. This was far too personal, too intimate. It had to be her mother, of course. Dammit, why hadn't Emily said something? Did she know the baby wasn't his? Is that why she'd kept quiet? He would drive up to the Cape the next day and make Emily tell him everything.

He recognized the new Plymouth on his driveway as soon as he turned into his street. The Boston detective, Sergeant McDowell. Hope leaped in his chest. They'd found Claire. Alive. She had to be alive. The hope died soon enough. McDowell wasn't there with good news. He'd come to bring Tom in for an interrogation that made it official: Tom was the chief suspect in the disappearance—and possibly the murder—of his wife.

Now, in retrospect, Tom realized how ridiculous it had been to think that the police could have brought any kind of charge and made it stick. But then, in that small gray, smoky room, it seemed all they'd needed was a motive. *So your wife had a lover and got knocked up. You found out and went a little crazy . . .*

Tom stared out the window of the DC-10 into the darkness. When Emily finally told him about Claire's abortion, he'd realized she assumed the baby was his, that she'd be horrified to know otherwise. She thought Claire

127

had been afraid to risk having another retarded child. Yes, he would have a talk with Emily. But how could he ever tell her the truth?

For the past eighteen years, whenever Kevin McDowell sat in a bar, people kept a nervous distance. Something in the way he moved, something in the way he talked—whatever that something was that told them he was a cop, it had disappeared, and McDowell felt as exposed as a naked turtle.

The old broad on the next stool twisted arthritic fingers in raddled orange hair and told him how she earned her nightly ration of booze by giving cut-rate blowjobs. On the other side two giggling faggots shared a joint and gossiped about picking pockets in Quincy Market.

Dick Twohy came in, crossed the room to join him. The fags and the whore drifted away, crawling back under their rocks.

"Guess I've lost it." McDowell stubbed out his cigarette, shook another from the pack.

Twohy signaled for a beer. "Lost what?"

"The touch. The cop smell. You know why? Simple. Let 'em screw who they want, murder, rob. I don't give a shit anymore." He ordered another double vodka and they went to sit in a booth.

Twohy talked about the weather, politics, the Sox's latest series in New York, some frigging wallpaper he and Peg were planning to hang.

"Tell me about the Chinatown hit," McDowell said.

"Christ, Mac. I came to have a friendly drink."

Safely away from the bars near the station house. Well, he couldn't blame Twohy for that.

"We can drink and talk at the same time. Galvin kicked me out of the office. He can't switch off my brain, too."

Twohy shook his head. "You just don't get it, do you? Sure, Galvin's an asshole, but he's doing you a favor, Mac. You ever hear of burnout? You don't back off, buddy, you're gonna make like a Molotov cocktail."

"Right." McDowell emptied his glass, ordered another drink, lit another cigarette. "Now, tell me about the gooks."

Twohy threw up his hands. "Nothing to tell. No suspects, no leads. Now, can we give it a rest?"

"Just put it in the files, huh, Dick? Case pending. Well, what the hell. Plenty of unsolved cases. We all got 'em."

"That's right. We do. We're not supercops, Mac. We just do the best we can."

"And too bad it's not good enough." McDowell downed the vodka. Might as well have been water. No effect at all. He waved for another. "I had this one case—ever tell you about this one? Came so close to breaking it." Claire Blanchard and his gut feeling about the husband. "Never found a body, so Homicide wasn't interested, but she's dead, sure as hell. They got a cottage—this lake, up in Vermont. I called up there, tried to get the locals to drag it, maybe bring in some dogs to search the woods. Think they'd do it? No probable cause, they said. Probable cause, hell. Budget, that's what it was. Always the fucking budget."

"Mac, you tried. You did all you could."

"Hell I did." The dark oak bar slipped sideways, righted itself. A million reflections in the mirrored wall, all edged in red. "Should've gone up there. Put on some heat. Why didn't I go up there, Dick?"

"Because you had a shitload of other cases. Or something else was breaking and you couldn't leave. Or it was the goddamn budget. Listen, Mac. Are you listening? Forget all this. See a shrink. Take a vacation. I don't know. But you can't go on like this.''

''A vacation,'' McDowell said dreamily. ''Yeah, maybe you're right.''

''Now you're making sense. Listen, I gotta get home. Peg'll throw out my dinner if I'm late again.''

McDowell waved him off, went home himself, packed a bag, packed his gun. Then he drove for a long time, no place in mind, just drove. Past Harvard Yard, along the Charles, with moonlight gleaming on smooth black water.

Sometime before dawn he hit the turnpike heading northwest, still not knowing where he was going until he saw the green and white sign listing a choice of destinations. The last place on the list was Brattleboro, Vermont.

16

Lizzie hugged Leon and drifted, body thin as smoke. Up in a big plane that flew backward, wings flapping slowly, and then Mr. Blanchard came and pushed her through a tiny window and she fell a long, long ways. She saw the ocean and palm trees and Vista View Elementary and Buddy Duffy's house, and then she was in her own house, in her own bed.

Somebody stood in the door to the hall—light shining behind his back so she couldn't see his face, but it had to be—"Daddy," she said. "Hi, Daddy."

Only it wasn't Daddy. It was something with a face like runny Jell-O and a mouth spilling white worms as he whispered, *I found you, Lizzie*.

She screamed and screamed and Mr. Blanchard reached down from the sky with long Gumby arms and grabbed her. The plane flapped its wings and she was back at Gramma's house, holding Leon, changing from smoke to a real body.

"Bad dream," she whispered. "Bad dream, Leon."

Leon purred and snuggled against her. Not Leon—Berry, warm and furry, working his sharp little claws in and out against her arm. Berry . . . he shouldn't be here. She stroked him and tried to remember why. Because . . . because . . .

Berry yawned and stretched and slipped out of Lizzie's arms, jumped off the bed. "No, come back," she said, but it was too late.

He stood there, reached down, picked up Berry.

His face was almost real now. But the hands holding Berry were claws like the eagle she saw one time on TV when it caught a scared little bunny.

The claws tightened and she shut her eyes and put her hands over her ears so she wouldn't have to hear Berry's cries and the sound of crunching bones.

Lizzie's screams jolted Joanna like a cattle prod, sending her heart racing, adrenaline pumping. Dear God, not again, she thought as she ran for her daughter's room.

Lizzie sat rigidly in bed, staring. The unearthly wails raised fine hairs on the back of Joanna's neck. She muffled the terrible sounds against her breasts, rocking Lizzie and smoothing her hair.

"It's okay, baby. It's only a dream, a horrible dream. Wake up, Lizzie, please wake up."

Gradually the screams turned to a sob-racked babble. The Bogeyman. And the cat again—dead, Lizzie insisted so convincingly that Joanna was shaken.

What if the child *were* having some kind of premonition? What if the cat really *were* dead? A stray dog, a car in the parking lot—maybe she should call Miles and ask him—Sweet Jesus, will you listen to yourself? she thought. This was not a premonition. Lizzie had been having the damn dream in one form or other for months now.

The whole thing was her fault. Losing her temper yesterday over the incident with the tree. And, of course, the way she'd been deliberately avoiding Miles. She knew how anxious Lizzie was about the kitten. How could she have been so self-centered?

A survival instinct, she decided, painfully learned. At this point her happiness with Tom was a tentative, fragile thing, and she instinctively wanted to keep it secret and protected. So she had ignored Lizzie, and now—

"—Berry was crying, Mommy, and the Bogeyman h-h-hurt him so bad and then—"

I can't *stand* it anymore, Joanna thought. Lizzie's agony was a pain in her own heart, twisting and tearing.

"Listen to me." She smoothed back tear-soaked wisps of hair from Lizzie's forehead. "The other day you dreamed the same thing and Mommy told you Berry was all right and he was. Remember?" Lizzie nodded slowly. "Well, he still is and we'll go over to Mr. Angstrom's in a little while so you can see for yourself, okay?"

"O—kay." Lizzie, soaking wet from sweat and tears, shivered in the cool morning breeze that fluttered the curtains.

A warm bath and a rubdown with a fluffy towel, dry pajamas—then Joanna took Lizzie to bed with her, holding her close. Lizzie dozed fitfully, but Joanna was wide awake.

She wasn't sure what time Miles opened the stand. Nine, she thought. Maybe nine-thirty. Every day except— Lord—except Monday. The stand was closed today. She'd have to call Miles at home. And if he wasn't there—if he'd locked up and gone away somewhere on his day off—

I'll figure out something, she promised. My fault—the whole thing's my fault.

If she had been paying attention to Lizzie instead of being so caught up in her own feelings, so damn—horny, that was the only word for it. She certainly couldn't use love as an excuse. She hardly knew Tom Blanchard. What she felt for him at this point was plain old lust.

But I could love him, she thought. I could.

The memory of Saturday night washed over her—God, so sweet. The lovemaking, of course, but they had talked, too, in a mutual rush. About growing up—her childhood in Vermont, his in Boston with summers at the cabin near Brattleboro. High school, college, and there, as if both had drawn a line, the memories stopped. This far and no further. Pain and secrets had no place in that first happy coming together.

Their brief conversation in his car that night after their first dinner seemed isolated, a quirk of circumstance. Would they ever be able to talk about the past again? Or like two survivors in a leaky lifeboat, would they have to spend their time bailing just to stay afloat? If he called her again—*if*, she thought bitterly. My God, she wasn't even sure of that much.

And she had no time to worry about it now. Lizzie had to be her first concern. Maybe the two of them should go away for a few days, do something different. She didn't have a lot of money to waste, but a day or two might be worth it, especially if it distracted Lizzie from this morbid thing about the cat. She ran through a list of possibilities in her mind. Lots of historical places around. Lizzie was too young to understand much of it, but Plimoth Plantation with its re-creation of colonial New England might fascinate a child. And they could stay someplace by the sea, at least for a night. Lizzie would like that.

Oh, right, Joanna. A little cotton candy, saltwater taffy. That will fix everything.

She looked down at her sleeping child. Lizzie's E.T. pajama top hiked up to show a curve of rib beneath the delicate skin. Under spun-silk hair her skull looked thin, awkwardly vulnerable on the fragile stalk of neck. Her lashes fluttered and Joanna could see rapid eye movement under the closed lids.

Another dream? Oh, baby, what kind of demons have moved into your mind? Whatever they were, they wouldn't be exorcised by a trip to the seashore.

Careful not to disturb Lizzie, she slipped out of bed and went downstairs. It was early, but she looked up Dr. Henderson's number anyway, determined to call before she lost her nerve in a tangle of rationalizations. So, no more beating around the bush. The best child psychologist in the Boston area, that was the recommendation she wanted.

Dr. Henderson's service told her that he'd gone away for a few days. If it was an emergency, another doctor was taking his calls.

Joanna hesitated. "No. No emergency. Thank you."

If she was going to ask a stranger for advice, she'd go to the top. She called information for the number of Children's Hospital in Boston. The best person on their staff, she was told, was a Dr. Rachel Klein. To her surprise, Dr. Klein was free at ten o'clock the next morning.

"A cancellation," her receptionist said. "Shall I put you down?"

The appointment made, Joanna went to look for a map to refresh her memory of Massachusetts expressways. She could drive in tomorrow morning, but that meant a very early start and running into commuter traffic. The sensible thing was to go today and stay overnight. After dinner, she decided, to avoid the rush hour and to keep to a minimum those useless hours of motel time. And thinking of motels . . . she reserved a room at a Holiday Inn near the hospital.

She ought to let the police know she'd be away, especially after the vandalism. She left a message with Officer Stimson to pass along to the chief, saying she'd be gone overnight.

That done, she made coffee; sipped it while she organized her thoughts. Should she call Walt? Well, yes, she should, but she wasn't going to. And Mom . . . she was due to check in tonight, so Joanna would miss her call. Which was probably just as well. If Ruth had even a hint of this . . . and how long could Joanna keep it from her? She'd call back again and keep on calling. What if the doctor wanted to keep Lizzie in Boston . . .

Time to worry about that tomorrow, Scarlett.

Right now she was going to keep her promise to Lizzie. Miles answered on the second ring and listened while Joanna told him that Lizzie had had another bad dream about the cat.

"Poor baby," he said. "Is she all right?"

"She went to sleep finally after I promised we'd come

check on Berry." She had a sudden image of arriving at the stand and finding a box of small, mangled corpses. "Miles, I hate to ask you and I know it sounds silly, but if you could go down and make sure the kittens are okay before I bring Lizzie—"

"I don't have to," he said. "I just saw them and they're fine." He explained that the kittens had been climbing out of the box and he was afraid that something would happen so he'd brought them up to the barn last night.

"Well, thank God." Good Lord, she really *had* been afraid that Lizzie was having premonitions. "Is it okay if we come over later?"

"I have a better idea. We did have kind of a dinner date, remember? How about a picnic instead? I'll bring the kitten along and Lizzie can play with him to her heart's content. What do you say?"

"I'm sorry, Miles, but I can't, not today." Silence, and she knew exactly what it seemed like—a brush-off. "It really does sound nice, it's just that Lizzie and I are going away and—"

"You're leaving?" There was an odd tone in his voice—something she didn't recognize that made her uneasy.

"Just for a day or two. I thought I'd take Lizzie to Plimoth Plantation or maybe to Boston—" To see a shrink, only she wasn't going to tell him that, of course. Why did she have to explain anything to him? "I just wanted to—to get away for a while."

"I see. You're going this morning, then?"

"Well, no. Later today."

"Then you'll have to eat lunch. Come on, Joanna. It'll be good for Lizzie. She won't worry about her cat while you're gone."

That made sense. And how long would it take to pack an overnight bag? "Okay, if you'll let me bring the sandwiches and we can be home by three."

They agreed that he would pick them up at eleven. When she asked where they would go for the picnic, he said, "A surprise. Someplace very special, I promise."

She went to check on sandwich ingredients in the refrigerator, but Lizzie called from upstairs, her voice edged with hysteria. It took a while to convince her that Berry was safe and sound and that they would see him very soon.

"Darling," Joanna said carefully, "after the picnic, later on today, we're going to take a trip."

"Are we going home?"

"No, we're going to Boston. Lizzie, all these terrible dreams you have—when you try and tell me about them, I know I don't understand. But there's a special kind of doctor who knows all about bad dreams. We're going to see her tomorrow."

"I don't want to go to Boston." Lizzie's eyes looked huge in her pale face. "Can't we see Dr. Bob instead?"

"No, baby, he's on vacation, and anyway, you'll like this doctor, I promise you. Now, come on, if we're going on that picnic, we've got lots of things to do. And Lizzie . . . this is private family stuff, okay? We won't talk about it to Mr. Angstrom."

"Okay," Lizzie said.

A cool north breeze had dropped the temperature enough so that Joanna decided on jeans and a blue-checked shirt, tan cords and a Smurfs T-shirt for Lizzie.

After she settled Lizzie with scrambled eggs and orange juice, she hunted up Mom's old picnic basket. The original plastic dishes had long since given way to paper plates and styrofoam cups, but the tablecloth was there, Mom's favorite yellow splashed with daisies. There was enough ham and Swiss cheese for her and Miles. Lizzie would rather have peanut butter anyway. She added pickles and carrot strips, noting that the refrigerator was pretty bare. She took some hamburger from the freezer for dinner just as the telephone rang.

Tom, arriving at his hotel after the red-eye to Los Angeles. "Oh, I'm so glad you called," Joanna said.

"I don't have much time." The distance in his voice had nothing to do with signals bouncing off satellites. "I just got off the red-eye and I'm pretty wiped out. I have to leave again in a few hours."

She felt cold and knew it wasn't just from holding the frozen meat. She put the hamburger down on the counter and stared out at the bright wash of sunlight in the back-yard. She'd been right about the barriers coming up when he left her yesterday morning. Why did she have to be right all the time, dammit?

"Well, then, you'd better get some sleep. Lizzie and I have a lot to do anyway, so I should get off the phone." And who needs you, fella? "We're leaving later today, taking a short trip, maybe down to Plimoth Plantation."

"That sounds wonderful." She was sure there was relief in his voice. "I'm glad I called before you left."

The back of her throat hurt, but she said brightly, "As a matter of fact you just caught us. An old friend is coming by in a few minutes to take us on a picnic. He and I—we go back a long way."

"I see. I'd better not keep you, then. Have a good time, Joanna. Talk to you soon."

Hot tears rushed to her eyes as she hung up the phone. *He and I go back a long way . . .* the lie of a desperate adolescent. God, did she actually expect him to be jealous? Get with it, Joanna. One-night stands, casual liaisons— that's the way the game is played. Who needs forever? She had forever with Walt.

She wiped her eyes on a paper napkin and slammed the lid on the picnic basket. To hell with it. She just got out of one no-win situation. She didn't need another one. Anyway, she had neglected Lizzie long enough. Her main concern during the next few days was to take care of her daughter.

Angstrom Acres might be closed on Mondays, but Amos Fowler walked in that direction at the same time as usual. Regular habits kept a man functioning properly—meals, bowels, exercise. Let your schedules slip and they might as well start warming up your bedpan in the nursing home.

It was cooler this morning, thank God, and he moved easily, invigorated by the brisk edge to the air, savoring the familiar weight of the Colt Special against his hip. After all these years the leather of the belt holster fitted as though it had been molded to his skin. He'd rarely fired a weapon in the line of duty, and most of the time it was the twelve gauge he brought out when he meant business. Nothing like a shotgun to put the fear of God into people. But he believed a man should never carry any kind of weapon unless he was prepared to use it and that he should be as expert in that usage as possible. He might not wear the pistol routinely anymore, but the day might come when he'd need it, and by God, he would be ready.

At the edge of the woods near his property line, he

detoured to a small clearing where he'd set up a target range—bottles and cans on stumps and a big piece of plywood with supports nailed to the back to keep it upright. On the board, heavy black lines outlined the figure of a man.

Fowler sat down on a log and loaded his revolver. The woods had the warm, yeasty smell of early summer and rang with birdsong. He put on a pair of tempered sunglasses, got in position, assumed the Weaver stance and began firing.

Cans flew. Bottles smashed. He stopped to reload. The woods stank of cordite and were eerily silent. This time he concentrated on the board.

Aim for the heart. Head's too small for accuracy. Miss the heart and you stand a good chance of hitting a lung, the stomach, vital organs. A gut shot may not stop a man cold, but it sure as hell slows him down.

The deafening volley ended and he went over to inspect his marksmanship. A lot of holes in the wood, but he had them memorized and could tell immediately how many times he'd hit the target. Five out of seven. Pretty damn good. Like to see that pissant Lankersheim do as well.

When he ran out of shells, he holstered the gun and resumed his walk. It was warming up and he was sweating by the time he reached the point where he ordinarily would leave the woods and angle across an open field to the junction of County 15 and Old Mill Road.

Damn stomach was acting up again, so he chewed on a couple of Rolaids and sat down on a stump to rest. He was about midway between the produce stand and Angstrom's house and barn. The wooden shutters of the stand were closed and locked. Nothing moving at the house either. He noticed the pickup was gone.

Much as he liked target practice, it was a poor substitute for bracing Miles. Feeling vaguely disappointed and more tired than usual, he got up, walked slowly back into the woods and plodded homeward.

Five minutes later Miles Angstrom's pickup, carrying Joanna and Lizzie, drove past on County 15, heading for the mountains.

17

A warm breeze through the open window of the pickup lifted Joanna's hair and floated strands around her face.

"Too windy?" Miles asked.

"No, it's okay."

Actually the breeze was the only pleasant thing about the outing, that and the way Lizzie sat between them, cuddling a skittish Berry, her face radiant.

"Honey, I really think I ought to hold him now."

"No, Mommy. I can do it. Please."

Joanna put a hand on the cat's haunches just in case he decided to bolt. Having him jump out the window was the last thing Lizzie needed.

She shifted on the thin bench seat and stared out at a tiny village rushing past, so distinctively New England that it might have been straight out of the Disneyland Circle

Vision film, *America the Beautiful*. She tried to remember all the places for picnics in this area. A surprise, Miles had said when he picked them up. Someplace special.

Sorry, we can't go. Those were the first words that popped into her head when he knocked on the door. But it seemed such a stupid thing to say when she was standing there, picnic basket in hand—or at least ready on the hallway table—and Lizzie had been so excited.

Joanna glanced over at Miles. He was dressed casually, in his usual well-washed jeans and a light blue plaid shirt, long sleeves rolled up to his elbows. He looked and smelled as though he'd just stepped out of the shower, and his pale brown hair still had comb tracks. He gripped the steering wheel, leaning forward slightly . . . keyed up, she'd sensed that right away. Was this quasi-date really that big a deal to him?

In Lizzie's lap Berry meowed, questioning, nervous. Joanna could feel his bunched muscles and his tail twitching. *I know just how you feel, cat.*

Considering everything that had happened in the last twenty-four hours, it was no wonder she was upset. The ugly gouges in the old maple, Lizzie's—what? Dreams? Hallucinations? Then the call from Tom—not to mention the thought of tomorrow's session with Dr. Klein . . .

"Miles, where *is* this place we're going? You did promise we'd be home by three."

"Don't worry. I know you're anxious to get away." That note in his voice again and an oblique, bright stare. "Relax, Joanna. Your hot date in Boston will wait for you."

Hot date?

Jesus, she was sick of men. Bloody, indifferent Tom

144

and now a jealous Miles. "You're right, Miles, he will. I'd just like to beat the rush-hour traffic."

She felt a surge of satisfaction as his jaw hardened and a flicker of pulse beat in his temple. "Now, exactly where are we going? I really don't like surprises."

"To my cabin," he said.

Hadn't Amos Fowler mentioned Miles's cabin that day at Angstrom Acres? That nasty scene . . . one more thing to make her wish she'd stayed at home.

"Is your cabin made out of logs, Mr. Angstrom?" Lizzie asked. "Are there any bears?"

Miles's jaw softened. He smiled down at the little girl. "No bears, I'm afraid. It's just a little place made of stones—like the way they made the stone fences. But there's lots of woods and a creek. You can catch tadpoles. Would you like that?"

"What are tadpoles?"

"Good God, Joanna, how could this child grow up not knowing about tadpoles?"

Because she's been raised in a planned community of concrete and ground covers with a father who thought a big outing was for her to sit in Daddy's BMW waiting for him to wrap up his latest deal.

The question was rhetorical anyway. Miles was already launched into an explanation of the life cycle of frogs. Her anger seeped away. Miles so obviously wanted to be with her and Lizzie. If she had her head on straight, his jealousy might even seem endearing. Poor Miles didn't know how lucky he was that she wasn't attracted to him. He'd had enough grief without getting mixed up with her problems.

Ahead was a sprinkling of buildings, too small to be a

town. Miles turned off County 15 and drove past a service station, a grocery, a few houses strung out beside the road as it narrowed and headed into the low mountains. A stream raced by, paralleling the shiny asphalt. Thick stands of birch and oak edged small meadows, the lighter green darkened here and there by pine trees.

Another house and in a field next to it, Joanna saw a red-haired boy throw a stick for a dog whose coat was a lighter shade of red. She felt a start of recognition. Silly. Lots of boys and dogs around—but how many in matched sets? Had Lizzie noticed? No, she and Miles were onto minnows and dragonflies.

The little girl looked so happy, so *normal*. Maybe this Dr. Klein was a big mistake. Maybe all Lizzie needed was time and love. Once a psychiatrist started digging around in both their heads . . . God, she hated the thought.

The truck climbed sharply and her ears popped. More pine now and fir, closing in and shutting out the sunlight. Birch bark looked ghostly white against the dark evergreens. Miles seemed to have exhausted the subject of polliwogs and insects and concentrated on the winding road.

The kitten had finally curled into a fluffball, so Joanna felt it safe to take her hand away. She slipped her arm around Lizzie, turning slightly, and felt the child snuggle into the pelvic curve against her stomach.

Tomorrow . . . Oh, Lizzie, what have I gotten us into?

Berry felt soft and warm and surprisingly heavy against Lizzie's legs. He slept with a buzzy sound almost like snoring. He really was all right, just like Mommy promised. Last night when the Bogeyman came and stood by her bed . . . He *had* been real and Berry had been real and Berry's bones had crunched when the Bogeyman squeezed him, but now Berry was here and he was okay. How could it all be true?

Maybe the doctor would know, the special doctor they were going to see in Boston. Mommy said she understood all about bad dreams.

Lizzie hoped the doctor would believe her. That she'd figure out a way to protect her and Mommy and Berry. She wished they were in Boston right now. She wished they'd hurry up and have the picnic and go home and . . .

Mr. Angstrom reached out and ran a finger along Berry's head, between his ears and down the bumpy backbone. Mr. Angstrom had long fingers with short, shiny nails. She thought she felt Berry shiver.

Suddenly she felt all hollow inside, her ribs like a bony cage and her heart a trapped bird fluttering around, trying to get out. She looked up and Mr. Angstrom was watching her, smiling a little as if he knew a secret. His teeth were shiny, too, and so were his eyes. They had funny white rings around the black dot like a wolf's eyes she'd seen on TV. Even when he looked back at the road, she could feel him watching her.

"Are you cold, Lizzie?" Mommy said. "Miles, would you mind closing the window?"

He took his hand off Berry's head and put it back on the steering wheel while he rolled the window up. Then he braked and turned down a road that made the truck bounce. Dark trees crowded around, scraping the truck's roof. Lizzie's bird-heart beat very fast as they drove out of the trees and stopped. She shut her eyes tightly. Maybe if she tried real hard, she could go to sleep and then she'd wake up and Mommy would say, "It's a dream, Lizzie. It's just another bad dream."

But Mommy wasn't saying that. She said, "I think she fell asleep," and Mr. Angstrom said, "Let me take her, Joanna. I'll bring the cooler if you can manage the basket and the cat."

Lizzie tried to wriggle away, but it was too late. He picked her up and started walking away from the truck toward a little house made out of ugly gray stones. There was an open space around it like a yard where nobody ever cut the grass. Black trees grew on the edges, their branches reaching out to touch the house.

He took a key from his pocket, unlocked the door and pushed it open. It was dark inside and it smelled like animals lived there—snakes and tigers and big ugly birds that ate dead things. She wanted to yell to Mommy, please please *please* let's run away and hide, but she couldn't make her throat work right.

Mr. Angstrom said, "Well, here we are. Come on in," and carried her into the place where the Bogeyman lived.

18

THE BOGEYMAN

Joanna's heart sank as they entered the dismal little house. A special place, he had said. Well, maybe it was special to him, and given a good cleaning and airing . . . it would still be a dump.

The combination living room and kitchen was small with low ceilings, full of a dim chill, and smelled of mold and dust. An Early American sofa and a wing chair defined the right-hand side of the room, sagging in front of a soot-blackened fireplace with an old steamer trunk serving as a coffee table. On the opposite wall a kitchen filled the far corner with an open cupboard, an ancient propane stove, a wall-hung sink. In between sat a dusty table. There was only one window paned with old bubbly glass.

Berry meowed loudly and began trying to climb Joanna's shoulder, his claws needle sharp.

"Ouch," Joanna said, picking him loose and putting him down on the rough-planked floor. The kitten scampered through a doorway opening into a bedroom off the kitchen.

What had Chief Fowler said to Miles that day at the produce stand? *Funny how you keep holding on to that place.* Now that she'd seen it, she definitely agreed.

"Just put everything over here." Miles left the cooler on the floor beside the table.

Lizzie drooped in his arms, head on his shoulder, watching Joanna with sleep-dazed eyes. Poor baby, last night had finally caught up with her.

Joanna placed the picnic basket next to the cooler and said, "I'll take her now, Miles."

"No, that's okay. I don't mind." He sat down on the sofa with Lizzie in his lap. "Why don't you unpack the food?"

He actually expected them to eat in here? God knows what kind of bugs called the place home, not to mention mice and other assorted vermin.

"It's pretty dirty, Miles. Why don't we have our picnic outside?"

"I'd rather not. Can't you just dust off the table? It would mean a lot to me." He smoothed a wisp of Lizzie's fine blond hair and said quietly, "It was the last place we were together—Bonnie and me and Sarah Ann."

Lizzie looks very much like Sarah. The realization left a cold, uneasy trail through Joanna's mind.

Miles had been drawn to Lizzie since that first day at the produce stand. Was he going through some kind of—what did they call it? Delayed stress syndrome? A reaction connected to the fact that Lizzie resembled his lost child?

150

"Look," she said, "this wasn't such a good idea. Lizzie's tired and—"

"I don't understand you, Joanna. We came all this way and now you want to leave before we have lunch. What exactly's bothering you?" There was a shine to his eyes, a watchfulness that sent alarm skittering up and down her spine.

Amos had most of the farm dug up, looking for the bodies . . . Joanna remembered her mother's words, monstrous in the soft twilight that night on the back porch. *He still thinks that Miles . . . did something . . . to Bonnie and little Sarah Ann.*

"Joanna, I asked what's bothering you."

"Nothing." Her throat was so dry the word came out in a croak. "I just—Lizzie didn't sleep much last night and—"

Grab Lizzie and run for the door. No—too far back to the nearest house—oh, God, he mustn't see the panic on her face. She turned to the table, took napkins from the picnic basket and began blindly wiping the dusty wood.

"That's more like it," Miles said. "I'm starved."

Food, that was a good idea. Some people acted strangely when they were hungry. Low blood sugar changed personality—that was a proven fact.

She flapped the tablecloth into place, took out paper plates and napkins. The routine act settled her nerves a little. Why was she getting so upset anyway? Miles hadn't actually done or said anything that was so frightening. Maybe it was her own body chemistry out of whack. Just coffee for breakfast and she'd been spooked since yesterday. As far as Amos Fowler's suspicions—an old man's senile obsession, that's all. The thing to do was calm down, have the stupid picnic. They'd be home long before three and she'd have a good laugh at her jitters.

As she unpacked sandwiches and soda pop from the cooler, she glanced at her daughter. Lizzie seemed okay—a little too pale and her eyes still heavy with sleep, but she sat placidly. Joanna knew if she wasn't careful, Lizzie would pick up on her anxiety. The child was a little lightning rod, attracting every spark of emotion.

Berry came in from the bedroom, detouring to sniff the hearth. He left paw prints around an old black poker and a cracked bellows, then, nose to the floor, began tracking along the wall. She hoped fervently he wouldn't find a mouse. She couldn't deal with a limp little body in the cat's mouth right now.

"Now, isn't this nice?" Miles carried Lizzie over to the table, hitching up a wooden chair with his foot. "How about it, Princess? I brought along some root beer. Would you like some?"

"Okay," Lizzie said dully.

Joanna took cans of A&W from the cooler and began unwrapping sandwiches. She smiled at Lizzie. *Everything's going to be all right, baby. I promise.*

The eye contact seemed to rouse Lizzie. She said, "Mommy," urgently, leaning toward Joanna, but Miles restrained her with a big hand firmly splayed at her waist where Lizzie's Smurfs T-shirt had ridden up.

The sight of his fingers against Lizzie's soft skin was too much for Joanna. To hell with rationalizing.

She put down the food and reached out. "Give her to me, Miles."

Before she could touch Lizzie, Miles grabbed Joanna's left wrist. "Lizzie's just fine where she is." He squeezed until Joanna gasped with pain. "Why do you have to spoil everything? I just want to have a nice, quiet lunch. Is that asking too much?"

The petulant tone contrasted with the vulpine set of his face as he squeezed harder. Joanna could feel her bones grinding together. "Miles—don't—"

He let go. She staggered backward, her calves bumping into a chair, and sat down abruptly. The pain still pulsed up her arm to flower brightly in her head.

"Mom-mee." That Look, Lizzie's pupils dilated, staring darkly. "It's *him*, Mommy, it's *him*, and oh Mommy Mommy *Iwannawakeupnow*."

Him. No mistaking that emphasis, not after all these months of hearing Lizzie describe her phantom monster.

"It's okay, darling." Joanna managed a rictus of a grin. "You fell asleep and had another bad dream." *And it's still going on, baby. We're both in the middle of one of your nightmares.* "Be a good girl, Lizzie. Please, darling. We'll go home soon."

"*Lizzie's* always a good girl," Miles said. "She's just hungry. We both are. We're having lunch here, Joanna. Remember?"

"Yes, of course."

The pain had receded, but her left hand was numb and the right wasn't much better, shaking badly as she passed Miles a plate of food and a can of soda. He *was* crazy. Should've listened to her instincts . . . grabbed Lizzie and run. But if she ran and he caught them . . . needles of feeling returned to her hand, reminding her of his anger.

A weapon . . . she needed a weapon. But what? Nothing in the basket except plastic knives and forks. Not even a can opener. The poker lying on the hearth . . . oh, sure,

Joanna. Just stroll on over and pick it up. Even if she had a .357 Magnum, what difference would it make? As long as he held Lizzie in his arms . . . She had to play it cool now. Do nothing to provoke him.

Outside a cloud passed over the sun, and the room darkened. She picked up a sandwich, pretended to nibble. Lizzie just stared at the whole-wheat wedges oozing peanut butter. Miles wolfed down a thick ham and cheese, ate a whole dill pickle, letting the juice run down his fingers all the way to his elbow. Only a few blond hairs on his arms, she noticed. Nothing at all like Tom. She had a sudden piercing memory of the dark fur of hair on his chest and stomach, soft against her cheek.

Tom . . . on his way to Honolulu by now. Tom, I need you.

"You're not eating, Princess," Miles said to Lizzie. "Better finish up if you want to go down to the creek and catch some tadpoles."

"I don't want to catch tadpoles," Lizzie said. "I wanna go home. Please, please, I wanna go home."

"It is getting late, Miles." Careful. Careful. He was a time bomb and she had to snip the leads to the detonation device. "Lizzie didn't sleep much last night, so she's pretty cranky. Why don't I just clean up here and we can get started back—"

"I know what you're doing," Miles said. "You don't give a damn about Lizzie. You just can't wait to go to Boston so you can screw your boyfriend."

"Miles, for God's sake! Please don't talk that way in front of Lizzie."

"Oh, you're really worried about Lizzie." A puritanical

gleam in his eyes, witch-trial bright. "She's right there in the house while you're fucking away on the back porch."

Oh, my God, it was him. He stood behind the maple and watched and . . . She saw the savaged tree bark, the sap thick as blood . . .

Lizzie began to cry, big tears bursting from her eyes and a strangled *"Whu-whu—"* erupting from her mouth.

"There, there, darling," Miles said tenderly, rocking back and forth.

Lizzie's sobs quieted, but her streaming eyes fastened on Joanna, full of a terrified knowledge too enormous to verbalize. Joanna wanted to snatch Lizzie away, to run, but she was so dizzy with fear that her body didn't respond to the frantic summons.

"Please," Joanna said, "please, Miles. Let me hold her. She's so upset—"

"Of course she is. No wonder. It's your fault, Joanna. Your fault."

She felt hysterical laughter rising in her throat. The same thing she'd been telling herself for some time now turned into a new, hideous truth. Her fault . . .

"You're right. It is." Agree with him. Pacify him. She choked back revulsion as he caressed Lizzie's shoulder. He did care for Lizzie. Maybe—please God, maybe—she could appeal to that feeling. "I acted badly—made a lot of mistakes. I know that now. But my trip to Boston—I'm not going to see anybody—not a boyfriend, I mean. I'm taking Lizzie to a doctor."

"A doctor."

"Yes. I told you about Lizzie's nightmares. The dreams about the cat and—and other things. They're getting worse. So I called Children's Hospital and made an appointment.

That's why we're going to Boston, Miles, to see a doctor for Lizzie. Dr. Rachel Klein. She's the best child psychologist on their staff."

His face was flat, unreadable. She could sense the wheels turning behind that narrow skull . . . tumblers falling into place. He finally nodded. "I see."

Relief flooded Joanna's body. "I'm glad you understand, Miles."

"Oh, I understand," he said. "Of course."

"Then if we could just go home now . . . I've got so much to do. Packing—and then the drive—I have to go tonight. Lizzie's appointment is tomorrow—first thing tomorrow morning."

"A lot to be done," Miles said. "Yes, I can see that now." He stood up. "Let's go find Berry, Lizzie, while Mommy cleans up."

Giddy with relief, she watched him go off toward the bedroom, holding Lizzie's hand and calling, "Kitty. Here, kitty."

Lizzie's eyes stayed fixed on her mother as he pulled her along. Joanna tried to signal reassurance, mouthing, "It's okay."

She grabbed up plates and leftovers, stuffing everything into the basket. If she kept her head, everything would be all right. His crazy outburst, triggered by seeing her and Tom together, seemed to be over for now. The best thing to do was to have everything ready as soon as he came out with Lizzie and the cat. Things would be better when they got out of this place, out into the sunshine. She'd keep him calm somehow, and then once they were safely home, she'd call Chief Lankersheim or Amos or . . .

Her peripheral vision caught movement behind her. She turned just as Lizzie wailed a warning.

A dull thump on the side of her head. Then sparkles of blinding light . . . her body shifting, splitting away . . and Lizzie . . . screaming . . . screaming . . .

19

A portion of Ruth's mind stayed constantly on the alert these days, listening . . . for God knows what. That was why she noticed the metallic stutter in the Winnebago's engine before Matt did.

"What was that noise?" she asked.

"I don't know. What did it sound like?"

"Sort of—oh, like chirping." Not at all accurate, but she found it impossible to describe anything mechanical.

"Probably a squeaky fan belt." Matt was a Saturday afternoon mechanic, convinced that his ability to change spark plugs and air filters made him a complete authority on engines.

"Stop worrying," he said comfortably. "Enjoy the view."

There was lots of view to enjoy. Another ubiquitous lake,

sapphire-faceted in the afternoon sunlight, tall firs edging flower-starred meadows. Matt seemed intent on taking every back road in Ontario. Right now they were on a hundred-mile detour along a strip of patchy asphalt marked on the AAA map with a faint broken line. Who were the idiots that keep saying mankind was running out of open space? They'd never been in the Canadian wilderness, that's for sure.

"How soon before we get back to Route 17?" Ruth asked.

"Three—four hours. Sometime before sundown."

"That's a big help," she said tartly. This far north, twilight lasted until ten.

"We're not exactly punching a time clock, Ruth." He spotted the twenty-fourth moose they'd seen that day, slowing to a crawl to stare at the huge, bulbous-nosed creature who stood at the edge of the lake and stared right back.

When Matt accelerated, the engine noise grew louder. "Did you hear that?" he asked.

"Of course I hear it. I just told you about it."

"Well, why did you say it was a chirp? That's not a chirp. Listen to it."

"Oh, Matt, for heaven's sake. How do I know what it *sounds* like? What *is* it? What's going wrong?"

"Might be a bearing in the water pump. I'll have it checked out in Dryden."

"When will that be? You know Joanna's expecting to hear from us tonight."

"We'll get there when we get there," Matt snapped. "It's a hell of a note having to plan this trip around your phone calls home."

"I don't want her to worry," Ruth said defensively.

Matt muttered something about "minding your own business," but Ruth ignored him. As a matter of fact, she thought she was showing considerable restraint, limiting her calls to every two or three days. Matt might believe Joanna's Little Mary Sunshine routine, but every instinct told Ruth that something was wrong. Joanna talked too much and said too little. Would Joanna tell her if Lizzie was worse? Ruth doubted it. During the past years with Walt, Joanna had become skilled in hiding the truth, even from herself.

The chickens were coming home to roost, and a couple were perched in Ruth's own backyard.

Ruth remembered the first time she met Walt Kerso. He came home with Joanna one weekend, and they all had dinner at the country club. Several of the Harts' friends dropped by to be introduced and afterward told Ruth how lucky Joanna was. "A dreamboat," one of the women sighed. "A real catch."

A master's in business from Wharton, an endearing grin, always the right thing to say at the right time—Ruth chided herself for sensing an amoral taint beneath the charm. Parents never thought any man was good enough for their daughter, did they?

Joanna got engaged on Valentine's Day and set the wedding date for late June. Ruth saw very little of Walt during those hectic months, but try as she might she couldn't put that nagging doubt out of her mind. Something about the way he looked at other women, the way he looked at *her*. Ruth knew she was fairly attractive, but she was, for God's sakes, Joanna's mother.

Ruth had friends who screamed and cried and fainted

whenever their children did things they didn't like. Ruth, observing these emotional manipulations, often felt superior. A thoroughly modern mom, she had cut the cord, allowing Joanna to be her own person, to make her own mistakes.

Now Ruth gripped the armrest, staring out the camper's wide windows, and thought she'd made a terrible mistake. She had known with deep intuitive certainty that Walter Kerso would break her daughter's heart. If only she'd said so, loud and often. Oh, yes, if only . . .

More than likely, of course, Joanna was too much in love to listen. Ruth would simply have destroyed the relationship with her daughter. Still, logic aside, it was the possibility that haunted Ruth, the fact that she might have made a difference in Joanna's life if she'd heeded her instincts.

She had that feeling again. That maternal urge to wade right in, to protect her child. Only this time she had no idea what the danger was. She only knew one thing. She should never have left Joanna and Lizzie alone.

Joanna hovered on the dividing line of consciousness. She smelled damp sour earth . . . a dream, of course. Like the one she'd had the morning her parents left. Any minute now she'd wake up to the sound of rain splattering hot soil, the thrashing of maple leaves against her bedroom window.

She sensed other, darker layers of the dream, the kind you never want to remember. A contorted face. That black rush of something slicing toward her . . .

She moaned and opened her eyes to a gray dimness, full of distorted shapes and shadows. The smell intensified.

Not a dream. Real . . . moist soil against her cheek, reeking of mold. She tried to sit up. Pain hammered her skull, searing, icy. She vomited weakly, then lay back down, riding out the waves of agony.

Drifting.

Oh, Jo, did you bump your head? Mamma will kiss it and make it all better.

Is she still falling out of trees, Ruth?

. . . somebody hit me . . .

Miles . . .

Miles hit me.

He had the poker in his hand, the one from the hearth. Lizzie cried out a warning but it was too late. He was already swinging the poker and Lizzie kept screaming . . .

"Oh, no, Lizzie . . . Lizzie."

She tried to stand, an impossibly complicated action that got her only as far as her hands and knees. If he'd hit Lizzie, too . . . Choked with dread, she looked around, expecting to see a limp little body, the delicate curve of forehead cracked like eggshell. Lizzie wasn't there. Joanna's relief was short-lived, swamped by another vision of Lizzie alone and hurt, crying, her life's blood seeping away.

Joanna got to her feet this time before the dizzying whirl began. She felt her knees buckle. Then she was outside herself for one long moment, a coolly observing eye noting the frailty of the human structure.

"I see you, Lizzie."

He lifted the corner of the bed, pulling it away from the wall to reveal Lizzie's hiding place, but when Lizzie looked up, it was only Mr. Angstrom standing there. "Come on, Princess. We're going for a ride now."

Obediently she crawled out. She'd been having a terrible dream, but she couldn't quite remember the details, only that the Bogeyman had been here in Mr. Angstrom's cabin. She had fallen asleep in the truck, she remembered that. Mommy and Mr. Angstrom must've put her in here for a nap. She was glad it was time to leave.

"I wetted my pants," she said miserably.

"That's all right," Mr. Angstrom said, taking her hand. "Don't you worry about it."

"Are we going home now?" It hurt a little to talk. In the dream she'd screamed so loud, the sound tearing her throat. In the dream . . .

"We're going to pick up a few things," Mr. Angstrom said. "You need some dry clothes."

So maybe they were going to Gramma's house and maybe Gramma and Grampa would be back from their vacation and maybe . . .

He led her toward the open doorway into the cabin's other room. Her heart beat heavily, the sound booming in her ears. In the dream . . .

The Bogeyman hit Mommy, a loud sickening thump, and Mommy fell down and . . .

The room was empty. Gramma's picnic basket sat on the table and Mommy's purse was on one of the chairs.

"Where's Mommy?" Lizzie whispered.

"She's taking a nap."

His hand had a dirty streak across the knuckles, Lizzie saw. There was dirt on his pants, too, and a long dirty wisp of some kind stuck to his shirt. He had a funny smell, like mushrooms. Not the kind you eat. The kind that grew in the corner of the park where the sprinkler leaked and the ground was always smelly and damp.

Something thick and hot filled Lizzie's chest, squeezing all the air from her lungs. In the dream . . .

In the dream the Bogeyman's runny skin had turned to normal flesh and she looked at him and knew he'd become a real person: he'd become Mr. Angstrom and he said awful things and hit Mommy and it wasn't a dream, wasn't a dream . . .

"Come along, Princess," Mr. Angstrom said. The Bogeyman said. "Don't dawdle. I've got a lot to do."

When Joanna opened her eyes again, she knew time had passed. She didn't know how much time. But somehow during that period of unconsciousness her mind had assembled what she'd seen, sorted it, reached conclusions. She was in a room with a low, unfinished ceiling, a dirt floor. A slit of window too narrow to crawl through. Crusted with filth, it let in a little weak light. Basement . . . no, a cellar, smelling of fungus and decay.

Around her loomed piles of sagging cardboard boxes; the skeleton of a rusting bed frame; a rocker, the back spindles cracked and twisted askew; a coatrack sprouting antlers. Antlers? Spiders had abandoned the room, leaving webs that looked old, dust-clogged, like strips of Spanish moss.

She turned her head cautiously, unwilling to lift it and risk that mallet strike of pain with its accompanying vertigo. Lie still and think. Lizzie wasn't down here, she remembered that. Oh, God, let that be a good sign. And Lizzie wasn't screaming anymore. Surely she'd hear if Lizzie were screaming. No human sounds at all in the tomblike silence. Just the drip-drip of water somewhere and furtive rustlings that she didn't want to identify.

So . . . assume that Lizzie was all right, that Miles wouldn't hurt her. She had to believe that or otherwise she'd go crazy.

Lizzie was safe, then—up there—in the cabin. Unless Miles had taken them someplace else. No, how could he handle her limp body and a terrified child? This cellar must be below the cabin, although it was too small to extend beneath both rooms. She saw thick boards nailed on a wall to form the rungs of a ladder and above it, between crude wooden beams, the faint outline of a trapdoor.

A way out . . .

Oh, right, Joanna. Can't even lift your head, so what good is a trapdoor?

Well, the dizziness wouldn't last forever. She pushed away thoughts of concussion and hairline fractures. She'd go slow, take it easy. She rolled over, levered herself up an inch at a time. Expecting the pain, she was able to block it a little. The effort drenched her in sweat. On hands and knees she rested, taking deep breaths of air that felt heavy and useless as though the dank odors had replaced vital oxygen.

When she felt, not stronger, just more convinced she could handle the exertion, she crawled over to the boxes and pulled herself upright, using the cartons for support, the cardboard caving in at her touch. The headache coiled at the base of her skull, ready to strike. Her heart beat raggedly and she could taste bile in her throat. Standing, she realized the ceiling was about six feet from the floor. She'd only have to climb a step or two on the ladder to push open the trapdoor. But would she dare? Silence didn't guarantee that Miles wouldn't be there, waiting . . . waiting with the poker in his hands.

Thump thump thump—she froze as dust puffed from the ceiling, punctuating the sounds. Footsteps. *He was coming.* Lie down, pretend to be unconscious—no, the sounds were getting louder, moving toward her away from the trapdoor. Then she heard a loud *ka-THUNK* almost directly overhead that had to be the front door of the cabin closing, so she had to be beneath the main room.

If the front door was located there, then the narrow window must look out to the front of the cabin. She found a toehold on one of the crumbling boxes, lifted herself the few inches necessary to peer through the dirt-frosted glass. A mole's-eye view, through the weeds, but she could make out part of Miles's pickup, then movement.

Somebody—Miles—like looking through a pop bottle— but yes, thank God, he was carrying Lizzie. They got into the truck and she heard a distant rumble, felt it transmitted through the ground, as the engine started.

She watched the pickup drive away. Lizzie . . . Lizzie looked fine. Looked fine but there were so many ways to hurt a child . . . no, please. Lizzie had to be all right.

Joanna turned from the window, looking toward the steps that led to the trapdoor. Now was the time to get out—while Miles was gone. Escape . . . go for help.

She worked her way around the room past the broken furniture. Move a foot. Rest. The hat rack did have antlers: a stag's head hung on a curving hook, glassy eyes staring. The pain in the back of her head pulsed, bright as a banked fire. How long had Miles been gone now? Her internal clock was broken, just like her poor skull.

An eternity later she reached the steps, pulled herself up

until her hair brushed the ceiling. She could see the trap-door plainly now, but she couldn't tell how it opened. Clinging to the rough wood with one hand, she reached out and put her palm on the nearest edge of the door. Pushed.

The door moved—just the tiniest movement, but it showed that the door did open in that direction. She pushed with all her strength, forgetting the pain until it hit with a vertiginous swirl, toppling her from the ladder. As she fell, she knew with cruel certainty she'd only been fooling herself, that Miles knew all about barn doors, that he'd taken great care to lock this one and she'd never had a chance to open it and get away.

20

Miles watched the speed limit carefully as he drove back to the farm. He carried precious cargo: the little girl who sat beside him, wrapped in a blanket, her seat belt tightened. Still pale, with that drowsy look he knew was shock. She hadn't even asked about her kitten when they left the cabin. Good thing, since he had no idea where the animal had gone.

His heart lurched even now as he thought how close fate had come to playing another cruel trick on him. He was sure he'd locked the cabin's bedroom door, but suddenly Lizzie was there, screaming as he swung . . . he could still feel a resonance in his scapula from the shock of the poker making contact. He'd never meant to hit Joanna, just to scare her. But she'd made him so furious. Bad enough to lie to him, but to use Lizzie as an excuse . . .

Lizzie was a perfectly normal little girl. Anybody could see that. She'd wet her pants earlier but that was certainly understandable. Sarah's things would fit her. He had saved everything, could never bring himself to dispose of them, so clothes were no problem.

Beside him Lizzie stirred as he slowed for the junction of County 15. "Are you okay, Princess?" he asked, but she turned away, looking out the window at the stands of pines flitting past.

She'd be all right. Children have a natural resilience, and he'd be there to take care of her. That's what he had to concentrate on now. Forget about Joanna. Take Lizzie and vanish. It happens all the time. He, of all people, ought to know that. He'd have the last laugh on Amos Fowler, too, as a little bonus.

Once they were safely away, he'd call Mort Lankersheim and tell him where to find Joanna. No chance of her getting out, not with the trapdoor locked and the old steamer trunk pulled over the opening. Not that she deserved much consideration.

This thing about taking Lizzie to a doctor . . . how gullible did Joanna think he was? She was dragging the child off to Boston so she could go whoring after her boyfriend. So it was her own fault for stoking his anger. All these years fighting for control, of trying to keep his promise to Papa . . .

"My little angel," his mother always said, and he was. A beautiful little boy who never gave her a moment's trouble. It was his father who noticed how Miles rushed to watch the neck twisted from Sunday's chicken, who saw how Miles stood and stared at a pig being hoisted for slaughter, his eyes alive with eagerness for the blood to flow.

Henry Angstrom recognized the darkness and dealt with it the only way he knew how. *There's the devil's own beast inside you, boy, his father said as he uncoiled the whip.* No matter how well Miles hid them, Henry always found the corpses of frogs, barn cats, the neighbor's black goat. *You got to build a cage, boy. Build it strong and keep the beast inside.*

Miles hunched over the steering wheel, remembering that first shock of leather cleaving him in half. *I tried, Papa.* God knows he'd tried.

He'd only lost control once in all these years since his father died, a lapse that cost him—cost him dearly. Mustn't think about that now. He'd tried too hard to forget those terrible images that burned in his brain, and he'd promised, never again. He swore it on Papa's grave. And kept his word—even with Amos goading him—until he realized that Joanna had played him for a fool.

How could he ever have been so taken in? That first day when she and Lizzie came to the farm stand, his heart went out to Lizzie, naturally, but he'd been touched by Joanna, too. Joanna, so obviously hurt with this pathetically thin little shell around her. The rumor mill was already working. Her husband left with another woman, had been screwing around for years. God knows Miles understood what it was like to be betrayed.

He saw it all clearly: a slow courtship—an out-of-date word but perfect here—understanding and affection deepening into love. He was at least twelve years older than Joanna, but men married younger women all the time.

He'd make a good life for all of them, especially for Lizzie . . . Lizzie, his daughter, his sweet little girl restored to him like a miracle.

Good Christ, he was stupid. Taking care not to rush things. Even after Lizzie had supplied the name that day at the farm stand—Blanchard, Tom Blanchard—he'd convinced himself things would work out, that they'd all be together. And all along Joanna was seeing Blanchard . . . fucking him. Just like Saturday night.

Maybe he wouldn't call the police after he and Lizzie left. It would serve her right. Down there in the cellar, all alone . . .

No, he told himself sharply. He *would* call Lankersheim as soon as he and Lizzie were far enough away. That's what Papa would want him to do.

Lizzie was sleeping now, the odor of urine strong in the cab even with the window down. He could smell his own sweat, too. They both needed a bath. He'd put Lizzie in the tub while he packed.

He slowed as he passed the sign reading "Angstrom Acres, 2 miles." He'd never wanted to be a farmer, but he'd seen the necessity of it. A degree of isolation, hard physical work, discipline. He looked at his precise, fruitful rows. The bugs would finally win—grasshoppers, cutworms, potato beetles. The weeds would take over. Never mind. He'd have Lizzie, that was the important thing.

Just past the farm stand, he turned into the long driveway bordered by mossy stone walls. The old house and barn sat under a canopy of ancient maple and beech a half mile off Old Mill Road. No animals anymore except for the cats. He used the barn for farm equipment and storage. The house was two stories high, freshly painted white siding with dark green trim. It looked just the same as it had when his parents were alive.

He parked the truck and got out. Birds chirped and wind rustled the cornstalks. He couldn't see anybody in the fields or the woods beyond, but the back of his neck prickled as he imagined Amos Fowler behind some distant tree, watching.

He opened the passenger's side of the pickup and unfastened Lizzie's seat belt. "Wake up, Princess. We're home."

"Home?" Her eyes widened, then filled with tears. "But I thought we were going to Gramma's house."

"Oh, you'll like it here much better. Come on, now. You need a bath. Then I'll make us some soup. Won't that be nice?"

"Not hungry."

He had to pull her along, inside, up the stairs to the bathroom. While he filled the tub, he stripped off her shirt and started to help with her pants.

"Don't wanna bath, don't want one." She twisted away and wedged herself into the corner between the toilet and sink cabinet.

"You're dirty, Lizzie," he said sternly. "And you smell bad. Come on out of there and get undressed."

She shook her head, sullen and stubborn. "Don't have to. Mommy said. Nobody's s'posed to touch me. Not if I don't want them to."

Touch her? Good Christ, Joanna had warned the little girl about child molesters, and Lizzie thought that he . . .

Feeling sickened and vaguely guilty, he said, "You can do everything yourself. I'll go outside. But you have to take a bath."

He drew the shower curtain across the outside of the tub, explaining to Lizzie that once she was in the water he'd come in to get her dirty clothes and bring her some fresh things.

From the boxes in Sarah Ann's closet he took lace-edged panties, a sky-blue pinafore. They smelled of mothballs but that couldn't be helped. While he was at it, he took out more clothes for the trip. Frilly dresses, a bundle of hair ribbons. What a beautiful little doll, people always said about Sarah. Lizzie would be just as pretty. He'd dress her up, take her places. Once he found them a safe place to live . . .

A big city, that much was obvious. People in the country were too nosy. Chicago, maybe. Dallas. He would go to the bank, cash a check, take the negotiable bonds from his safety-deposit box . . .

Damn! He looked at his watch. Past three and the bank was closed. Now they'd have to wait until tomorrow to leave.

Maybe that wasn't so bad. Actually it might be better, giving him time to think and make some plans. Have a good meal, a good night's sleep. Not so good for Joanna. She'd have to spend the night in the cellar alone. He could go back out there, take her some food.

His breathing quickened. Such a skinny thing, but she'd felt warm and round and lush when he carried her to the cellar. So helpless . . .

No, he couldn't take the chance. Let her go hungry. Little enough punishment for a whore.

He picked up the stack of clothes and started to his bedroom, pausing on the way to listen at the door to the bath.

Not a sound. Exasperated, he pushed open the door. He was tired of catering to the child. If she wasn't in the tub by now . . . No dirty clothes on the floor and he didn't have to look behind the curtain to know the tub was empty.

He dropped the clothes and ran downstairs. Hallway, living room—no sign of her—the dead bolt on the front door still in place, so she hadn't left the house that way. He heard a sound from the kitchen.

Lizzie stood on a chair at the counter with the telephone in her hands, punching out a call on the push buttons. Before he snatched the phone away, she began shrieking, "Daddy, Daddy, help us, pleaseplease help us—"

Miles put his hand over her mouth and held her while she flopped like a rag doll, beating her heels on the shiny tile floor. He started to slam down the phone, heard a voice and put the receiver to his ear. "Sorry. Your call cannot be completed as dialed—"

Miles hung up. "You didn't get through, Lizzie. All you got was a computer."

All the fight left her. When he took his hand from her mouth, there was a red mark on her face, and her eyes were dazed, hopeless.

"That was a very bad thing you did, Lizzie," he said softly. "Very bad. I was going to make us a nice dinner and you could've slept in Sarah's room tonight. But now . . ."

Too much of Joanna in the child just yet. She wasn't to be trusted. Tonight was no problem, but tomorrow . . . he could lock her up someplace while he went to the bank, but what if somebody stopped by? He didn't get a lot of visitors; still, people had a way of dropping in unexpectedly.

"There's nothing else to do," he said.

Blood sang in his head, and the watchful tension in his chest relaxed like a door opening.

"There's just nothing for it," he said. "We have to go back to the cabin."

21

After a series of ominous clinks and clanks, the Winnebago shuddered like a wounded elephant, backfired, and all the instrument panel lights glowed red.

"Don't tell me *that* was a fan belt," Ruth said as Matt shut off the ignition and braked to a stop.

Looking betrayed by the machinery, Matt climbed down from the camper and began a slow inspection. Ruth followed, glancing nervously up and down the road, slapping at black flies. The shoulder was too narrow to park off the pavement, but there was good visibility . . . Ruth suppressed the thought: at least in daylight. The road narrowed into dense woods a mile or so ahead, plenty of time for an approaching car to see their predicament.

Matt, on hands and knees, peered up into the oily undersides of the camper.

"Well?" Ruth said.

"Nothing leaking." He got up and dusted off his pants.

"What does *that* mean?" Ruth demanded.

Ignoring her, Matt opened the engine compartment. "Keep your eye out for cars."

That was about all Ruth could do as she paced around. Not that there were any cars to see. As a matter of fact, they'd only passed one other vehicle in the past half hour—or was it longer? A cool north breeze broke the lake's mirror surface into a short chop. Ruth shivered and went for her sweater.

After fifteen minutes of poking around in the Winnebago's innards, Matt wiped his hands on an old towel. "Might be the carburetor. Or the fuel pump."

Which meant he didn't know what was wrong. Would it kill him to admit it? "What do we do now?"

"Wait till somebody comes along and get a ride to town. It's not as though we're stranded out here without food and water, Ruth. How about some coffee while we wait?"

Coffee! Well, it wasn't such a bad idea at that. "Do you really think we're safe sitting halfway out on the road like this?"

"Probably a good idea to put out some emergency markers," Matt agreed.

Before he got the reflective triangles in place, a Blazer drove up. The four-by-four was loaded with camping gear and a family of five who offered to send help from a fishing camp about ten miles away.

"Not a lot there," the driver said. "But Dan's a pretty fair mechanic and he's got a Power Wagon fixed up for towing."

Dan Hardin was a short, muscular man with a bushy mustache and fish scales on his boots. By the time he'd rigged a temporary hitch and pulled the Winnebago back to the camp, Ruth wished they'd had time for the coffee and maybe a snack. She was hungry and tired, full of misgivings as she looked around at the dilapidated buildings.

A World War II airplane hangar acted as general store, garage and—from the smell—was used to store bait. An old Mustang, several boats and an automobile engine sat around in various states of repair. No room for the camper, so Hardin left it outside. Good thing because Ruth wanted no part of the rough cabins that straggled off past the dock. She intended to spend the night in the camper.

Three big dogs, lean as timber wolves, came running when they arrived, then loped off toward the docks where a fishing party was cleaning piles of bass and lake trout.

"I'm gonna have a bunch a thirsty guys on my hands," Hardin said. "Come on and have a beer. I'll take a look at your problem first thing tomorrow."

Matt accepted promptly. Ruth trailed behind, overwhelmed by the raw energy and powerful stench. At least there were power poles marching off toward civilization. She hoped one of the wires strung on the T-cross was a telephone line.

When asked, Hardin seemed mildly affronted by the question. "A course," he said. "Over there." He hiked a thumb toward an ancient pay phone on a far wall, adding, "If it's working."

Prophetic words. All Ruth got was staticky hum and a lot of empty echoing line.

*   *   *

When Joanna was a teenager, she'd had her appendix out, and once she had a very high fever with the flu. She'd discovered then how the mind can slip its mooring and wander off. That had to be what was happening now. She was in the Maple Grove Community Hospital having a phenobarbital fantasy. Any minute Dr. Henderson would come in, demanding to know why she wasn't taking better care of herself.

She pretended as long as she could, until the sensory input made it impossible. The pain in her head had settled to a dull throb. Her right knee ached and she'd bitten her lip. She tasted blood, felt the sharp edge of a tooth, chipped in the fall from the ladder. She opened her eyes.

A shaft of sunlight pierced the gloom in the cellar; dust motes tumbled in the weak glow. The sun was going down, shining through the window. *I'm going to be here in the dark. Alone in the dark. And Lizzie . . .*

She got up and went to the window, realizing as she climbed up on a box to look out that she was shaky but the dizziness was gone. No sign of the truck—unless Miles had parked out of her range of sight. She listened carefully and could hear no sound from the cabin overhead.

She had to get out—but how? Break the window . . . oh, right, Joanna, and then what? Impossible to squeeze her rib cage through that narrow slot, and nobody for miles to hear her calls for help. The walls—a charge of dynamite might do the trick. Only one way out. She crossed over to the crude stairway.

Hope surged as she stared up at the trapdoor. She'd been in bad shape before. The door might not be locked, just too heavy for her to open in her weakened state. Awkward, too, standing on the stairs. A box, that's what she needed, so she could exert all her strength to push the door straight up.

When she leaned over to pick a carton off the stack, the vertigo hit, her brain slipping around freely like gelatin in a bowl. She clung to the cardboard mound until the room righted itself.

Something's wrong with me . . .

Never mind. Don't think about it. Concentrate on getting out of here. Afraid to bend over, she squatted and pushed a box along the dirt floor. The flexing action made her knee hurt, but she was beyond caring.

Climbing onto the box was like standing on a sponge. She shifted around to get her balance, then put both hands on the trapdoor, pushed. The door gave—that maddening quarter of an inch. Stuck . . . maybe that was it. She pushed in short furious bursts until her strength ran out. She sagged down to the floor. Tears flowed down her cheeks, and her whole body trembled.

"Damn, damn . . ."

Just one word from her and Mom would never have gone on the trip. Why hadn't Joanna admitted how scared she was? Two days since Mom had called. Surely she would phone tonight, and when nobody answered . . . she'd assume they went to dinner or a movie or a drive or—

Joanna *felt* the truck returning before she heard it, a vibration transmitted though the earth.

Miles. He'd realized what a crazy thing he'd done so of course he'd come back to let her out.

She waited, mouth dry, a mixture of elation and dread knotting her stomach. Footsteps, Miles's voice—impossible to understand the words but surely his voice—and Lizzie's, a thin piping. She smoothed her hair with shaking hands, tried to brush the dirt from her jeans.

More sounds—impossible to translate—a distant pounding. Growing darker in the cellar now. What was he doing? He wouldn't just leave her down here . . . would he?

She stifled the impulse to go and bang on the trapdoor. No sense taking a chance of provoking him. More pounding and then after a while, a louder, scraping noise. Finally the trapdoor opened and Miles looked down.

"Well, don't just stand there. Come on up." He watched, not offering any help, his eyes bright, secretive.

Joanna could see the edge of the steamer trunk near the opening. He must have pulled it over the trapdoor. No wonder she couldn't move the door. She negotiated the steps carefully. When she climbed onto the cabin floor, she leaned heavily against the trunk as though to steady herself. The trunk didn't budge. Her dismay was quickly forgotten when she saw Lizzie sitting on the sofa.

"Mommy!"

Lizzie came running and hurled herself into Joanna's arms. Joanna held her tightly, scarcely daring to believe that she was all right.

"I want you to clean her up," Miles said. "Yourself, too, Joanna. You're a mess. There's no hot water. You'll just have to make do." He gestured toward the bedroom. "In there. I left some clothes for Lizzie."

Joanna saw then what some of the pounding had been—a bright metal hasp nailed to the outside of the bedroom door. A padlock hung there, and when she and Lizzie were inside the room, she heard the lock snap closed.

Her knees too rubbery to stand any longer, Joanna sank down on the bed with Lizzie on her lap.

"Mommy, he h-h-hurt you. I saw him—I saw—"

"Shh, it's okay now. I'm fine, baby, just fine. Are you—did he—do anything to you?"

"No." She told Joanna about riding in the truck to the farm, about Miles wanting her to have a bath. "I told him—about being private. Like you said."

"Good, baby. You did just right."

"When he went away, I sneaked downstairs to call Daddy. But he came and saw me and he got really mad and—" Lizzie pressed her face against Joanna's breasts. "I tried to remember Daddy's number. I tried so hard. He would've come, Mommy. He would've come and saved us."

"Yes, of course, darling." Would you, Walt? If Lizzie had managed to reach you, would you have come? "You were awfully brave, Lizzie. I'm so proud of you."

"I peed my pants," Lizzie said mournfully.

"That's okay." Joanna could hear Miles moving around in the other room. She stroked Lizzie's hair and looked around. A small dark bathroom shared the common wall. There was only one window, but it was certainly large enough if she could open it.

As though reading her mind, Lizzie whispered, "He put nails in it."

Joanna saw the shiny nailheads driven into the sash. That explained the rest of the pounding. The panes were too small even for Lizzie to climb through. "Yes—well, then—maybe we'd better do what he says and get you cleaned up."

"I don't wanna wear that stuff, Mommy. It smells."

183

Mothballs, Joanna realized as she looked down at the little blue dress laid out on the bed. A dress that must have been packed away. Sarah Ann's dress.

"You're not exactly a rose yourself," she said lightly. "Come on."

She caught a glimpse of herself in the wavy mirror as she stripped off Lizzie's corduroys and underwear. All eyes and cheekbones. Her hair was a fright wig and her skin pale, streaked with dirt. She soaked a washcloth and began giving Lizzie a sponge bath.

"Listen, darling, I know this is all very scary, but you're going to have to be brave a little longer. Mr. Angstrom—well, he's sick, Lizzie. Very sick. I think—if we're careful—he'll realize what he's doing and take us home."

"No, he won't." Lizzie shivered, goose bumps raised along her skinny little thighs. "He's just like I dreamed. He's going to do awful things—"

"No," Joanna said fiercely. "Now, you stop talking like that. This will all be over soon—tonight. You hear me? But you have to do what I tell you, Lizzie." Her head began to hurt and she could feel her strength ebbing away at an alarming rate. "Just be very nice and do whatever he says. Try not to act afraid. Let me talk to him, okay? Okay."

Lizzie stood silently as Joanna slipped on the beautiful little pinafore, but Joanna could feel the child cringing. Was she making a mistake to think she could talk to Miles? What she really wanted to do was bash his head in as soon as he opened the door. Good luck, Joanna. The furniture in the room consisted of a painted chest of drawers and a bed frame holding the mattress. Given enough time and the proper tools, she might be able to disassemble one of them. Right now she was limp as a noodle and there was nothing in the room to use to swat a fly, let alone knock Miles senseless.

"You about ready in there?" he called from the other side of the door.

"In a minute."

Was there anything else she could do? She tried to think of all the TV shows she'd seen all those nights she'd been alone, waiting for Walt. All those private eyes in impossible situations. Throw something in his eyes—that was a typical ploy. A handful of Comet would be perfect, but the bathroom was bare except for a sliver of soap, the washcloth and one thin towel.

She washed her face and finger-combed her hair. Maybe later—in the kitchen. She'd wait and see, grab any opportunity that came along. Some kind of cleaner, hot coffee, knives. Could she really use a knife? *If I have to . . . maybe . . .* Reasoning with him was still her best and most likely way out.

From the next room came the sound of hammering. Lizzie ran over and pressed against Joanna's leg. "Mommy?"

"All right, baby, he's probably just—just fixing something—" Fixing what?

The sound of a key in the padlock. "Joanna?" Miles called.

She smiled at Lizzie and took the little girl's hand. "Ready, tiger?"

Miles opened the door—cautiously, Joanna noted. A strong smell of fried chicken wafted in and Joanna realized suddenly that she was starved. No wonder she was so light-headed. She hadn't eaten all day. Three boxes from Kentucky Fried Chicken sat on the maple table.

"Look who I found outside." Miles gestured to the floor beside the table where Lizzie's white kitten greedily lapped gravy from a paper plate.

"Berry!" Lizzie ran over and sat on her heels, petting him and scolding.

Joanna started to follow, but Miles's hand closed around her upper arm. No mistaking that cruel pressure as he steered her to the sofa. "Lie down," he said softly.

"What?" A lump of dread, as palpable as the hunger, rose in Joanna's throat.

"Do you want Lizzie to be upset again like she was last night? Now, do as I say."

He gave her a little shove and Joanna fell back, the motion violent enough to start that sloshing inside her head. All she could do was lie there, cursing the weakness, while Miles picked up something from the floor and attached it to her right ankle. Some kind of leather thong, cinching tight. When he motioned her to stand up, she saw it was fastened to a length of chain bolted to the wall near the front door. The hammering she and Lizzie had heard . . . and now she was tethered like an animal.

"Miles, please, you can't do this."

"Can't I?" Excitement burned in his eyes.

He likes this. Oh, Sweet Jesus, he feeds on this.

Across the room, Lizzie stared at her mother for several seconds, then went back to petting the cat, rejecting what she'd seen or pretending it never happened.

Would Lizzie ever recover from this? If it ended soon, before there was irreparable harm . . . "Let me talk to him," Joanna remembered saying to her daughter. Reasonable words. *Stupid* words. But now talking to him really was all she could do. When he yanked her up and steered her to the table, pushed her down on a chair, she saw he'd calculated the length of the chain so that she couldn't go any further.

"Soup's on," he said merrily. "Come on, Princess."

He directed Lizzie to sit next to him and began opening boxes, taking out little containers of coleslaw and potatoes. The greasy, spicy smell of the chicken sickened Joanna now, and she gripped the edge of her chair, fighting nausea.

"Eat," Miles said. "What do you like, Princess? A drumstick? A wing?" He piled a little of everything on plates and put them in front of Lizzie and Joanna.

Across the table, Lizzie's eyes were enormous, imploring. Joanna picked up her fork, nodding for her daughter to do the same. She forced herself to eat a few bites. Miles poured milk for Lizzie, opened cans of Budweiser. Joanna didn't want the beer but she was still thirsty so she sipped a little, the fizzy liquid stinging her lip.

"Isn't this nice?" Miles said. "Just the three of us."

"Nice," Joanna said, feeling the strap cutting into her ankle, her mind trapped, too, racing around in a closed loop trying to find something to get him to let them go. Only one reason would worry him: Somebody was going to miss her and suspect something was wrong. And she'd neatly put the lie to that herself. They weren't even supposed to be home. She and Lizzie were leaving for Boston for an anonymous motel room. But Miles didn't know that. He thought she was going to Tom.

You have to let us go because Tom will miss me.

She remembered that moment when he hit her with the

poker and knew she could never mention Tom. So reason with him. Wasn't that what she'd told Lizzie she would do?

"You can stop this right now, Miles," she said carefully, conscious of Lizzie sitting so close to him. "It's not too late. Just take us home."

"And I suppose you won't ever tell anybody anything." He finished a chicken leg, then cracked the bone.

"I—" She knew the terrible risk, knew she would never be able to tell the lie and make him believe it, but she had to say it anyway: "I promise you I wouldn't."

"Right." He sucked out marrow, wiped his hands on some paper napkins and urged Lizzie to eat.

"Not hungry," Lizzie said.

"Well, then, I think it's time you went to bed."

Lizzie began to shake her head. "No—no—I want Leon—I want—"

"It's all right, baby," Joanna said quickly. "You'll have Berry to sleep with. Go ahead and take a little rest. Please, darling." *Please don't make him mad.*

Miles took Lizzie off with a monstrous little farce of bedtime hoopla, leaving Joanna with only a few feverish moments to scan the room. There was nothing within her reach that she could use as a weapon. Miles had prepared well. Rings in the dust on the end table marked spots where a few knickknacks had stood. Even if she could've reached the fireplace, the poker was gone.

He came out of the bedroom and locked it. "Let's sit down, Joanna."

She took a hesitant step and stopped. Just where the flap of material around the bottom of the sofa split at the sofa leg she saw the dull black point of the poker. Hidden there. Waiting for him to catch her off-guard.

"I meant what I said before, Miles. Take us home. We'll pretend this never happened. I mean it—please. For God's sake—"

He crossed the space between them and wrapped his arms around her, pinioning her brutally against him. His face, inches away, shone with an excitement that turned her blood icy.

"I saw all the things you did to your boyfriend Saturday night, Joanna. Now you're going to do them to me."

She arched her body, wrenched away. "You fucking *creep*. I'll never—ever—"

He doubled up his fist and hit her in the middle of her breastbone. Stunned, she stayed upright, just hunched a little as air rushed from her lungs. Fighting to breathe, she knew she'd guessed wrong again. He hadn't planned to use the poker. Just his fist, smashing into her left temple, sending her spinning off into the blackness.

22

TUESDAY

For years now Miles needed an alarm clock only when daylight saving time interfered with the natural rhythm of things. He always awakened at five, give or take a few minutes, so it was doubly disorienting to be jarred from a heavy sleep by somebody banging on the front door downstairs and the sight of his bedside clock reading 7:05.

For an instant he thought he was at the cabin and Amos Fowler was outside. His heart echoed the loud thumping.

"Mr. Angstrom. Mr. Angstrom, you at home?"

It was Timmy Lafferty, of course, ready to go to work. Miles lay there, his mind racing. The farm, the produce stand—none of it mattered now. Maybe Timmy would get tired and go away. But if the stand didn't open, people were bound to wonder why, especially Amos, and Timmy would talk. People were so goddamn nosy, somebody was bound to come to check on him. Better to keep things as normal as possible.

He rolled off the bed, feeling grimy, smelling his own sweat. He'd slept in his clothes, when he finally slept. He yelled, "Coming," to Timmy and went downstairs to open the door.

"Jeez, are you all right?" Timmy eyed him curiously.

"Not feeling too well. A bug, I guess."

"What about the stuff from the market?"

Miles stared at him as though he were speaking Greek.

"You didn't go to Brattleboro?" Timmy asked.

It was Tuesday morning, Miles realized. He went to the produce market in Brattleboro on Tuesdays and Fridays for all the extra vegetables he didn't grow.

"Overslept," he said. "We'll just have to make do. Why don't you get started on the cucumbers, Timmy. I'll be there in a few minutes."

"You sure you're up to it?"

"I'll give it a shot. You know where the tractor keys are."

He made double-strength instant coffee with hot water from the tap, then went down to work for a frantic half hour, carelessly ripping tomatoes from the vines and yanking up handfuls of radishes. As soon as the stand was hastily stocked, he gave Timmy the cash box and went back to the house to shower and shave.

He had to be at work when Amos arrived. Give the old bastard one reason to be suspicious and he'd be following Miles around like a bloodhound. Everything had to go well today. He'd go to the bank just as soon as he could and then drive to Springfield. He'd decided to go there and buy a used camper for cash, taking no chances of anybody recognizing him. He hated to leave Lizzie alone in the cabin for so long but it couldn't be helped.

She'd be all right. Locked in the bedroom, but he'd left plenty of food, milk and juice and pop in the cooler, and the bathroom was right there. Besides that she had the cat to keep her company and he'd brought some of Sarah's coloring books and crayons.

Sarah could always sit for hours, happily keeping herself occupied. Lizzie could, too.

How long before she forgot about Joanna? It was bound to be hard for the child, he expected that. At least she wasn't hysterical last night, but she wasn't responsive either; just stood like a little statue while he made up the bed in the cabin with clean linen and didn't say a word when he helped put on her pajamas and tucked her in with a kiss.

Time, it would take time. Children forget. Away from here she would forget easily. They'd have a new identity. He'd be Henry; his daughter would, of course, be Sarah Ann.

Ruth took a lawn chair and a Dick Francis mystery and sat under a pine tree while Matt and Dan Hardin poked around in the Winnebago's engine. The turpentiny scent of pine resin couldn't quite overcome the stench from the fish-cleaning block down by the lake, wafted her way occasionally by a vagrant breeze.

Hardin made his diagnosis in record time. "Timing chain," he said. "Damn lucky you didn't do some major damage. I can fix it but we'll hafta send Cass for the part."

"How long will that take?" Matt asked.

"A few hours. I can have you on the road by four. Meantime, whyn't you take a boat out? Catch some bass."

"Couldn't we go into town with Cass?" Ruth asked.

"Well, sure, if you really want to, I suppose."

"*I* don't want to," Matt said. He was still mad at her for running back and forth to the pay phone last night, dragging him along because she didn't want to go alone into the raucous beer-drinking crowd that hung around the store. "You can go if you like. I'll stay right here and go fishing."

Ruth imagined driving for hours with Cass, a sullen young fellow who stank, she was sure, of marijuana. Chances were good that she'd miss Joanna at home during the day anyway. If the camper was repaired by four, they'd be in Dryden tonight and she could call then. Meantime, she would keep trying on the pay phone.

She agreed to stay at the camp but adamantly refused to go out fishing with Matt. Privately she gave Cass Joanna's phone number in Maple Grove, money for long-distance charges and an extra five dollars for making the call.

Hurts to breathe. Hurts to think.

Lizzie and I . . . having dinner. That's it. A nice dinner . . . waiting for the phone to ring . . . for Mom to call.

Waiting and waiting . . . Lizzie and I . . . having dinner and . . . my leg was chained to the wall.

Joanna cried out and opened her eyes.

She was back in the cellar. She could see around the gloomy little prison, so it must be morning. She'd cheated the night. All that worrying about being down here in the dark. See how nice everything works out?

The stag's head, tilted on the hat rack, stared down at her with one glassy eye. Poor old deer. Dear old deer. Had your problems, too, didn't you?

She touched her rib cage, searching for sharp edges, bones broken or detached. She couldn't feel anything obvious. There was just the terrible soreness and the fact that every breath brought a twinge of pain.

Could she sit up? She found she could by rolling to her side and bringing her knees up, moving slowly. She stared at the quality of the dim illumination and suddenly wasn't sure that it was morning. How many hours had she lost? Maybe it was more than hours. A day . . . longer . . . She had a raging thirst and she needed to go to the bathroom.

At least Lizzie had been spared the trauma of seeing what happened to her mother . . . a small comfort. Miles was with Lizzie now. *A crazy man's with my baby.*

Joanna listened for sounds in the cabin above. Nothing. He had probably taken Lizzie and gone away again. Even if she could drag herself over to the window, she knew she couldn't manage to climb up and look out to see if the truck was there. Not now anyway. Maybe later. She'd be stronger after a while and then she'd look.

Right now she had to think. How could she have been so stupid trying to reason with him? She wouldn't make that mistake again. And to push him away like that. *You fucking creep* . . . saying that was the worst mistake of all.

Why hadn't somebody seen his madness? But, of course somebody had. *Amos had most of the farm dug up, looking for the bodies.* Her mother's words. Had Amos Fowler been right about Miles all these years, or was he part of the crazy-making process—the old man's relentless hounding coupled with grief finally sending Miles over the line?

She shivered and lay back down, still curled up in a fetal position. Chaining her up, and now this . . . She began to weep. *Please, God—somebody help me.*

Tom . . . why would he suspect anything was wrong? She was off on a picnic, having fun, and then going away for a few days. No, not Tom. But Mom would call. And keep on calling. Then she'd worry and get in touch with somebody. A neighbor? The police . . . oh, God, Mom would call Chief Lankersheim and he'd reassure her that everything was just fine, that his office had heard from Joanna herself that she and Lizzie were taking a little trip.

Who else would worry? Nobody. Certainly not Walt.

Nobody was going to help her.

She dried her face on the bottom of her blouse and sat up. She could either blubber all day or figure some way to get out of this mess—not just for her own sake, but for Lizzie.

She took care of her physical needs first, just the act of moving involving more pain that she would ever have thought possible. A corner of the dirt floor served as a bathroom, but there was nothing she could do to relieve her thirst. The thought crossed her mind that people did drink their urine to stay alive. She shuddered. Miles would be back in a few hours. Of course he would be back. She did look for a water line connected to the kitchen and bathroom and found it. Not that she had any idea how to get any water from it, but just knowing the location was somehow comforting.

She realized she'd never really examined the cellar thoroughly and began a slow search. When she was too dizzy to stand, she crept around on all fours, finding nothing useful. After allowing herself a short rest she made a start on the boxes. Old composition books, letters, magazines, mouse droppings. She left the cartons and reconsidered the castoff furniture. The rocker yielded two spindles, already used as the main course for an army of wood beetles and about as dangerous as Swiss cheese.

"Well, old friend." Joanna steadied herself against the coatrack, brushing fingertips against fur that felt like an old hairbrush. The heavy iron stand had a wide base, keeping it upright against the one-sided weight. There was only one other hook besides the one holding the deer head, and it was firmly bolted into place.

She had trouble getting a pickle jar open. How would she ever remove one of the hooks? And she certainly couldn't tuck the whole coatrack under her blouse and take it with her.

Exhausted and discouraged, she sat down on the floor and looked at the angle of sunlight coming through the window. Late afternoon and she was running out of possibilities.

Except . . .

The poker. She sat very still, heart knocking against her bruised ribs. She assumed Miles had hidden the poker under the sofa, but suppose he hadn't? He must've had his hands full after he hit her. A hysterical Lizzie, herself like a sack of potatoes. If he dropped the poker and somehow it slid across the bare floor . . .

Okay, so all that was true. He wasn't going to just sit there while she took a swing at him. Somehow she had to distract him . . . somehow?

You know what he wants, Joanna.

The thought of his hands on her body sickened her, but the revulsion was tempered by anger, a steady core of rage fueled by degradation and pain, the constant worry over Lizzie. How could sex with Miles Angstrom be worse than this? Sometime during that sexual frenzy, when his guard was down along with his pants, she'd give him a practical demonstration of that saying: She has me by the balls.

. . . *and then I'll pick up the poker and* then *I'll* kill *the son of a bitch* . . .

She rested, stoking her rage, listening for the truck. Only once did she permit the thought to slip back, the darkest thought of all, that maybe Miles was never coming back.

Miles waited while the teller looked at the form that would cash in his CD. There were two people in line behind him, both saying good morning to a new arrival. Over by the big pot that dispensed free coffee, old Maud Delsey helped herself to a cup, sobering up.

"You understand there's a big penalty for early withdrawal, Mr. Angstrom?" The teller was Dana Holt, two years out of high school. He remembered her working at McDonald's, a giggly buxom girl who always mixed up his order.

"I know about the penalty. Whatever it is—I don't really care."

"Well, if you're sure." She studied the form. "You marked cash on here. Didn't you mean to transfer the money to checking?"

"I marked cash because I meant cash."

"That much money—I have to get it approved." She

locked her cash drawer and took his forms over to Hiram Cates, the manager.

Miles could feel the stir of interest in the waiting line. Damned snoops. Talk about living in a goldfish bowl. He rubbed his sweaty palms on his jeans. He had to have the cash to buy the camper, but turning in the CD was a mistake. He should've taken one of his bearer bonds to Springfield, someplace where nobody knew him.

Hiram and Dana conferred, then Hiram waved him over. His desk was located beyond the coffee station, where Maud watched avidly.

Miles didn't wait for the civilities. "Hiram, if there's a problem—"

"No problem. It's just that ten thousand dollars—to tell you the truth, Miles, it puts us in a bind. Not that we don't have the money," he said hastily. "But it's payday at Dakin Mills." So many folks in town who worked over there and would be expecting to cash their paychecks today, you understand. "Be happy to give you a cashier's check, Miles. It's a lot safer anyway."

Miles felt sweat on his back. Maud was taking in every word. Soon tongues would wag all over town. He just hoped Amos didn't hear the gossip. The old man had hung around the stand longer than usual this morning, and Miles was sure he suspected something.

"Miles?"

"What did you say?"

"I said would you like a cashier's check?"

"I—" A cashier's check was safe, wasn't it? Just like cash. But the bank must keep some kind of record—a serial number, something that could be traced. "Listen, why don't we just forget it. I mean—what with the penalty and all—not as if I really needed the money. Another investment—but maybe I'll think about it some more.''

"Good idea." Hiram stood up and held out his hand. "See you on Friday."

Friday? The Jaycee lunch, Miles remembered as he hurried outside to his pickup. By then he and Sarah would be far away. Sarah . . . no, he meant Lizzie. He and *Lizzie* would be far away. He would just take the bonds to Springfield—his hand froze on the door handle. The bonds were still in his safety-deposit box. He'd forgotten all about them. That meant he would have to go back inside, face the scrutiny of all those damn busybodies . . . he jumped into the truck and headed out of town.

After a while he realized he was driving toward Springfield. If he hadn't bungled everything, he could be in the city in an hour. Since he didn't have the bonds or the cash, there was no sense going in that direction. He turned around and started back. There would be a turnover of customers in the bank by now. If he waited another fifteen minutes, Hiram would be out for lunch.

He slowed as he entered the town limits, came to a stop in front of the colonial graveyard where huge old oak trees shaded the street. A few tourists wandered up the hillside through the thin slate markers, snapping pictures. Miles felt as though the basic element of time had changed shape, these few minutes passing in slow motion while the day as a whole whirled by.

Too jumpy to sit, he got out of the truck and entered the cemetery through a wrought-iron gate. The sun beat down with a yellow intensity, air barely stirring under the roof of oak branches as he walked over the hill. The dates on the grave markers kept getting more recent, the rows laid straighter. Tourists never went beyond the 1800s up the slope of the second low hill. Over that second rise he was alone in the green stillness.

Enough time had passed now. He could go back to the bank. Instead he walked out into fierce sunlight, two rows over, ten markers down. This was the last time he'd ever come here. He couldn't leave without saying good-bye. Briefly he stood beside his mother's grave. She'd died when Miles was fifteen, still calling him her good little boy. The lettering on the adjacent marker read: Henry Angstrom, 1899–1974. Miles went down on one knee, touching the lettering. The gray slate was smooth, cool to the touch.

The sun burned through his shirt into his skin. Suddenly he could hear the hiss of the whip. He set his teeth against the cry that welled up in his throat. Mamma mustn't hear. As long as she didn't hear him, she could pretend it wasn't happening.

. . . He's out again, boy. The devil's loose . . .

He gripped the thin slab, pressed his head against the stone.

It's different this time, Papa. I swear it is. I stopped in time. Not like before . . .

A year after Papa died, a horrible year except for Sarah. That spring Bonnie took up pot throwing, leaving Sarah with him in the afternoon while she went to Brattleboro for a class. She began making excuses not to sleep with him: a yeast infection, trouble with her period, the flu. All the while she almost reeked of sexual musk. He hired a baby-sitter for Sarah and followed Bonnie—to school and then to a motel, where she went with a skinny guy who looked like Al Pacino. The teacher, Miles found out later.

Miles had left her there with her lover and come straight to the graveyard, letting Papa help him keep the rage in check. He knew his control was too shaky that night, so he waited to talk to Bonnie. They were going to the cabin the next day. Once Sarah was in bed, he decided he'd tell Bonnie he knew, let her admit her mistake, forgive her.

Everything went terribly wrong. She said she was glad it was finally out in the open, that she loved her boyfriend. She wanted a divorce. She wanted Sarah. He hit her— *slapped* her, that was all—containing his rage even then, but the bitch fought back, yelling and swearing. He tried, just as he promised Papa he would, and he might have succeeded, he surely would have . . . if only Sarah had stayed in the bedroom . . .

He blinked and looked around, aware that the sun had shifted and the graves were shaded now. He shivered, unaccountably chilled, and got to his feet. His watch said 2:51. No time to go to the bank now. Strangely relieved, he walked back through the cemetery to his truck.

Lizzie would have to stay at the cabin another day, so he had to take out some food. He didn't like the idea of her being there all cooped up this long either. He went by the farm stand to tell Timmy he was closing early. At home he filled a cardboard box with Dinty Moore stew, chili, Saltines. Added apples, Fritos, cookies. He'd stop for ice and milk on the way.

He put the box in the truck and decided to do something that would get Lizzie outside in the sunshine. Might as well clean up the area around the cabin. He tossed some garden tools into the pickup and then drove off toward the mountains, feeling better than he'd felt all day.

23

Kevin McDowell opened his eyes and couldn't remember where he was or how he got there. He sat up and found himself staring at one of the old drunks who slept in the alleys on his first beat in South Boston, that same wild look they used to get when he roused them with his nightstick. Not some old drunk . . . himself, mirrored in a dresser across the small room.

He stumbled out of bed into the bathroom to sluice his face with cold water. His stomach roiled like the harbor during a storm. The wheezing rattle of the window air conditioner felt like a jackhammer working at the base of his skull. He switched the damn thing off and went to sprawl on the bed, hands pressed over his eyes.

Of course he knew where he was; he was just a little slow this morning, that's all. A motel room—not a detective for nothing. The cinderblock outer walls and the furnishings, early motel modern, placed the construction date in the fifties as accurately as a carbon 14 test. Out in the country—another memory block clicked into place. The turnpike late at night, the signs counting down the mileage. *Brattleboro, Vermont.*

He remembered taking an exit and promptly getting lost on some fucking country road, of driving for hours until he saw this blinking little sign, "M * T * L," and a neon arrow. No wonder he didn't know where he was. He had been *lost*, for Chrissake, not blacked out. Nothing to do with the bottle he bought from the desk clerk.

A fifth of Popov vodka—it sat on the nightstand, still half full. Whoever said vodka was tasteless hadn't drunk the stuff straight to settle a hangover. A definite petroleum flavor—diesel, he thought—but after a couple of shots he was able to stand the roar of the shower and then, relatively clean-shaven, to step out into the sunlight as long as he wore his Ray Bans.

He headed for the café attached to the motel. Black coffee and some food—he squinted at his watch. Three o'clock. Thank God he wouldn't have to smell eggs cooking. He ate some soup and a slice of apple pie with Vermont cheddar, smoked his first cigarette with his coffee. The paper place mat told him he was in Keene, New Hampshire, and provided a handy little map showing that he was approximately twenty miles east of Brattleboro.

Where was Blanchard's summer place? The place mat just highlighted the main routes and towns. After a third cup of coffee he went in search of a real map, finding one at an Amoco station. He took it into his car and spread it out across the steering wheel.

Hickory Pond, a tiny blue spot. Figuring getting lost, an hour, hour-and-a-half drive. And then what? He would walk into Blanchard's place and solve the three-year-old case with a flash of intuition?

He folded up the map and squinted against the sunlight reflected off the chromed windshield frame. Checking out the cottage was a loose end that had never been tidied up. So it was a bust. What the fuck, he'd look at a tree, catch a fish—vacation, wasn't that what Galvin wanted him to do?

Best not to go off half-cocked, he decided. In the village he found a grocery store, bought a waxed carton of orange juice, some potato chips, a couple of Flair pens and a pad of ruled paper. Since he had slept past checkout time, he would be charged for another day anyway so he went back to the motel. The room had been made up. He mixed a mild screwdriver and kicked off his shoes. Bunching up the pillows for a backrest, he sat on the avocado chenille bedspread and picked up the tablet and a felt-tip.

He worked most of the night, stopping once to go out for a steak and some cigarettes. When he was finished, he had a fairly good re-creation of the file on the disappearance of Claire Blanchard.

Lizzie sat on the floor in the cabin's stuffy bedroom and colored a picture of a little girl making cookies with her mother. The paper was yellow and brittle. She had torn one picture already, so now she was being especially careful. Lizzie didn't like coloring books or the coloring work sheets at school because no matter how hard she tried she couldn't stay inside the lines.

"I'm being very careful, Berry." The kitten chewed on

a chicken wing that Lizzie couldn't finish. "Mr. Angstrom said I have to."

Because of the heat, she wore only her Smurfs T-shirt and panties. She had put the pajamas in the chest with the other clothes. She could still smell them, but at least they weren't next to her skin with that strange sharp odor that made her nose burn.

Her hair was damp and her hands slippery with sweat as she made the mother's hair a light brown and gave her a pretty pink blouse. Just like Mommy's blouse when Mr. Blanchard came and they all went for pizza.

Mommy . . .

Using the dark brown crayon, Lizzie made a big bruise by the mother's mouth, put dirt streaks on her face and arms, drew a leather strap around her ankle.

Mommy . . .

After Mr. Angstrom left last night, Lizzie lay in the darkness for a long time. She hadn't been able to sort out everything, but she knew that Mr. Angstrom was mad at Mommy because of her. If she'd been a better girl . . . they wouldn't even be here, they'd be home in California. She was sure Daddy left because of her and of course she was the reason Mr. Angstrom was hurting Mommy . . .

Now she stared down at the coloring book.

"Be a good girl," Mr. Angstrom had said. "Color me some nice pictures."

The page was ruined. She tore it out, wadded it into a little ball and threw it under the bed. She leafed through the pages until she found a picture of a daddy and a little girl going fishing. Working carefully, she gave the man light brown hair and gray eyes . . . just like Mr. Angstrom.

* * *

From the cellar window Joanna watched the pickup return and saw that Miles was alone. For a terrible moment she was sure that Lizzie was dead, and her knees gave way. Then she heard Lizzie's voice overhead and realized that her daughter must have been there all along, locked in the bedroom. She might have been able to communicate with Lizzie, but the possibility hadn't even occurred to her.

She got up and went to lean against the wall ladder, fighting the weakness that threatened to collapse her knees. She'd eat tonight, whatever Miles offered her, because she knew she must. She wasn't really hungry, just so thirsty that the back of her throat burned and her lips were cracked from dryness.

Finally she heard the steamer trunk being moved and then the door creaked open. She blinked against the bright light, squinting at Miles.

"You might as well come up," he said. "I wanted to get Lizzie out for some fresh air, but she can't think of anything but you."

Joanna climbed the steps slowly. The top of her head seemed detached, floating. After the closeness of the cellar, the air from the cabin was dense and rich. She smelled last night's chicken, soap, old ashes, the scent of drying grass and pine from the fields outside.

"She wet the bed again, too," Miles went on. It took a second for Joanna to realize he was complaining about Lizzie. "Sarah never wet the bed once she was out of diapers."

You never beat up her mother and kept them both prisoners, Joanna thought. *Or had he?*

Amos had most of the farm dug up looking for the

bodies . . . She faltered and he reached down, grabbed her arm and yanked her up the remaining steps. Off-balance, she fell against him. That soapy smell was his—freshly showered, wasn't he always?—but she could already detect the gamy odor of his perspiration. Instinctively she started to pull away but caught herself in time. The plan, remember the plan . . .

"Thanks," she murmured, easing back. "Lizzie—just an accident, that's all. Let me—I'll talk to her—"

"You do that. And get her cleaned up."

When he opened the bedroom door, the kitten streaked out, another stir-crazy inmate. He pushed Joanna inside and snapped the padlock closed. Much warmer in here and almost as stuffy as the cellar, she realized. A boxful of dirt serving as cat litter didn't help. Lizzie sat on the bed staring at her with big, frightened eyes.

"Mommy? Oh, Mommy."

Joanna sank down, gathering the child up, gasping as Lizzie squeezed her ribs.

"What is it, Mommy? Are you hurt bad?"

"Just—a little sore. Are you all right, darling? Mr. Angstrom—he didn't—" All the ugly possibilities tumbled through Joanna's mind.

"He said I was a bad girl. I took a nap and I went pee-pee again. I tried to be good, Mommy. I colored and everything—" Tears trembled on her lashes and splashed down her cheeks.

"Shh, that's all right. You're my good, brave girl. Listen, darling, Mommy's very thirsty. Could you bring me some water?"

The tepid liquid tasted of copper pipes and algae—it was wonderful. Using the bathroom, Joanna thought she'd never again take indoor plumbing for granted. She splashed her face in the sink, avoiding the mirror, then wet the washcloth and called Lizzie over. Beneath the green T-shirt with its silly Smurf face, Lizzie's tan had faded. She was so thin before and Joanna was sure she'd lost more weight. There were a few purplish marks on her upper arms and shoulder. Nothing, Joanna noted with relief, on her buttocks or thighs.

A few questions reassured Joanna that Miles had left plenty of food. "I wasn't hungry but I drank my milk. I hate this place, Mommy. Berry hates it, too. Did you see where he went?"

"Just into the other room, I think."

"I hope he runs away. I hope he does."

"Lizzie." Joanna cupped her face. "Tonight—I'm going to try to get us out of this, baby, but if—something—happens—"

Lizzie began shaking her head, but Joanna held her firmly. "Lizzie, listen to me. If you get a chance, run away, too, do you hear me? Just like you want Berry to do. Run into the woods and hide. Promise me."

Lizzie nodded mutely. Joanna held her close. "I love you, remember that. I'll always love you."

"Joanna," Miles called, and knocked on the door. "Are you finished in there?"

"Just about." She gave Lizzie another hug and said, "Go get a dress to wear, something pretty. We're going to play a game tonight, darling. We have to pretend we're having a good time. Understand?"

Lizzie nodded. Such a little girl to comprehend such a terrible necessity.

While Lizzie dressed, Joanna washed her face and arms,

brushed at her jeans. She longed for a bath, a change of clothes. How could Miles possibly be attracted to somebody who looked and smelled the way she did?

That wasn't what turned him on, of course. He liked the feeling of power, of having her at his mercy. She gripped the edge of the sink, calling up her anger. Whatever it took tonight, she would do . . .

She submitted meekly to his cinching the strap around her ankle, comforted by the sight of the poker tip beneath the sofa's fabric flap. When he steered her roughly to the table, she leaned on him, letting him feel her helplessness. Here I am, Miles, your whipped little dog. Ready to roll over and play dead—or any other fun games you can think of.

Lizzie sat at the table, watching, the pointed face pinched, her eyes enormous. She had done what Joanna asked, selecting a lilac dress lavished with nylon lace. A bad choice, it hung sacklike on Lizzie's skinny little body, and the color turned her skin sallow. She looked like a street urchin dressed in discarded finery.

Miles took a can of stew from a brown grocery bag. Joanna stared at the jagged edge of the lid peeling up from the can opener. Was it sharp enough to slice flesh? She'd never find out. After dumping the stew onto paper plates he put the lid inside the can and out of reach on the sink.

Berry hadn't escaped, after all. Lured by the smell of the food, he came to investigate the bag, then jumped up on the sink. Miles pushed him off roughly.

"I can't heat this up," Miles said. "Out of propane."

"That's okay. It looks wonderful."

If she hadn't been ravenous, she'd never have managed to swallow the cold lumps of meat and potatoes coated with congealed gravy. Berry rubbed against Joanna's ankles, sniffing the leather thong. Remembering her thirst and hedging her bet against another dreadful day in the cellar, Joanna drank the can of beer he gave her and asked—humbly—for another. The alcohol gave her an immediate buzz. Not enough to get her drunk, just to dull the reality of the monstrous charade of a meal.

"Finish your carrots, Lizzie," Miles said sharply. "You eat like a bird."

Obediently Lizzie lifted the plastic fork to her mouth just as Berry leaped into her lap. Peas rolled off the fork, falling onto the lace-trimmed yoke of the dress.

"Dammit." Miles seized the cat by the scruff of the neck and hurled him to the floor.

Lizzie gave a wail of alarm but Berry was only dazed. He scrambled up and ran off to hide. Miles scrubbed at the brown smear on Lizzie's dress with a paper napkin, muttering, "Now look what you've done—making a mess—"

As Lizzie cringed away, Joanna tried to think of something to distract him. "It's gotten a lot warmer, hasn't it?" Surely the weather was a safe topic. "You look as though you were out in the sun today, Miles."

He turned on her savagely. "It's none of your business where I was. Seems to me you've got a hell of a lot more to worry about than how I spent my day."

"I'm sorry, I didn't mean—I'm sorry." She didn't have to fake the tears rolling down her cheeks. They mingled fear, frustration and a growing outrage at the whim of fate that put them in the hands of this madman.

"As for you, young lady," Miles said to Lizzie, "if you can't behave yourself, you can go on to bed."

"Mommy—"

"It's all right, darling."

Lizzie stood up slowly, then scooted around the table to give her mother a last desperate hug.

"Remember what I told you," Joanna whispered, then added aloud, "Go on now. Do what Mr. Angstrom tells you."

"Take that animal with you," Miles ordered.

As the door closed behind Lizzie and the kitten, Joanna remembered the horrors of the night before, and her confidence vanished. The clicking shut of the padlock sounded like a gunshot in the silent room. She clenched her fists, fighting the tears that threatened to come now in a bitter flood.

"Why don't I clean up the table, Miles?" Her voice was properly fawning, just a little thick around the edges. She stood up, began stacking the dirty paper plates. All her nerve endings prickled, tracking his movement as he crossed the room.

He came up behind her and put his arms around her, his elbows effectively locking her arms in place while his hands closed around her breasts. He pushed her up against the table and she could feel him against her, hard with excitement. She willed herself to relax, trying to ignore the pain that radiated from her breastbone, the sharp edge of maple digging into the front of her thighs. She mustn't cry out, frighten Lizzie.

If he shifted just a little, she could reach back and . . .

Slowly she moved against him while he kneaded her breasts. His breath whistled in her ear.

"Are you ready to be my whore, Joanna?" he whispered harshly.

"Yes—I—want to—" she choked out.

He squeezed viciously, sending pain snaking down her arms, up her shoulders. She screamed, forgetting Lizzie, as he spun her around and sent her sprawling. Her head banged against the floor and light danced on the back of her retinas.

He straddled her, pinning her down, his eyes bright, implacable. "I don't like whores, Joanna. That's what Bonnie was—what you are—" His hands on her shoulders moved up to her throat.

She struck out wildly, felt a solid connection. Some warm liquid spattered her arm as he grunted with pain. He released her to clutch his face, but for a second she just stared at the blood leaking from his fingers—from his nose, she realized.

She wriggled away, made a crablike lunge for the sofa, scrabbled beneath it. The poker was cool, heavy in her hands. So heavy—one swing—one chance. He saw her coming, so the edge of surprise was lost. She slashed at him with all her strength, knowing as she swung, she was too weak, far too weak. He raised bloody hands and grabbed the poker.

Then he grinned, a delighted gleeful grin hideous in the blood-spattered face, and took the weapon. She backed away, raising her arms to protect her head, so the first blow splintered her right arm just below the elbow. White-hot streamers of pain overloaded her nervous system so she really didn't feel the blow that snapped her left femur or the glancing blow on the side of her head that shifted the precarious balance in her head and sent the world cartwheeling away . . .

* * *

. . . moving . . . flopping . . . an unstrung puppet . . . oh mamma mamma i hurt so much . . .

. . . darkness, a sense of being enclosed in something soft, rough-textured. No motion now, just a sound, repeated over and over, a sound she'd heard before . . .

She is in California and she is in the backyard and there is a rosebush in a black container, a hard plastic container— Double Delight, the petals creamy white, pink on the edges. The sweet spicy scent perfumes the air as she starts to dig.

. . . the sound stopped. Pain again, a crimson flood, and she was falling . . . falling . . .

. . . the sound again and now she knows . . . she knows. The sound is a shovel sliding into earth.

24

Ruth listened to the distant ring of the telephone in her house in Maple Grove. A full two minutes, just in case Joanna had the television on too loud or had already fallen asleep. Maybe this wasn't her phone ringing. It could be a wrong number. All those circuits in between, how could you trust them when they only worked 2 percent of the time? A hundred attempts today to get through to the operator, she'd kept track, and this was the second time she'd succeeded.

"Your party doesn't answer," the operator said.

"Would you please redial the number? Somebody should be home."

Another two minutes. The operator firmly suggested trying the call later.

Slowly Ruth hung up. Having established a link to

Vermont, she hated to break it. Outside, a long golden twilight burnished the lake. Raucous laughter drifted up from the cabins along with the smell of frying fish.

Cass had returned late with the news that the timing chain for the camper was out of stock and had to be ordered from Thunder Bay. As for the phone call to Joanna, Cass reported she wasn't at home but kept the money for toll charges as well as the five dollars. Of course he might have lied about making the call, but somehow Ruth believed him.

She could understand Joanna and Lizzie being out during the afternoon. They might've gone shopping, for a walk, to a movie. But it was ten o'clock in Maple Grove now; long past Lizzie's bedtime. Where were they? She could see Lizzie sleepwalking, falling headlong down the stairs; a drunk driver on the curves of Old Mill Road, the awful sound of howling tires and rending metal . . .

She grabbed the receiver off the hook. She'd call the Maxwells. Surely they would know if something was wrong. From the telephone came a hissing noise, like tapping into a windstorm. The Maxwells' number—what was it? While she tried to remember, Dan Hardin came in from the garage and rang up totals on the cash register.

Ruth hung up. No use calling the operator if she couldn't remember the number. It was unlisted but she'd have it in her address book back at the camper.

"Sorry, Mrs. Hart." Hardin took cash from the drawer and counted it. "I'm closing up now. No luck?"

She shook her head. "Have you reported this line to the telephone company?"

He looked surprised. "Always been like that. You learn to live with it."

Ruth thought about arguing as he locked the door behind her. It would only take a few minutes to go for the address book, but Hardin was an intractable man, she'd learned in the last twenty-four hours. He wasn't likely to listen to her and she couldn't depend on Matt to back her up.

Matt was determined to wait out the delivery of the part right here at the fishing camp rather than pay an expensive tow into Dryden. He was perfectly content to catch bass and read. But Ruth had made up her mind.

Sometime tomorrow somebody would be going into town. When that opportunity came, she was hitching a ride even if it meant smelling marijuana fumes or riding in the back of a pickup. Tomorrow she was going to find a telephone that worked and get in touch with Joanna.

When the wheels of the 747 touched down at L.A. International, Tom knew there was no way he could continue the Honolulu run for another week. The headache had persisted. He was exhausted and drained, in no condition to have the lives of three hundred people in his hands. As soon as he deplaned, he reported in and asked for some sick leave. Then he checked into the Airport Hilton and left a wake-up call for 7:00 A.M. He would catch the morning flight back to Boston.

He thought about calling Joanna, remembered with relief that she and Lizzie were out of town. Soon, very soon, he would have to deal with his feelings about Joanna, but not now, not tonight.

Two Percodans helped him to fall into a sleep that was like being set adrift in black, uncharted seas. He dreamed he and McDowell were in the city morgue. Their heels clicked on the tiled floor, echoing off the hard surfaces in the room—metal tables, plastic chairs, the steel fronts of big sliding drawers where they filed away the dead.

He was going to look at another body. Not Claire's body. He knew that and McDowell knew that. McDowell was doing it again, calling him down to look at every drowned, stabbed, mutilated corpse that turned up, hoping he would break.

Tom could feel panic rising as the drawer rolled out. His breathing grew louder, a harsh panting. He started to run but McDowell pushed him forward, made him look and then he saw . . .

. . . Joanna . . . her slender body marble white, her face swollen, purple . . . Joanna . . .

There's another one, McDowell said.

This time Tom ran, an endless dream loop of gray-tiled passages, on and on, unable to escape, knowing that sooner or later he would have to look in the second drawer.

In a corner of the barn surrounded by bags of fertilizer, shelves stocked with weed killers, insecticides, oil and parts for the tractor, Miles took down an old lantern and lit it with shaking hands. When the mantle settled into a constant yellow glow, he hung it from a hook on a rafter and turned off the electric lights.

Summer heat, trapped in the barn, felt heavy in his lungs, pungent with the chemical odors and an ancient smell of horse urine. Runnels of sweat mixed with dried blood and traces of soil and leaf mold on his face and arms.

Nails driven into the wall held rolls of wire, rope, odd bits of harness and the black coil of an old whip. The leather stock was warm in his hand as he carried the whip over to sit on his heels in the lantern light.

"I tried not to do it, Papa," he whispered thickly. "I really tried."

You lie, boy. You do your dirty work and then you lie about it.

"You don't—understand—never did understand—how hard it was . . ."

Tired of the demands of her remaining litter, the big white mother cat stole in silently to investigate. She stopped in the shadows and sat, tail twitching, nose translating the man's scent and his strange, garbled cries. Then, ears laid closely against her head, she slunk away to squeeze through the crack in the old door, relieved to be out in the familiar terrors of the night.

Some gigantic weight pushed Joanna down, the pressure grinding shattered bone into raw nerve endings. The pain itself kept her alive, that pulsing arc like electrodes being shoved into her brain.

The smell was all around her, a loamy, fecund smell mixed strangely with an odor of wool. She remembered the sound of the shovel, the sensation of falling.

. . . a hole in the ground, a grave, and I am buried buried ohsweetjesus . . .

She wandered off into a nightmare. Caskets spilling bones, the inside of the lids raked with claw marks, skeletal fingers oozing blood . . .

Another jolt and she was back. She recognized the smell of wool, an old blanket like the one she and Dad used to take camping. She could feel the rough texture against her cheek, realized dimly that the blanket had kept the dirt off her face and trapped enough air to keep her alive.

Her salvation. Her shroud . . .

Instinct took over. The blanket had saved her life, but now it was a trap. Its restriction plus the weight of the dirt made movement almost impossible. She tried to raise her hands to push away the suffocating weight. A splinter of the fractured ulna in her right arm pierced tissue, muscle, skin, the pain so intense it was as though the sliver dug directly into her cortex. Helpless, all she could do was ride out the waves of agony.

Think, Joanna. Not much time. She could already feel her lungs straining. Slowly she wiggled the fingers of her left hand. Assured the arm wasn't broken, she began trying to free it. There had to be an opening in the blanket above her head. Panting with the exertion, aware of the oxygen she was using up, Joanna worked her hand up until it cleared the rough fabric.

Lungs bursting now, she scrabbled at the soil. Dislodged dirt ran down her arm under the blanket. Joanna felt it in her hair, trickling down her face. Coughing and sobbing in panic, she managed to turn away far enough to find a safe pocket while she tore at the earth above.

. . . the sounds of the shovel . . . how long had they gone on? Six feet deep . . . a standard grave—but surely he had been exhausted. Killing is hard work. *Almost* killing. Then carrying her from the cabin. Oh, God, *how deep?*

She is eleven years old, swimming in the country club's pool with her friends. A whole bunch of them, horsing around, somebody grabbing her legs and pulling her under. Mikey Matusak and he won't let go. Pressure builds in her chest, her heart's ready to explode.

"Let go, Mikey," she said thickly. "Le' go."

Just as darkness closed in, her hand broke through. She struggled feebly for a few more seconds, long enough to compact the soil around her arm and open a small air passage.

25

WEDNESDAY

Only nine o'clock in the morning but the sun beat down on Amos Fowler's head as he cut across Angstrom's fields toward the produce stand. Awful lot of pole beans still on the vines, he noted. Cucumbers, too, some of them turning to mush. There were five cars in the graveled parking area under the old walnuts. Quite a rush for this time of morning. Everybody trying to get a jump on the heat, he supposed.

He wrinkled his nose as he caught the scent of fermenting tomatoes and decaying greens. Under the shingled awning Timmy Lafferty dumped summer squash into one of the tilted bins, then rushed over to take money from a customer. Damn little produce and most of it still in the picking lugs. Miles was nowhere in sight. From the looks of it Timmy was handling everything.

"Where's your boss?" Amos nodded hello to Dora Maxwell, who was next in line.

"Sick." Timmy totaled Dora's purchases on a hand calculator and asked for two dollars and ten cents.

"What's wrong with him?"

"I don't know. A bug of some kind."

"Where's that nice spinach you usually have?" Dora asked. "And the fruit? I really wanted some plums."

"Sorry. Mr. Angstrom didn't go to Brattleboro yesterday." Timmy handed her change and added, "Guess he was getting sick then."

First day in years that Miles missed work, and it had to be hot enough to give you heat stroke. Amos leaned heavily against a table with a small pile of tomatoes and mopped his face as he watched Maud Delsey pick through the overripe lot.

"Saw Miles in the bank talking to Hiram," she muttered. "He looked terrible."

Be just his luck if the son of a bitch had something terminal. Up and die before Amos could ever nail him. The thought brought the taste of bile and a bubbling in Amos's stomach.

He popped a couple of Rolaids in his mouth and said to Timmy, "You be sure to tell Miles I was here."

Timmy nodded, looking harassed and wary. Amos set off toward home, pretty sure that Timmy would pass along the message. Kid damn well better tell Miles if he knew what was good for him. The air in the woods felt thick as syrup, and Amos walked slowly, stopping to rest a lot. Sweat soaked his shirt and ran down the back of his pants by the time he arrived home.

Hattie took one look at him and began flapping around

like a headless chicken, wanting to take his temperature, wanting to call Bob Henderson.

"Don't need a damned doctor," he growled. "I need a cold beer and a little rest, 'specially from you."

She let him be after that, hovering around in the kitchen doorway while he sat in the Barcalounger and put up his feet. The beer did the trick and he even closed his eyes for a few minutes. Feeling better, he got out of his sweaty clothes and showered before lunch.

He had another beer with his toasted cheese but passed up the peach cobbler. "Too damned hot to eat."

That was a perfect opening for Hattie to start in about air-conditioning the house but she was off on another tack.

"If you're feeling better, we could take a drive down to Springfield," she said. "You could use some shirts, Amos, and it'd be cool in the mall."

"Ayuh, it would but you can forget it. I got too much to do to go traipsing off to Springfield."

Restless, he prowled around the house. He thought about going out and shooting some targets, but it was too hot and anyway, he had practiced on Monday. Wasn't going to get rusty in two days, for God's sake. He decided to fix the latch on the back screen door and was out in the garage rummaging around for the proper screws when Hattie called him to the telephone, yelling to hurry up, it was Ruth Hart calling long-distance.

Pain awakened Joanna as blood pooled in the backs of her legs and her muscles spasmed. She moaned weakly. She could taste dirt, feel it coating the inside of her nose. But—alive—she was alive. She flexed the fingers of her left hand and they moved freely, outside where the sun

227

was shining. She could feel the warmth on her exposed skin, and even inside the blanket, beneath the foot of earth that imprisoned her, she could tell it was daylight.

The night was over, that terrible night. Miles was finished with her now. Dead and buried. That's what he thought. Or had he known she was still alive when he brought her here? Could he really be so monstrous? Oh, yes . . . yes. Lizzie knew, saw him coming over and over again all those nights. ESP, after all; she never needed a shrink. Oh, Lizzie, Lizzie . . .

Joanna pushed back dirt with the heel of her palm. In a circle, around and around. She could feel all the muscles in her arm, stretching, twisting. Pushing boulders would be easier. Or locomotives . . . a snap.

Lizzie was safe. For now—as long as Miles saw her as a substitute for Sarah Ann . . . everything always came back to Sarah Ann and Bonnie . . .

She slept—or passed out. She couldn't tell anymore. She woke up the next time because something tickled her cheek. Lizzie, playing games. No, God, no, of course not Lizzie. Something *crawling* . . .

Wide awake, she screamed and jerked her arm down, bringing an avalanche. The movement set off explosions of pain in her broken arm, her leg, her bruised ribs; her head throbbed violently, but all she could think of was that slithery, crawly *something* inching its way down her face.

She is eight years old, going fishing with her father, and they are digging for bait down in the corner of the backyard. Dad lifts the shovel, turns over the soil. Worms, dozens of them. Fat, pinky-brown, shiny . . .

Her hand was useless anyway, trapped outside the blanket. She scrubbed her cheek hard against the rough fabric until the wriggling stopped.

Sobbing with revulsion and despair, she realized she'd sealed the opening. Pushing her hand free again, she moved her arm back and forth, firming the soil, and felt that precious trickle of air. Her face was slimy but to press it against the messy blanket . . . Oh, God, she had to get out. Beneath its surface crust the earth was alive, just like that crawling mass that Dad dug up all those years ago.

"Shows the earth is good," he had said. "They're nature's garbage disposal."

. . . *the worms crawl in and the worms crawl out* . . .

She could feel them, soft, squirming. Bugs, too; big fat beetles, ants, maggots—finding all the places her skin was broken, pierced by shards of bone . . .

. . . *the better to eat you, Joanna* . . .

She worked in a frenzy, scraping her skin raw, freeing her arm to the elbow just in time because once the piles reached a certain height the dirt just fell down again. Now she began a tedious process of pushing the piles back so she could start again. Room enough now for the motion of her arm to pull the blanket from her face.

Calmer, she told herself that the prickly feeling in her lower body was not insects. She was numb from lying in one position for so long. Could that cause permanent damage? How much more damaged could she get? Graveyard humor. She giggled with a kind of helpless hysteria.

Thinking it was probably a good idea to stimulate circulation, she moved her right leg as much as she could. The left—the motion started that white-hot pulsing, every beat echoed inside her skull.

She drifted, sailed away, outside it all . . . *a fine mess you've gotten us into this time, Joanna* . . .

Blue sky overhead . . . why hadn't she noticed that before? Beautiful blue sky. So what was a few bugs? If she'd been a little weaker, unconscious a little longer, she'd still be buried.

The sun shone down into her little peephole. Noon. Just as well she was lying down. She'd never be able to stand up, her head hurt so badly. So thirsty, too, mouth and tongue swollen. She knew she'd voided herself like a baby while she slept . . . ah, God . . .

She dug again, sure she could hear a breeze soughing in the trees, and then she glimpsed branches. Evergreen, pine or hemlock. She could smell the resinous odor.

Where was Miles now? Selling radishes and tomatoes at the stand, acting as though nothing had happened? Would he dare look Chief Fowler in the eye?

Now she remembered what Miles had said. *I don't like whores . . . that's what Bonnie was—what you are.* He tried to kill Joanna. He thought he *had* killed her. What had he done to Bonnie? She must have run away. She'd have known about his temper, so she took Sarah and left. Because if she hadn't . . .

Joanna couldn't stop the thoughts now. They had their own terrible momentum. If Miles had killed his wife, then he must have killed his daughter, too. He worshiped Sarah but he'd killed her. If his own daughter wasn't safe . . .

Frantically she searched her memory. So many pieces missing. Whole chunks of time unaccounted for. How long had Miles worked on the graves? Was there one grave? Or two?

Lizzie . . . oh, Sweet Jesus, Lizzie here, too, all this time . . . buried . . . *dead* . . .

"Liz–*zeee* . . ."

Lady watched the Frisbee sail through the air, then she galloped off, matching the speed of the plastic disk until it hovered and turned. She leaped—too late—couldn't hold on and the Frisbee ricocheted off to land in a patch of goldenrod. Carrying it to the boy, she eyed him anxiously to see if he was displeased.

"You almost got it, girl."

He patted her head and she wagged her tail, joyful. She'd grown again in the past few weeks, a sudden spurt that upset her coordination. Things that had held her weight now collapsed when she jumped on them. She often fell over her own feet. "Get *down*, Lady," everybody said. "Get down, you overgrown lummox."

"Okay, Lady, try it again."

Another near miss and the Frisbee veered off into the trees. Lady bounded after it. Distracted by the crazy quilt of scents on the ground, she stopped several times to sniff. They were further into the woods today than they had come for a long time. The odors recalled the memory of the rabbit, that glorious chase, the clearing with its strange dark smells.

Picking up the Frisbee, Lady paused, cocked her head and stared off into the trees. A sound—too far away for the human ear, but Lady heard it. "L-l-l-l-e-e-e."

Noticing her alert position, the boy trotted over. "What is it, girl?" He listened. "I don't hear anything."

She looked up and whined hopefully.

"Oh, no. No way. I've gotta go to the dentist and Mom will have a shit fit if I'm late."

Tucking the Frisbee under his arm, he headed toward home. Lady lingered, her ears up, listening. "Come on," he said sharply.

Her whole world revolved around this slight red-haired boy in his threadbare jeans and stained T-shirt. His word was law. Reluctantly she turned away from the voice that seemed to be calling her name.

26

There was a spring in Amos Fowler's step as he left the Dodge Charger on the Harts' driveway and walked up to the front door. Almost like the old days when he didn't have to fix screen door latches just to have something to fill the time.

"I'm so worried about Joanna and Lizzie," Ruth Hart had said. The details came out in a rush, the Harts' breakdown, being stranded, the poor phone service. She had gotten a ride into Dryden and checked into a motel. "I tried calling the Maxwells but they're not home. I knew if anybody could find out what's going on, it was you, Amos."

Him, not Lankersheim. When Amos was police chief, he took care of his people, knew them by name, was never too busy to go that extra mile to reassure them.

He stooped to retrieve today's *Boston Globe* that lay in the edge of the grass. While he waited for Joanna to answer the doorbell, he saw the edge of another rolled paper under the foundation planting of juniper. No sign of life in the house. He went over and pulled out the newspaper. Yesterday's *Globe*. He looked around but didn't find any more.

He walked around back just in case Joanna and Lizzie were outside. Nobody. And he'd bet money nobody had been around for the two days indicated by the uncollected papers. There was a feeling about the place—deserted, *waiting*.

Ruth had described the location of a spare key. In one of those magnetized key cases, stuck behind a drainpipe. Better than a flowerpot but any determined thief would find it. He rapped loudly on the front door before he unlocked it.

The odor hit him as soon as he went inside. "Judas," he muttered, reaching for his gun and then remembering he no longer carried the weapon on his hip. Reflex, anyway. Too late for a gun when something smelled like that.

Still, he walked warily, his heart thumping. Jesus God, what could've happened? And how would he ever tell Ruth?

When he saw the plastic-wrapped package of hamburger on the kitchen counter and realized the meat was the source of odor, he was too relieved to feel foolish. Three green bottle flies buzzed around the package. His hand trembled slightly as he took out his handkerchief to mop his head. How long had the hamburger sat there? Two days? At least that from the state of putrification.

He checked the freezer, found similar plastic-wrapped

packages. So, say Joanna had taken out the meat to thaw. Then why hadn't she cooked it?

He searched the house room by room. The towels in the bathroom had been used, dry now. So was the soap. Beds were made, a stuffed lion sat on the one that must be the child's—Lizzie's. Toiletries, toothbrush in place and suitcases in the closet.

"You sure she didn't go away for a few days?" he'd asked Ruth, who'd admitted that it was possible but Joanna knew she would call and worry if nobody answered.

People own extra toothbrushes and he had no exact count of the luggage. Only why would somebody go off and leave a pound of hamburger to stink up the place? Of course, she could've forgotten about the meat. Say it was a spur-of-the-moment thing, she's rushing around. Easy enough to do. He went into Lizzie's room and picked up the lion. One eye was missing, an ear rubbed smooth. Seams repaired in several places. Amos never had any children but he knew something about them and he couldn't imagine Lizzie going away without the toy.

He set the stuffed animal back in place and finished searching the house. Nothing. Downstairs he put the tainted meat in a trash bag and took it outside. He supposed the next thing to do was to go to Lankersheim and tell him what he'd found, but by God, he hated the thought. He doubted the man would put out an APB. Amos had to admit grudgingly that he probably wouldn't himself at this point. If he had one more piece of solid evidence to justify his uneasiness . . .

He went searching for a garbage can and found it—and that additional evidence as well. Ruth Hart had described the car Joanna drove, Ruth's own Chevrolet station wagon.

She even gave Amos the plate number. There it sat in the garage, stone cold and dark.

So now there was nothing for it. Amos had been a cop too long not to go to Lankersheim. "Don't have to like it," he muttered, and headed back to the house. There was one thing he had to do, something he dreaded worse than going down to the police station.

"Tell Joanna to call me," Ruth had said. "Or else you call from the house. I'm going to sit right here and wait to hear from you."

Only one ring before she picked up the phone. "Joanna?"

"It's Amos, Ruth." He told her that Joanna and Lizzie weren't there but played down his suspicions. No need to panic at this point.

"But where could she be?" Ruth asked. "I even called her husband just to make sure she hadn't gone back to California. Something terrible has happened, I just know it."

"Now, Ruth, you just hold off on your worrying until I do some checking. Meantime, you make up a list of all your relatives and friends around here she might be visiting. I'll call you back later."

The list was mostly to give Ruth something to do to feel useful. Could be as simple as that. He hoped so. But he had a bad feeling—a cop's bad feeling—that Ruth was right.

Miles dreamed that Sarah was crying out in her sleep. He was the one she always wanted when she had a bad dream. He started to get up and go to her, but suddenly everything was all wrong. Instead of his and Bonnie's bedroom, he was at the cabin. Bonnie shouted at him, a fishwife—yes, her mouth was huge, fishlike, the words like air bubbles that popped in his face.

Make sense, dammit. He grabbed her shoulders, shook her until her head wobbled back and forth. He put his hands around her throat to steady that crazy motion . . . then Sarah was there pounding his leg with her fists, crying, *Stop it, Daddy. You're hurting Mommy.*

He tried to push her away but she wouldn't let go, kept hitting him, and then she sunk her teeth into his leg. Terrible pain and he reacted instinctively, letting go of Bonnie with one hand and reaching down to grab Sarah . . . his fingers in the soft hair . . . she lifted so easy, thistledown, dandelion fluff, sailing away . . .

He woke up, heart pounding, to a room full of stifling heat and yellow hot sunlight pouring through the open window. He groaned and covered his eyes. Sarah . . . he'd never meant to hurt Sarah. He just wanted to get her *off* him, that's all. Bonnie's fault, the goddamn whore, not only admitting she'd slept with her ceramics teacher, saying she *loved* him, she was going away with him, getting a divorce, taking Sarah. Even Papa would've understood his rage. He'd forgotten about Sarah—she was supposed to be asleep—my God, why hadn't she stayed asleep?

He sat up and stared at his trembling hands. He could feel her hair, silky fine; the weight of her fragile body. After Bonnie was finally quiet, he found his little girl by the stone hearth, her head tilted at an odd angle, cool to the touch. He got a blanket, wrapped her up, held her, but she only got colder and colder.

They were still there, in the cabin. Soon, he'd go down and call Chief Fowler. *Put the beast in a cage*, Papa said, and now he really would be, locked up forever. Strangling Bonnie . . . anybody could understand that . . . but Sarah . . .

Nobody has to know . . .

The thought must have been there all along, for it leapt up fully blown. A grave in the woods, Bonnie's car abandoned at a nearby airport, himself as the bewildered victim. He was sure he could manage it all—except the most important thing: putting his baby in a hole in the ground and leaving her there . . .

Stomach heaving, he bolted to the bathroom and threw up, watery bile that burned his throat. A pile of filthy clothes lay on the tiled floor. He remembered taking them off, standing in the shower, scrubbing himself over and over.

His mind felt like a cogged wheel slipping crazily.

Digging . . . he'd been digging . . .

Bonnie and Sarah . . . already buried. The decision made, acted upon. *Any news, Miles?* People kept asking him that and shaking their heads, *Poor Miles*, when he left a room. *Poor Miles*, they'd said it for years now.

Years . . .

Another cog. And then he remembered Joanna.

Armed with detailed directions from the county clerk's office, McDowell thought he'd found the turnoff to Blanchard's cottage. Only the third try. Not bad out here with no street signs and all the treelined back roads that looked exactly the same.

He wiped his nose again. His eyes were running, too. An allergy or a cold, he wasn't sure which. All this fresh air—what was so fucking wonderful about it?

In the yard of a house on the corner, a woman weeded a

flower patch. She stopped and watched him as he made the turn. Shit, just what he needed. A suspicious neighbor calling the police. He stopped and called "Hello, there" out the window. She came over carrying some kind of gardening tool, long with a notch at the end. A plain, dumpy woman. Late thirties, he guessed, but wouldn't put money on how close that was.

"Hi." He gave what he hoped was an engaging grin. His George Peppard grin. "Please tell me if I'm heading for Tom Blanchard's cottage. Tom gave me directions but I must've really screwed up because I've been driving around for hours trying to find the place."

"It's just up the road. Tom's not there right now. Did he know you were coming?"

"Well, sure." He made a production of blowing his nose. "He kept saying I ought to use the place. Now I've got this cold I can't seem to shake so I thought if I got away for a few days and rested up—" He didn't have to fake the sneeze.

"I'm sorry. I didn't mean to sound so suspicious." Her cheeks colored a little. She really did have a pretty face. Flawless skin and big Bambi eyes. "It's just—well, Tom hasn't had much company since Claire—"

"Oh, yeah, such a damn shame." Casually he turned off the engine. "Were you really close friends?"

"No, not—close, exactly. But we've known Tom and Claire for years."

"You and your husband, you mean?"

"Yes. Jack. Jack and I—well, we keep an eye on the place for them. That's why I was being nosy."

"Don't apologize. Everybody should have neighbors like you. Now that I think of it, Tom did say I ought to stop by and let you know I was around, but with this damned cold—you ever have one like that, where everything seemed to just go right out of your head? I mean—I know Tom told me, but I can't remember your name.''

''Donna. Donna Greene.'' She didn't seem surprised that he'd forgotten. ''Well, I hope you have a good rest.''

No offers of hot tea or chicken soup? So much for country hospitality. Dammit, why couldn't she be the gossipy type, running on a mile a minute? Unable to think of a way to steer the conversation back to Claire and Tom, he started the car.

''Sorry I didn't get a chance to meet your husband. Maybe he'll come by the cottage when he gets home.''

McDowell drove slowly up the skinny asphalt road through overhanging branches. Like a green tunnel. The thought made him uneasy and he was glad when the road ended at a small cottage on Hickory Pond. No fancy architecture, just a simple little house, the wooden siding painted a light green that fit right in with the pines. He parked in the shade and got out. The trees gave off a hot dusty smell and made him sneeze again.

Pine needles crunched as he walked around toward the lake. He recognized the pier, the one in the picture. Tom and Claire sitting there, smiling—he often wondered who took the photo. Probably the Greenes, Jack or Donna.

How hard would it be to get into the cottage? He could've asked Donna for a key, pretended he'd forgotten to get one from Blanchard or misplaced it. But no sense pressing his luck. These places usually had cheesy locks.

This one was no exception. Thirty seconds with a lockpick. He'd learned from a pro. Fast Willie, they called him, till he developed the shakes and had to turn stoolie to keep himself in booze.

Inside, the cottage was pleasantly cool. Older than he'd first realized and homey. It reminded him of a lodge up in the Catskills. His father had worked there, security, one whole summer when McDowell was twelve. The same maple furniture, heavy and comfortable. Tweedy platform rocker and the sofa covered in a brown print full of birds—quail, that was it, with the little feathers sticking up on their heads.

A bit dusty but he was sure somebody had been here recently. Blanchard or the neighbors? A cluster of pictures on an end table, one of them a gold-framed duplicate of the photo in his files. He'd studied it so often he thought he could see beyond the sparkling sunlight, Claire's beautiful smile. A lot of grief there. He knew of some, could only guess at the rest.

How did he do it, Claire? Quick—McDowell hoped so. The lady had suffered enough.

Unfamiliar faces in the rest of the pictures. An older couple, the woman with Claire's oval face and blond hair. One on the pier, Blanchard and another man with a string of trout. The man had a crutch under one arm.

McDowell prowled around the rest of the cottage, finding nothing. He hadn't expected bloodstains on the floor, but *something* had drawn him to this place. A hunch—no good cop ever scoffed at the feeling that sometimes led him where logic didn't point.

The refrigerator was running. No food but a couple of bottles of beer. McDowell opened one, took it out on the veranda that overlooked the lake, lit a cigarette. He'd only planned to come in and have a look around. But, what the fuck, he might as well stay. If the Greenes checked him out with Blanchard, he'd flash his badge, claim it was official. If they didn't . . .

His first partner in the detective squad told him something he never forgot. "Best way to know your suspect is to walk around in his shoes for a day."

So he'd walk around in Blanchard's shoes, study his notes and see what happened.

27

The young deputy looked up, startled, when Amos strode into the police station. He hadn't set foot in the place for years, not since Lankersheim made it plain he didn't need any help from doddering old fools.

"Chief Fowler—I mean—" The boy colored at the slip. Well, he'd lived in Maple Grove all of his life and most of it the old man had been the chief of police. "Can I help you, sir?"

"Ayuh, like to talk to Lankersheim." Amos could see him through the glass door of his private office—Amos's private office—sitting in front of a computer terminal.

The boy said the chief was busy—stumbled over giving Lankersheim the title, Amos noted with satisfaction—but he would buzz him . . . Lankersheim was just as surprised to see Amos, and he obviously planned to give him short shrift, leaving the computer on, the green screen full of figures.

"Budget," Lankersheim said. "Town Council meeting next week."

He wiped his glasses while Amos told him about Joanna Kerso. "If you'd come to me first, I could've saved you some trouble." Behind the smeary lenses, his eyes had a malicious glint. "Mrs. Kerso went out of town for a couple of days. She called and asked us to keep an eye on the place."

"When was this?"

"I don't remember, but Stimson will have it on the records. He can give you the exact date."

"And you don't think it's peculiar her car's still in the garage?"

"Not especially. A friend picked her up or a neighbor gave her a ride to the bus station."

"Well, I don't like it. I've known Joanna since she was knee-high. She's not the kind of girl who worries her mother to death."

"You *knew* her," Lankersheim pointed out. "A long time ago. Maybe these days she doesn't report all her moves to her mother. Look, if she hadn't called, it'd be different, but she did, so—"

"Well, since you don't intend to do anything—being so *busy* with your budgets and all—I guess I'll do some checking around myself."

"Sounds like a good idea."

His hearty endorsement didn't fool Amos for a minute. Get the old pest out of his hair, that's what he wanted. Amos's stomach bubbled as he stalked out to check with Stimson about Joanna's call.

"Yessir, I took it myself." Stimson rustled papers. "Here it is. Said she would definitely be gone Monday night, possibly Tuesday. Guess she was a little nervous after what happened the other night."

"What was that?"

Stimson described the vandalized tree in the Harts' backyard, guessing it was the work of kids. Amos went to see for himself.

He stood looking at the gouged bark of the old maple for a long time. Mostly the sap had solidified, sealing the cut, but the wounds still looked fresh. Uneasiness settled like a rock in his stomach, adding to his indigestion. Stimson was probably right. A bunch of juvenile delinquents out having fun. But, by God, he didn't like the looks of it.

Chewing on some Rolaids, he let himself back inside the house and left a prominent note for Joanna. Now pray God she came home to see it. Never being one to depend on the Almighty, Amos went out to investigate.

The dirt piles were ready to topple again. Joanna tried to throw the earth she scooped from around her shoulders over the piles. The effort drained her, shortening the work periods. Her nails were all broken, blackened; her raw hand bled.

She hadn't thought it possible to hurt any more—wasn't there some threshold where pain leveled out, even became tolerable? A lie—invented by somebody who had never suffered anything worse than a hangover. The torn skin, her thirst-swollen throat and cracked lips, were added to the agony generated by broken bones and swelling tissue.

None of it was as bad as the thought that Lizzie was here, sharing her grave.

She remembered Lizzie's warm weight on her stomach, newly born, while the placenta was delivered—still attached, a part of her. The first time that rosebud mouth touched her nipples.

She can't be dead . . . cannot be . . .

While she worked, a cloud floated overhead, fluffy white, a pearly gray bottom. Welcome relief. Sun, then another cloud, this one darker. Maybe it would rain. Cool water on her face, in her mouth . . .

Turning the piles of dirt to mud, filling the hole . . .

Oh, dear God, please don't let it rain.

Miles stood under the shower scrubbing every inch of his hairless body with a bar of Lava soap. His mind had slipped into the groove he was fairly sure was the present. He still wasn't certain; his memories were so vivid, so mixed up as though somebody had reached into his head and stirred up the brain cells with a stick.

Bonnie and Sarah—that was in the past. Joanna—last night, had to be last night. He'd never intended to go that far. But she hit him in the nose, and then she picked up the poker . . . she'd meant to kill him. Was it any wonder he'd lost control? His blood raced as he remembered the feel of the iron bar hitting flesh.

Her eyes . . . that was the best, always the best . . . the stunned agony turning to surrender . . .

Drying his tingling pink skin, he caught sight of his face in the medicine-cabinet mirror. The bridge of his nose was puffy and one eye had turned black, a racoonlike ring. How could he leave the house looking like that? Sunglasses might help. After he dressed he found a pair, but his nose was so swollen they wouldn't fit.

He *had* to go out . . . somewhere. The bank, of course. He had to go to the bank and get the bearer bonds from his safety-deposit box so he and Lizzie . . .

Lizzie . . . how could he have forgotten about Lizzie? She was out there at the cabin all alone. She had the cat to play with and he'd left the ice chest full of food . . . hadn't he?

A loud knock on the front door make him jump. He ran upstairs and looked down from the bedroom window. Timmy—and Miles hadn't even heard the tractor. He called down.

"Mr. Angstrom?" Timmy craned his neck to look up. "I'm running out of stuff. Is it okay if I close up now?"

"Fine. You go ahead."

"What about the cash box?"

"Just leave it by the door," Miles said.

"Well, okay. Listen, are you all right, Mr. Angstrom? Should I call the doctor or something?"

"No—no, don't do that. It's just a touch of the flu. Have to stay close to the bathroom."

"Yeah, sure. Well—" He dithered from one foot to the other.

"Something else?"

"Yeah. I'm sorry but Chief Fowler said to tell you he came by—I mean he said I had to." Timmy left quickly for his VW bug parked beside the barn, calling that he hoped Miles would be feeling better tomorrow.

Amos . . .

Miles started downstairs to get the cash box. Amos, something about Amos. Then he remembered. Amos had a warrant and he was coming tomorrow to dig up the farm to look for Bonnie and Sarah. He wouldn't find anything and then maybe he'd leave Miles alone. Miles began shivering so violently he had to sit down on the stairs.

The old man would never give up. Never. He'd be digging at the cabin, too, except for the fact it was out of his jurisdiction.

A crunch of gravel outside. Miles sat frozen while footsteps approached the door. Knock-knock. "Angstrom?" Amos. He was here already. Maybe he had the other warrant. More thumping. "Angstrom! I want to talk to you."

Miles sat very still, scarcely daring to breathe. Finally Amos went away but Miles knew he'd be back tomorrow with the bulldozers.

Lizzie lay curled on the bed waiting for Mr. Angstrom to come back. He had been gone for a very long time. After Mommy stopped screaming last night Lizzie had been sure that this time Mr. Angstrom would come in and hit her, too. He'd been so angry when she spilled food on the dress. But then he'd gone away in the truck, so maybe he wasn't going to punish her, after all.

She wished he'd hurry up and come back. She didn't care if he did punish her as long as she got to see her mother. She was hungry, too. He hadn't left the icebox this time. Just some Fritos and Twinkies, which she'd shared with Berry.

The little cat pounced on a cricket in the corner. Lizzie hated the crunching sound he made when he ate the bug. She hugged her knees against her chest and remembered going to the San Diego Zoo last winter and seeing a huge turtle, how he'd drawn his head and legs into his shell. She closed her eyes and rubbed the edge of the pillow, pretending it was Leon. Then, turtlelike, she drew inside herself, too, closing her eyes and listening to her heart beating, a comforting boom that drowned out the frightening noises.

Cocooned against reality, she sorted through her memories and played all the nicest ones: she and Daddy splashing through waves at Huntington Beach, Mommy laughing as they decorated Christmas cookies, the swing in the maple tree as Grampa pushed her higher and higher, Mommy holding her and whispering, "Run away, Lizzie, promise me. If something happens . . . run away as fast as you can . . ."

28

By four o'clock Amos decided he could do everything else by telephone and went home. Hattie flurried around, clucking like an old hen, "Out in this heat, a man your age . . ." As he sank into his Barcalounger he had an uneasy suspicion that she was right.

"Oh, stop nagging, woman. Get me a beer. And bring the phone over here so I can reach it."

Sipping his Michelob, he reviewed the case. None of the neighbors had talked to Joanna; nobody had seen her leave. He'd found out pretty quickly that she had kept to herself since coming back to Maple Grove, not renewing any old acquaintances. He remembered her at the Fourth of July picnic being friendly enough but distant, too. Then he had remembered that the Harts were at the picnic with Miles Angstrom. Miles and Joanna?

Seemed an unlikely match but enough of a connection to go and question Angstrom. He knew the man was home. His truck had been there, the cash box from the stand sitting by the door. Left by Timmy? Now he yelled to Hattie for another beer and the telephone directory.

Timmy verified that Angstrom was at home. "I think he's real sick with the flu. He didn't even come down to the door when I left."

Man can still talk, Amos thought as he dialed Angstrom's number, but the bastard wasn't answering the phone either. Well, no sense putting it off any longer. He called Ruth's motel in Ontario.

He told her about Joanna's alerting the police that she was going away.

"Well, then," Ruth said, "maybe I am worrying about nothing."

"Probably, but—"

"But what? Is there something you're not telling me, Amos?"

"Now, Ruth, I'm sure it's nothing, but the car is still there in the garage."

"The car's there? Then how could she've gone any-place? Amos—"

"Maybe she went off with somebody—a friend. How about that list I asked you to put together?"

"I have it."

Amos could hear paper rustling. He wrote down the names she gave him. Only a half dozen, mostly relatives.

"This last one," Ruth said, "Joanna just met him re-cently. Tom Blanchard. Oh, Amos, now that I think about it, maybe that's what happened. I remember he had a summer cottage somewhere near Brattleboro. Maybe he came by and picked them up, took them up there.''

A good possibility, Amos had to admit. Ruth had no idea exactly where Blanchard's cottage was located. She told Amos he was a member of the flight crew when Joanna came back from California and gave him the name of the airline. Ruth was pretty sure he lived in Boston.

"All right, you sit tight," Amos said. "Let me see if I can track down this fellow."

No Blanchard listed in the telephone directory for any towns around Brattleboro. Several in Boston, none of them the right Thomas Blanchard. "Take me the whole damn night to get through all the suburbs," Amos muttered. Hell with that. He called the airline. A lifetime of being a cop put enough authority in his voice to cut through the red-tape bullshit. He had Blanchard's home number in ten minutes—and the fact that Blanchard had been on the L.A.–Honolulu flight since Monday. He was listed on sick leave as of today. No other number for him, maybe he was on his way home.

Well, if he was in Hawaii on Monday, he sure as hell wasn't with Joanna. Had he offered her the use of the cottage while he was out of town? Maybe he'd talked to Joanna since he left. Wouldn't hurt to check. A machine answered. Much as he hated the blasted things, Amos left a message.

Hattie brought him some supper before he called the rest of the people on Ruth's list. Leftover pot roast, just as tough the second time around. His stomach felt sour and gassy. He crunched some Rolaids while he made the calls. In an hour he'd exhausted all the possibilities—all dead ends.

Supposing Joanna *was* sitting at that cottage. Or Blanchard was on his way up there. Oh, Amos could find the place, all right. Not a hell of a lot he could do tonight but tomorrow he'd go around to the county seat, check the property records. Meantime, there was one other thing—

"Amos." Hattie crept up, scaring him half to death. "Amos, aren't you coming to bed? You must be all wore out."

"In a minute. Can't you see I'm busy here?"

Time to call in a favor. The *Brattleboro Reformer* was being put to bed, but the editor reluctantly agreed to pull a story from the front page.

Finally Amos couldn't think of anything else, so he went to bed. He rested but it was impossible to sleep. He kept turning things over in his mind. And no matter how many times he reviewed the case, he always came back to the same name: Miles Angstrom.

Letting himself into his apartment, Tom was struck by how much it reminded him of the airport terminal. Not the furnishings but the feel of the place, that anonymity of a way station inhabited by strangers. He wanted to throw some things in a bag and drive straight up to Brattleboro, but he knew he'd be better off to get some sleep and leave early in the morning.

The message light glowed from the answering machine. He rewound the tape, but all he got was a staticky hiss from the playback. Dammit, half of L.A. was shopping plazas. He should've remembered his machine was acting up and gone out to buy a new one. He wondered if Joanna had called. Probably not. She'd been going on a picnic with an old friend. More than a friend?

Their evening together—a one-night stand, maybe that's all it was. Maybe it was all he wanted it to be. No, that was jealousy talking, the wounded macho pride. Well, hell, why shouldn't Joanna cultivate old friendships—or make new ones? He certainly hadn't given her any reason not to.

How did he really feel about Joanna?

That dream last night—symbolic as hell, probably. It made him cold to think about it. So damn real . . .

He pushed away the memory and went through the mail. Another letter from Claire's mother. He skimmed it. An apology, and would he please reconsider their offer to finance a new investigation? Feeling drained, he went to bed and set the alarm for five o'clock.

Joanna stared up at a thin slice of moon veiled by clouds. The cool of the evening had been a blessed relief, but she was getting cold now. Most of the body's heat loss was through the head—wasn't that right? The earth around her felt cold, too, leaching out warmth.

Something crawled on her neck. She clawed at it—squishy soft and fuzzy—and threw it as far as she could. Her whole lower body itched fiercely. Oh, God, she was being eaten alive . . . no, she could not, would not, think like that. Think positive, Joanna. Like gangrene, losing a leg . . .

Oh, Mom, aren't you worried by now?

She should never have left California. Lizzie tried to tell her that. No, she should never have *gone* to California in the first place. Should've left Walt when Lizzie was born.

*   *   *

Two weeks before Lizzie was due, Walt had gone on an overnight business trip. Positively the last one for a while, he'd told her. She was so smugly, blissfully happy. Walt was breaking sales records and spoiling her rotten with flowers and presents. Once the baby came—a hard kick and when she put her hand against her stomach she could feel the outline of a tiny foot.

She was making a list when the doorbell rang, a list headed "Things to Do Before the Baby Comes." A woman demanding to speak to Walt. Ordinarily Joanna wouldn't have admitted a stranger but as soon as she saw the slender blonde something clicked in her mind. She knew even before the women blurted out her story. Walt's lover. She worked in a flower shop near his office. All of Joanna's roses and daisies and daffodils passed through her hands. When she finally left, Joanna smashed every vase in the apartment. Before midnight her waters broke and she had Lizzie alone, forbidding the doctor to try and contact her husband.

The following afternoon he charmed his way past a nurse. Tears ran down his face as he told her the lies that would become so familiar: He was so sorry, it would never happen again, he loved her. What could she do? She had a one-day-old baby who needed a father and, God help her, she believed him. She had let him take her and Lizzie home, and when Mom arrived the next day, Joanna never said a word.

Now she shivered and tried to tuck the dirt-stained blanket around her shoulders. In the dark woods cicadas sang; an owl hooted. So many furtive creaks and rustlings she couldn't identify. A little rest and then she'd dig again. The moon slipped out. Pale, lemony light. She drifted into a dream about another moonlit night . . . of Tom making love to her . . . oh, Tom . . .

Miles sat at the entrance to Old Mill Road and suddenly he had no idea which way to turn. There was a box of food on the seat beside him—Cheerios, raisins, a can of deviled ham, a package of extra-wide noodles. His nose ached and there was a sharp pain in the back of his head as though a skewer had gone through his skull.

He seemed to remember he was going to the cabin—no, that couldn't be right. He had to get up early tomorrow to open the stand. Besides, he didn't feel like that long drive. Whatever he was planning to do could wait.

He backed the truck into the gravel parking area of the produce stand, turned around and went home.

Joanna dreamed. Astride Tom . . . slippery flesh . . . sweet, hot delight . . . silvery moonlight, falling across Tom's white, hairless body . . . Not Tom . . . Miles, his lunatic eyes shining in the moonlight. She tried to pull away but he held her . . . squeezing her arms . . . splintering the bones . . .

She cried out and opened her eyes to darkness. Overhead, icy stars sprinkled the black, moonless sky. Chill night air settled in the hole, moist air that smelled of decaying leaves and mold.

Trying to adjust the blanket around her shoulders, she saw—no, *felt*—something watching her and froze, breath caught in her throat as she turned her head slowly. A rounded shape, black on black, crouched above her. A gleam of yellow eyes.

"Get away." Her voice was unrecognizable, hoarse, grating. "Get away from me." She grabbed up handfuls of dirt and threw them. "I'm not dead . . . not dead . . . yet . . ."

29

THURSDAY

Afraid to sleep, Joanna lay in the darkness. So cold. Freezing. Crazy—it was summer . . . hypothermia, that's what the coldness was called. The sleep of death. Maybe that's what brought the animal . . . were there wolves in Vermont? No, no, surely not. But whatever it was, she had to stay awake and keep it away. *I'm not dead yet . . . but soon . . .*

Movement, yes—activity to keep her blood circulating. The long muscles in her left arm screamed with protest as she began digging. Think of something . . . Lizzie. Lizzie wasn't here, wasn't dead. That mother/child bond, so strong, almost tangible. Surely when it severed, Joanna would *know*. But if Miles didn't kill her little girl, what was he planning to do?

If he was substituting Lizzie for Sarah, maybe he would

keep her at the cabin, dress her in his daughter's clothing
. . . but Lizzie was not Sarah Ann. Joanna remembered
Miles's anger when Lizzie spilled food on her dress. And
when Lizzie kept making a mess and wetting the bed and
crying . . . what would he do then?

As she watched the dawn, her thankfulness was mixed
with dread. The sun wouldn't stay behind the trees, gently
warming the air. When it climbed high, fueling her raging
thirst . . . she worked harder.

Her hand was blackened, swollen, like wearing a catch-
er's mitt. So used to the routine of scooping up soil, she
didn't realize at first that she'd touched something solid.
Rounded. Knobby. She dug frantically. A stick—oh, God—a
nice fat pine branch, a tool! She lifted her head, craning to
see as she pulled it free.

Dirty gray, longer than her forearm, broken on one end
to a sharp point. No mistaking what it was.

She had found Bonnie Angstrom.

The smell of eggs made Amos queasy and he felt exhausted even though he'd slept later than he had for years.

"More coffee?" Hattie looked lively enough. Sleeping
till all hours obviously agreed with her. "Don't you like
your eggs, Amos?"

"Too damn greasy." He pushed back his plate and
stomped off upstairs.

Even his bowels refused to cooperate. Feeling off-center
and irritable, he went outside, hesitated, then came back
in for the car keys. Late for his walk and too damn hot
anyway. But he didn't want to miss going to Angstrom's.

Timmy was at the stand, alone again. "I'm really getting worried about him." The boy was already dirty and

sweating. "He's acting really weird, Chief Fowler. You think I ought to call Doc Henderson?"

"Maybe so. You sure he's up there at the house?"

"Yessir. I talked to him. He *said* he was better, that I wasn't to worry. Maybe I'll wait till later today. If he's not better by then—"

Amos got back in the car, sat there staring up at the old farmhouse in its grove of maple and beech. Maybe the man was sick. But Amos didn't like it. Didn't like any of it. He started the engine and pulled out onto Old Mill Road. As he drove to the Harts' house, his mind kept plodding around in circles. Another woman and child missing from Maple Grove.

The child . . . he'd been thinking too much about Joanna. The right age, the same white-blond hair . . . Judas Priest, he'd seen it himself, that day at the stand. She even *looked* like little Sarah Angstrom.

Today's *Boston Globe* on the lawn and no sign of life at the Harts'. Inside only silence and the lingering odor of rotten meat. Amos went home.

"Ruth called," Hattie said as he headed for the gun cabinet. "You going shooting today?"

"Ayuh," Amos said grimly. "Probably am."

"More coffee?"

McDowell nodded, said thanks and went back to the sports page of the *Globe*. Must be something to this fresh-air shit, he decided, because he'd slept soundly and awakened hungry. Nothing in the cottage to eat, so he started driving toward Brattleboro and wound up in a truck stop along I-91.

The Sox had lost a heartbreaker to Chicago and two more

American League players had admitted sniffing a little coke to lighten their spirits. What else was new? Disgusted, he put the paper back on the ledge behind his corner booth. A trucker on his left immediately picked it up.

Sipping his coffee, McDowell debated going back to Blanchard's cottage. He had searched the place, tramped through the woods, stood on the pier and stared down into the water. Nothing. Not a single lightning bolt of inspiration. Jack Greene had stopped by after McDowell returned from getting a hamburger. The man in the picture with Blanchard, crutch tucked under his arm. He was missing a foot.

McDowell didn't ask but Greene answered anyway. "Vietnam." The one-word sentence was typical of his replies to the questions McDowell did ask. Old Jack was as close-mouthed as his wife.

Something there, but for the life of him McDowell couldn't think what it was and his makeshift file had been no help.

Now McDowell forked the last of the Pilgrim Special—corned-beef hash, fried eggs and muffins—into his mouth and pushed away the plate. So—what was next? Not knowing his plans, he'd tossed an overnight bag into the car when he left Boston. Did he really need to spend another night at Hickory Pond? Being there had stirred up something, but he still had no idea what the fuck it was. Well, hell, three years had passed; he couldn't remember everything. If he went back to Boston, talked Twohy into slipping the file out . . . yeah, that was probably the thing to do.

His mind made up, he signaled for a last cup of coffee,

lit a cigarette and rooted around on the ledge behind the booth for the front page. The *Globe* was gone. He came up with the *Brattleboro Reformer*. National news mixed with a lot of local stuff. An item halfway down read "Maple Grove Woman Sought." He skimmed over it until suddenly a name leaped off the page.

The muffins congealed into an indigestible lump in his stomach as the implication of the article hit home. A woman and her daughter missing since Monday. No cause for alarm at this point, but retired Police Chief Amos Fowler was seeking information about a part-time resident of the Brattleboro area, Tom Blanchard.

McDowell tore out the article and went to find a telephone. He'd better have a talk with this Amos Fowler.

"Miles, good morning." Hiram came over himself to let Miles into the bank vault. "Heard you were under the weather."

"Flu, I guess." Miles followed him back to the wall of safety-deposit boxes and handed Hiram his key. The sunglasses dug into his nose. An ice pack had reduced the swelling but it was still tender and sore.

"Hope you're feeling up to lunch tomorrow."

"Lunch? Oh, yeah. Well, I'll have to wait and see." No more Jaycee luncheons or Chamber of Commerce meetings or cooking hot dogs for the Fourth of July picnic. Miles was surprised at the pang the thought gave him.

Hiram made a little ceremony of unlocking the door and then standing aside while Miles pulled out the long metal box. "Let me know when you're finished."

"Won't take long," Miles said.

In the private booth he removed the bearer bonds, the

deed to the farm, his mother's diamond ring, a string of pearls—his present to Bonnie when Sarah was born. He'd brought a padded mailing envelope to put everything in.

Leaving the bank, he felt almost light-headed with relief. One more stop and he could leave Maple Grove forever. He parked along the street beside the cemetery and walked slowly through the slate gravestones.

Whatever was wrong with him, he was all right now. The flu—it must have been the flu with a high fever. He still had that shaky hollow feeling you get after being sick, but his head was clear now. As soon as he finished here he was going to check on Lizzie, then go to Springfield to cash one of the bonds and buy an RV.

He felt bad about leaving Lizzie alone so long. Still, it wouldn't hurt the child to go a little hungry. Maybe she'd learn to appreciate it when he was nice to her. She was going to have to change her behavior a lot. He'd see to it. She was too much like Joanna.

He reached the top of the second hill. This time of day his parents' graves were shaded. Down in the newer section a mower droned. The smell of cut grass blended with the scent of roses left on a nearby mound. He knelt beside the gray stone marker to make peace with his father.

Once she'd conquered her feelings of revulsion at handling the bone, Joanna quickly learned that it made an excellent digging tool. Before long she'd cleared the dirt around her upper body. The increased movement sent pain swelling through her broken arm. Then she could see the damage: a jagged splinter of bone sticking through the skin above her wrist, the flesh purple and swollen to her elbow.

The wound itself had an angry red look, oozing pus. So

dirty how could it not be infected? Somehow seeing it made the throbbing worse.

Sitting up? Impossible but she had to try. Breathing harshly, she put her hand flat against the ground beside her hipbone, elbow bent, and pushed tentatively. No way in the world she could lever herself straight up. She would have to twist her body one way or the other. Twisting toward the left would put less pressure on her injured arm. Steeling herself, she pushed again, turning. Bone fragments shifted, found new nerve endings to mangle. She moaned, fighting that terrible whirlpool that threatened to suck her under.

Finally upright, she hunched over, barely hanging on until the blackness receded. Then, slowly, she forced herself to look around the small clearing at the leaf-clotted ground. She could rationalize, convince herself that Lizzie couldn't possibly be dead, but if there was another fresh grave . . . Her breath rushed out, a great sob of relief at the sight of undisturbed leaves.

Lizzie was still safe . . . for now . . . please, God. Wielding the fractured tibia, Joanna resumed digging. She could feel her strength ebbing away, like sand through an hourglass, like time itself running out for her and Lizzie.

30

When he walked into the cottage, Tom had such a feeling of wrongness he thought for a second he'd wandered into a strange house. The thought passed quickly—of course it was his own cottage—but he couldn't shake the sensation that something was wrong.

The smell, he realized slowly. Not just a close musty odor. Tobacco smoke.

Jack came in regularly but he was especially considerate of nonsmokers and had never lit up a cigarette here in Tom's presence. Maybe he wasn't so careful when he was here alone. That must explain it, because there was no sign of a broken window or forced entry. Still, as Tom walked through the small cottage the feeling persisted that somebody else had been here.

Just your imagination, he told himself. And God knows

his must be working overtime considering his nightmares the last couple of nights. He'd dreamed of corpses again, of Joanna . . .

He opened up the windows, then went out on the deck. Leaning against the railing, he stared out at the lake. A breeze ruffled the surface, creating miniature whitecaps. A duck bobbed on the wavelets like a feathered cork.

Time to wrestle the demons. That's what he'd come for.

Claire . . . he should've followed his instincts and never left her alone here that summer. Their marriage might not have survived if he'd thrown his weight around, but a divorce—anything—was preferable to this.

Oh, goddamn you, Claire, what did you get yourself into?

He jammed his hands into his pockets and went down to pace along the water. Claire may have come here to think, but she also enjoyed going into Brattleboro. There was a thriving art community—poetry readings, concerts, plays. While he'd been waiting patiently, trying not to pressure her, she'd picked up some sensitive soul, brought him here, screwed him . . .

Demons, one. Blanchard, zip.

He couldn't get past the anger, that was the problem. That devastating sense of betrayal, worse because he couldn't confront her with it. Maybe that was the real problem all along. Peel back all the anguish, the uncertainty, the guilt. And what do you have? He was pissed off, enraged, mad as hell. And, by Christ, he had a right to be.

Furious, he stomped up and down the pier, then back to the house. By the time he'd climbed the steps up to the deck, the anger subsided and he felt cleansed somehow.

He went inside and picked up the picture, running his thumb over his wife's smiling face.

Poor Claire. Facing her own demons, alone. Who was he to judge?

I can forgive her. The thought startled him. He hadn't known until now that he needed to. Once started, the realizations became an avalanche. His inability to give up the search, to put his life with Claire behind him—somewhere deep down he'd been afraid if he gave up it was because of his anger.

And his feelings for Joanna . . . Anything real there? Or just a way of getting back at Claire?

Outside, tires crunched on pine needles; a car door slammed. Jack, checking up. Tom went to let him in, but it wasn't Jack who walked up to the cottage.

"Greene said you were up here." Kevin McDowell stood there, a folded newspaper in his hands.

He looked used up, Tom thought. Burned out. There was only one reason this man would've left Boston and come all the way up here.

"You found her," Tom said numbly.

"Who?"

"Who?" Tom stared at him, bewildered. "Claire, of course. Is she—dead?"

"You tell me." He walked in, walked over to the sofa, moving—Tom saw—with a sense of familiarity. He put down the newspaper, took out a pack of Marlboros, tapped out a cigarette.

"You were here, in my house," Tom said, indignant.

McDowell struck a match on his thumbnail, sucked in smoke. "Thought it was about time. Always did want to

269

come up here. It was the picture.'' He nodded toward the photo. ''Bad mistake, Blanchard, giving me that picture.''

''What the bloody hell are you talking about? If you think you're going to start that same old crap again—''

''Oh, no, not at all.'' He grinned, mirthless as a piranha. ''This is all new crap.'' He picked up the newspaper and tossed it to Tom. ''Middle of the front page.''

Maple Grove Woman Sought . . . Joanna . . .

Tom felt as though McDowell had hit him in the stomach. ''I don't—believe this.'' His ears echoed with a hollow ringing. ''This your idea of a sick joke, McDowell? Some new kind of police torture?''

''Don't be an ass, Blanchard.''

''It's true?''

McDowell's face said it was. Legs suddenly boneless, Tom stumbled into a chair. Again. It was happening again. Frantically he reread the short article. ''This says there's no cause for alarm, just that the family is concerned—'' He broke off, looking up at McDowell.

''Sound familiar?''

''Yes,'' Tom said dully.

That first article about Claire—not the exact wording but he recognized the tone. ''Why are they looking for me? Do they think she might be here?''

''Is she?''

''For Christ's sake! You were here before I was. I'm sure you did a thorough search. Did you find anything?''

McDowell hesitated, shook his head. Tom thought he saw the first chink in the cop's wall of suspicion. Tom got up, digging out his car keys as he headed for the door.

''Where are you going?'' McDowell asked.

"Joanna's missing. Where the hell do you think I'm going?"

In the car he had to make several tries before he got the key in the ignition. McDowell had followed, stood beside the car door as Tom finally started the engine. A roar, then the engine died. Tom tried again. A ripe smell of gasoline—flooded. He gripped the steering wheel, feeling as though he would explode into a thousand pieces.

"Move over." McDowell opened the door. "Your car's a damn sight faster than mine."

The hot yellow eye of the sun had climbed above the trees now. It glared malevolently at Joanna as she worked to free her injured leg. She was sure she could pull the right one out before the dirt was completely cleared, but the left ballooned her jeans, the fabric no longer blue but thoroughly soaked purple-red with blood.

Relieving the pressure on the swollen tissue might help the pain, but she had no way to rip the strong denim and, anyway, she wasn't sure she could stand the sight of what lay beneath it. The smell of the blood and the foul blanket made her stomach churn. She leaned against the side of the hole, tasting bile.

Overhead, three large birds circled, riding the air currents, watching. Scavengers, come to pick her bones. They'd been cheated of Bonnie Angstrom. The worms had beat them out. Joanna could see other parts of the skeleton protruding from the soft earth . . . a ball and socket, the slope of a clavicle. She had shuddered with the fear of finding other, smaller bones.

"Haf to—get—out—" Her throat was so swollen the words were a croak.

All she'd thought about until now was the digging. Actually getting herself out of the shallow grave had not been a consideration. Her good leg was still partially buried, useless. She knew she dare not waste the energy to remove the dirt. Clenching her teeth against the onslaught of pain, she began inching her way backward.

She was quickly drenched with sweat. A few precious inches and she stopped, panting. She'd drag her leg free and then what? She'd be against the end of the hole. If she could stand . . . oh, right, Joanna. And the cavalry might come galloping through the woods. Oh, God, how could she ever get out? The hole was at least a foot and a half, she estimated. Might as well be a mile and a half if she planned to lift her body straight up.

Using the old bone, she began pushing dirt back into the hole behind her, angling it into a crude ramp.

McDowell drove at top speed, erratically. Tom didn't care as long as they got to Maple Grove.

"This is crazy," Tom said. "How can this be happening to me again?" He stared blindly at a blur of green trees whipping past. "I didn't kill my wife, McDowell. I know that's what you think but it's not true. And this—Joanna—I swear to you—"

"Right."

One chink maybe but the wall still stood.

"Have you talked to the Maple Grove police? This Chief Fowler?"

"Retired police chief. That's his home phone in the article. I tried calling him but he wasn't there. Police probably aren't in on it yet."

Why didn't McDowell go directly to Maple Grove? Find

Fowler or go to the police to tell them about that desperate criminal, Tom Blanchard. Because he wasn't about to be cheated of nailing me himself, Tom thought grimly. So he'd come back to the cottage to look around some more, probably to question Jack and Donna.

Oh, the hell with McDowell and his stupid suspicions. It was Joanna he had to worry about. If he hadn't been so wrapped up in his own problems when they talked . . .

"My God, I called her on Monday, Monday morning. She said she and Lizzie were going on a picnic."

"Alone?"

"No. With a friend."

"She mention a name?"

Tom shook his head. "She just said he was an old friend."

"He. A man, then. Really narrows it down."

"Lay off," Tom said savagely. "All this time—you've never had anything to connect me to Claire's disappearance, have you? Why do you keep hounding me?"

"One thing about being a cop, Blanchard, you get lied to by pros." McDowell bore down on a Ford Econovan, whipped around it. "Keeping your little secrets—you're a real amateur, man. Somebody hides things from me, I always figure it's because those things'll make him look guilty as hell."

How could he make McDowell understand that looking guilty and being guilty were two different things? They entered the Maple Grove city limits and Tom was grateful that he could change the subject. They found a phone booth and McDowell tried to reach Amos Fowler again. He came back shaking his head.

"Still out. His wife said he did talk to the police. Let's see what we can find out."

Inside the police station Tom's name got them in to see the chief immediately. McDowell introduced himself.

"Just happened to be visiting," he said.

"Mort Lankersheim." A harried man who held out his hand but didn't offer them a seat. On a desk beside him a computer screen glowed greenly. "Amos was here, all right. And of course I know about the article. Everybody in town's been calling me up. I appreciate your coming by, Mr. Blanchard, but before you get in too much of a flap . . ."

He told them about Joanna's call saying she was going out of town. "She's probably having a good time, decided to stay over a few days."

With an old friend? *We go back a long ways* . . .

"This Fowler," McDowell said. "He a good cop?"

"In his day," Lankersheim said grudgingly. "Gets carried away sometimes."

"Still, there must've been something about this that bothered him." McDowell was pleasant enough, but Tom recognized that implacable edge to his voice.

Lankersheim admitted that Joanna was supposed to be gone one day, maybe two, and that Fowler had found her car in the garage.

"And you don't think that's enough to start looking for her?" Tom said.

"I think Mrs. Kerso's going to be mortified when she gets back and finds out about worrying everybody like this. And no, I'm not ready to commit a lot of time and money to search for somebody who's off on a vacation. Now, if you'll excuse me . . ."

Following McDowell from the station, Tom was overwhelmed with the same sense of helplessness he'd felt for three years now. The earth had opened up again and swallowed somebody he . . . loved? Yes, dammit, loved. At the car he paused, gripping the door frame.

"McDowell? Thanks for—everything—back there."

"Curiosity, that's all."

"That's not all. Something's wrong. I know you feel it, too."

"Yeah, well—can't hurt to talk to Fowler."

Fowler . . . the name sounded like a lifeline. The man had been a cop. Obviously he was already worried about Joanna. Tom would see to it that he pressured Lankersheim into launching an immediate search.

But Fowler still wasn't home. "Mrs. Hart keeps calling," his wife said. "Amos went off to do some shooting. Don't know what he's thinking of in this heat, a man his age . . ."

They calmed her down enough to find out where Fowler did his target practice and set off through the woods. Oppressively hot and so still you could hear every twig snap. No sound of gunfire and no sign of the old man in the clearing. McDowell picked up a bullet-punctured can, knelt to tilt up a wooden board with its outline of a man.

"He hasn't been here, has he?" Tom asked.

"I don't think so. No smells," he explained. "Cordite stinks."

So this was the lifeline Tom was counting on. An old man wandering off God knows where and every second precious . . .

"McDowell? You've got to help me find her."

275

McDowell stood up, brushed off his pants. "Out of my territory, chum. Why should I stick my neck out?"

"Curiosity. And—what you said earlier—about knowing I lied to you about Claire. I'll make you a deal. Help me find Joanna and I'll tell you everything."

McDowell stared at him, then nodded curtly. A pact with the devil. Tom just hoped to God it was worth it.

The boy tossed a stick a couple of times and Lady brought it back. "Not much fun," he said gloomily, snapping the wood in half.

He'd forgotten the Frisbee in his haste to leave the house. Lady eyed him anxiously, tail drooping. She'd been so excited about their walk this morning that she'd overturned a large potted plant onto the freshly vacuumed carpet, setting off a frightening session of yelling by the boy's mother. Lady still wasn't sure if the boy was mad at her, too.

"It's okay, girl." He squatted down at eye level and rubbed her ears. "But we'd better stay outa there 'til Mom cools off."

He found a larger branch and to Lady's delight set off into the woods. She plunged ahead while he set the stick whistling, decapitating seedling pine and fireweed. Sunlight spilled through the tall trees, dappling the woodbine and the soft forest floor.

Nose down, Lady quartered the area. A whole palette of scents painted mind pictures, sharp as vision. A rabbit here, a covey of quail, something bigger that made her senses hum. And then, finally, that darker scent, the one she'd smelled before. Stronger this time, filling her head.

She ran back to the boy, whined urgently, ran ahead, repeating this several times.

"What *is* it, girl? Oh, okay, go on."

He ran behind her as she tracked the scent, keeping up until the blood scent grew so intense she forgot everything except that wild call. Well ahead of him, she burst into the clearing.

A hole dug in the loamy earth, piles of dirt. She stopped, nose quivering. New smells overlaid the old. Fresh blood. Violence. Pain. She stood there, confused. The remembered odors down there in the hole, a fresh trail going off the opposite side into the woods.

The boy caught up. Panting, he stopped beside her, staring. Sweat trickled down his face, down his spine, suddenly turning icy. The same clearing they'd come to the time Lady ran away . . . he *thought* it was the same one . . . only why would somebody want to dig it up? And what was sticking out of the dirt?

He wanted to bolt for the woods but he climbed down slowly, saying, "Come on, girl," wanting her with him, certainly not wanting to go down there alone. Lady sniffed rapidly, nose touching the gray curving *thing,* and then began to dig.

Rounded bone, eye sockets . . .

"Holy shit," he whispered as the skull grinned whitely up at him.

31

Ruth couldn't eat breakfast. She paced the small motel room, sipping coffee, willing the phone to ring. An hour's time difference in Maple Grove. Where in the world had Amos gone? Why didn't he call?

He'd found out something, something terrible. Joanna was in the hospital, she and Lizzie hurt, dying . . . Ruth snatched up the phone and got the information operator to ask for the Maple Grove police station.

"Oh, yes, Mrs. Hart." Mort Lankersheim didn't sound happy to hear from her. He hadn't heard anything about Joanna and he had no idea where Amos was. He added, "I'd like to have a word with him myself."

"You are looking for my daughter, aren't you?"

"She's not officially missing yet, Mrs. Hart."

"*Officially* missing? My God, you're *not* looking for her."

"She told us she was going away, wouldn't be back till Tuesday, maybe Wednesday, so—"

"You listen to me, Mort Lankersheim. I don't care about your damn rules. Something's happened to Joanna. You either start looking for her or I'm going to call everybody on the Town Council and raise so much hell—"

"All right, Mrs. Hart. Calm down. If you're that concerned, then of course I'll investigate."

Anger subsiding, her knees weakened and she sat down on the bed. "I'm sorry. I didn't mean to lose my temper." She drew in a shaky breath. "I gave Amos a list of names—friends, relatives. I think he reached most of them except for a man named Tom Blanchard."

"Blanchard was here," Lankersheim said. "A little while ago."

"At the police station?" Her heart sank. "Then he hadn't seen Joanna?"

"No, I'm afraid not."

"I'd like to speak to him myself. Do you know where he was going? Did he leave a number?"

"He was looking for Amos. I gave him directions. You might be able to catch him out there."

Ruth called immediately. Hattie said Ruth had missed Tom but promised that if he returned or Amos came home, she would have them call. Sick with frustration, Ruth began pacing again. If only Matt were here. She'd tried to reach him several times, only to be told the line was out of order. A big surprise that was. She could probably get through if she kept trying but she didn't dare tie up the phone. I can't stand this, she told herself. To be so far away, so isolated . . .

The phone rang. Tom Blanchard, sounding just as worried as she was. "Mrs. Hart, I have a—friend with me, a detective with the Boston police, and he's agreed to help look for Joanna. He's going to pick up the other extension." Since they couldn't locate Amos, Tom wanted to hear everything Amos had reported to her.

She told them what little she knew. "I think he was holding something back. Just the way he sounded, like he didn't want to frighten me."

"Mrs. Hart—" The detective, McDowell, with a businesslike tone to his voice. "It might help if we retrace Chief Fowler's steps. I'd like to go to your house and look around."

"Yes, please do." She told him how to find the key, made Tom promise to call later.

The maid came to make up the room. Ruth still had no appetite, but her stomach was upset from nerves and too much coffee, so she decided to get a sandwich from the adjoining café, making the maid promise to answer the phone and take a message. Ruth was back in fifteen minutes with tuna on rye and a carton of milk. The maid shook her head, no, no calls, eyeing her curiously. Ruth sat on a lawn chair just outside the door and picked at the food while the woman vacuumed.

Why on earth had she ordered tuna fish? The smell began to make her nauseous, so she gave the remains to the departing maid to put in the trash. Taking the milk back inside, she sat on the edge of the bed, waiting. When the phone finally rang, it was Matt, sounding crabby.

"This damned thing. I must've called twenty-five times. What's going on, Ruth? Why'd you stay in Dryden?"

She told him about Joanna but the habit, long engrained, of smoothing things over made her add, "It's probably nothing, Matt. The police think I'm being paranoid."

"But you think something's wrong. You've thought so for days now."

"Yes," she said miserably.

"I'm going to get somebody to drive me into town," he said. "You find us a flight from Thunder Bay, sweetheart. If something's happened—pray to God it hasn't—but if there's even a chance, we belong at home."

Wrong way. Must be going the wrong way.

She'd been crawling for hours, it must be hours. Surely the sun had climbed higher. Hotter, so much hotter, even in the green denseness of the woods. Her whole body burned with thirst. A creek, Miles had said. How could Lizzie grow up without knowing about tadpoles?

But there was no creek, no sound of running water, no smell of mossy stones. Liar. Son of a bitching *liar*. She collapsed, chest heaving with dry sobs. She'd have to go back to the clearing and start over, choose another direction.

There had been several faint trails into the trees. She'd chosen this one because the footprints Miles left in the soft earth seemed to point this way. And there had been blood, too, dried splotches on some broad-leafed vine.

Once decided, she had to focus her whole energy on crawling. Her one attempt to stand—a disaster. Even if her head had stopped whirling, her leg wouldn't support her weight. Right elbow, left knee . . . a poor inchworm she made. She'd stuffed her broken arm inside her shirt to keep it from flopping, but there was nothing to be done about her leg. A great red tide of pain with each movement, often sweeping her under. So easy to lose her way, her memory full of short circuits.

Took a wrong turn, Joanna. Must have. Have to go back, start over, have to get to Lizzie . . . and then what? If Miles was there . . . one more blow, that's all it would take. She could feel the fear draining her strength. If she thought about it, she would give up, lie down here and die. Concentrating, she started to push herself up on her elbow and then she saw it, a dark brown blob on the pine needles.

Like Hansel and Gretel she'd marked the path to the witch's house—with her own blood when Miles carried her through the woods.

Amos stopped in the edge of the woods, catching his breath. Ahead in the clearing the old stone house looked abandoned with its weedy yard and bubbly-glass windows shining blankly in the sunlight. Miles's truck was gone from the farmhouse, he'd driven by to check. Just in case Miles was at the cabin Amos had left his car at the turnoff, hidden behind some bushes, and walked in. Unnecessary, it seemed now. Miles wasn't here.

Amos propped the heavy shotgun beside him, leaned against a tree, wiped his streaming face. All these years he'd wanted to come here and search—damn fools on the Town Council. Didn't think it at all peculiar that Angstrom let him dig up the farm but slapped on a restraining order to keep him away from the cabin. If Amos was right and that murdering son of a bitch had struck again . . .

Taking shells from his pocket, he loaded the gun and

approached the cabin slowly, scanning the area for any sign of the pickup, listening for the sound of the engine coming up the narrow road. He heard something, stopped. Two crows squabbled on the rooftop. Rustlings in the woods. His heart beat raggedly as he reached the front door. Locked. He was already in violation of a court order, so what the hell. Using the gun butt, he smashed a window, knocked out all the glass shards and squeezed inside. A combination living room and kitchen. A door in the wall on the left, padlocked shut. Storeroom? He edged over to listen but heard nothing.

Angstrom had been here. There was a big red and white cooler sitting beside a maple table, a cardboard box with some food, a lot of scuffed footprints in the dusty floor. The place smelled of old mustiness and a newer odor of greasy chicken, garbage.

Something shiny caught his eye. A length of chain attached to the wall. Some kind of leather thong at the other end. The hairs on his neck rose. Dark stains on the wood floor. He bent for a closer look, smelled a familiar coppery scent, knew it was blood. A poker lay there, gore-encrusted.

"Ah, Christ," he said.

He felt old and tired. His arm ached from the weight of the gun. He put it down on the floor at the back of the sofa, rubbed his arm. Hattie was right. He was too damned old for this and anyway he was too late . . .

Then he heard the sound again, the same one he'd heard outside, distinct now. A meow, coming from behind the locked door. Amos hurried over, afraid to hope.

"Joanna? Joanna, you in there?"

Silence and then a thin piping, "Mommy?"

The child, by God! "Lizzie? Lizzie, honey, hang on. I'm going to get you out of there."

He looked around for something to pry off the padlock. The poker. No time to start worrying about fingerprints. Inserted in back of the metal hasp, it worked perfectly, levering the nails from the wooden molding.

The little girl, eyes enormous in her pale face, huddled beside a bed holding a white kitten. She shrank away as he approached. Her hair was damp, matted, her arms matchstick thin.

"Lizzie?" He knelt down, not touching her. "Remember me? Chief Fowler. I'm a friend of your grandma and grandpa. I'm a policeman." Well, he was. Always would be. "Your grandma was real worried so she sent me to look for you."

"Gramma?"

"Yes. You don't have to be afraid anymore, honey."

Lizzie nodded slowly. Shock, Amos knew. But otherwise she looked okay except for some bruises on her cheek and her arm. Of course, God knows what else that sick bastard had done to her. The cat howled loudly, wriggled from her arms and ran out the door.

"Lizzie, can you tell me about your mother? Do you know what happened to her?"

"He hit her," Lizzie said. "She was all purple and black—and I heard him hit her some more—" She stared at Amos as though she'd seen him for the first time. "Are you a real policeman?"

"I sure am."

"Then please, I want you to arrest him and put him in jail and hit him the way he hit my mommy—" Tears spilling from her eyes, she scrambled up into his arms.

"Don't you worry, little one. I'm going to see to it he never hurts anybody again." Amos patted the frail shoulder clumsily. Too late for Joanna but at least the child was safe. "You come on now, honey. Let's get you home."

"Mommy, too," Lizzie said. "She's in the basement."

Miles drove up the winding road squinting at the sunlight reflecting off the chromed windshield wipers. His nose had begun to swell again so he had to take off the sunglasses. After the session with Papa, he felt purged, empty, a little light-headed.

Papa had forgiven him when he explained that what happened to Joanna really wasn't his fault. Miles had promised, never again. This time he could keep his promise, he was sure of it. He'd have a center to his life once more. Lizzie.

A bag from McDonald's sat on top of the box next to him, filling the pickup with the aroma of onions and french fries. Still plenty of time to drive to Springfield today. If the banks had closed, he'd get a motel, cash one of the bearer bonds first thing tomorrow. A problem, having Lizzie along, but he couldn't risk leaving her at the cabin any longer. People were getting suspicious. Amos . . . had he come to the house or had Miles dreamed it?

His hands felt slick on the steering wheel. No sense taking chances. He'd figure out a way to deal with Lizzie. The court order would keep the old man away from the cabin. Still . . .

His stomach rumbled, so he ate a couple of french fries, licking the salt from his fingers. He was hungry but he'd wait and share the rest of the food with Lizzie. She'd like that.

He slowed for the narrow road, made the turn, then took his foot off the gas as sunlight glinted on something in the bushes. He coasted to a stop, looking in the rearview mirror. Something back there.

He got out and walked back. Tire tracks in the grass and in the bushes . . . a blue Dodge Charger, as familiar as his own pickup.

32

McDowell hesitated before opening the door, chilled by a sudden vivid memory of that apartment in Boston, the Thu Duc Tien family, headless corpses, gouts of blood . . .

"What is it?" Blanchard asked anxiously.

"Nothing."

A solid old New England home. Why the hell was he so spooked? He turned the key, pushed open the door. Oak floors and antique furniture glowed. Everything was in perfect order, but the warm silence was tainted by a faint odor, as though something had crawled off under a baseboard and died.

"Now what?" Blanchard said.

Impossible to explain what it was like just to get a feel of a place, so he simply said, "We'll take a look around.

You've been here before, so if something looks unusual, sing out.''

Famiy pictures on the wall in the entryway. A candid shot of a slender woman sitting on the grass holding a little girl in her lap. Both fair, the child's hair white-blond, the woman's darkening to brown. Smiling—not the big phony, say-cheese kind of smiles. Shy, even a little sad.

"Joanna and Lizzie," Blanchard supplied.

The kitchen was tidy. A cup, two bowls, a few glasses in the dishwasher, rinsed but not clean. A collection of African violets wilted on a counter.

"She didn't ask anybody to come in and water," McDowell said.

On the kitchen table lay an Auto Club map of Massachusetts, folded open to the inset of the Boston area. Was that where she was planning to go? If so, why leave the map at home? Unless, of course, she drove in with somebody else, someone who knew the roads.

He headed upstairs, Blanchard following. Bedrooms told a hell of a lot more about people than any other place in the house. Things shoved into closets and under the bed. Sex, hang-ups, messy secrets. The Harts led a tidy, comfortable life. The master bedroom had a king-sized bed and lots of drawer space. A nineteen-inch Sony with earphones and a bookcase fully stocked. In Joanna's bedroom Blanchard stood, looking around.

"Well?" McDowell said.

"I was never in here. I *wasn't,*" he said to McDowell's skeptical look.

He'd admitted he and Joanna were lovers, so where had they made out? Remembering the picture downstairs, McDowell felt a twinge of envy.

While he checked the closets, Blanchard touched things as though searching for some psychic impression.

"You know if any suitcases are missing?" McDowell asked.

Blanchard shook his head.

"You're a big fucking help," McDowell said.

No way to tell if her clothes were all here. Toiletries and makeup—looked like everything, but there was no law against having duplicates for traveling. In the child's room the same kind of inconclusive feeling except for a stuffed lion on the bed.

Blanchard picked it up. "Lizzie had this with her on the flight to Boston." He had told McDowell how he met Joanna and her daughter, the little girl's fear of the plane. "She slept with it. She wouldn't've left it here, not if she was going to stay overnight."

If he was any kind of cop, Amos Fowler had been through all these same steps. A check with the neighbors verified that Fowler had talked to them. Nobody had seen Joanna on Monday or noticed her leaving. They'd all read the story in the Brattleboro paper and asked anxious questions.

"We haven't found out anything," Blanchard said as they returned to the car. "This is all a big waste of time."

"Routine police work. Most of it seems like a waste of time but it's got to be done. I sure as hell wish we could talk to Fowler."

Weird the way the old man had vanished. When they arrived back at Fowler's house, his wife still hadn't heard from him. She hopped around like an anxious bird, straightening pillows, looking out the window. "I can't imagine where he's gone. It's almost lunchtime and he didn't even finish his breakfast. I keep telling him he ought to slow down but you think he'd listen? You're sure he's not out there in the woods? Maybe he fell down or—''

"We didn't see him, Mrs. Fowler. Are you certain he was going to practice?''

"Well, he said he was.''

"He said, 'I'm going to do some target practice.' ''

"Well—no. Not like that. He took down his gun and I asked him and he said—he said he *probably* was.'' She sat down on a tapestry-cushioned chair, looking as though she might start crying. "He *had* to be going to practice because otherwise—''

Blanchard started to say something, to voice the obvious probably, but McDowell gave him a warning look.

Strolling over to the gun cabinet, McDowell said, "Maybe your husband said something earlier about where he was going. Why don't we go over it and see if you remember something.'' The cabinet was unlocked, the key still in the door. Careless. "Just take your time.''

"We slept late,'' Hattie said. "And he didn't eat much, been worrying all night. He was tossing and turning and—'' She broke off, shaking her head.

McDowell opened the gun cabinet. Quite a collection of firearms inside. A Colt .38, police issue, well cared for. Several other pistols. A rack held a .22 rifle, an old Springfield. One empty space.

"He didn't say much of anything,'' Hattie went on. "Just went off to the farm stand like he always does and then he came back and got his gun.''

"Which gun did he take?''

"The big one. The shotgun.''

For target practice?

"He went to get Joanna," Blanchard said.

"Shut the hell up," McDowell said quietly. Something the old lady had said hit a wrong note but he'd missed it. "Did he talk about Joanna at all?"

"No." Hattie's mouth trembled and her eyes were bright with tears. "And he didn't say anything about where he was going. I told you he just went out like he always does and then he came back and—and that's all that happened."

McDowell moved behind a Barcalounger and stood looking down at the green simulated-leather upholstery. Fowler's chair. A faint impression of the old man's body, a stain at the top of the chair where his head had rested. A lingering smell of hair oil and cigar smoke. Standing there, McDowell could *see* Amos Fowler as clearly as though he were seated in his favorite chair puffing a Roi-Tan.

Stubborn. Hard to live with. But also dedicated, shrewd, with the instincts of a bloodhound. Busy with the investigation, cranky and tired, he had still taken the time to follow his routine—

"This farm stand," McDowell said. "He always goes there?"

Hattie nodded, suddenly tense.

"He brings home fresh vegetables every day?"

"No." Her face crumpled. "No, he—you have to understand—he still thinks he's the chief of police—silly old fool. Badgering poor Miles—going off—shooting—"

A few more questions and McDowell had the story from her. He heard Blanchard suck in his breath when Hattie told about Miles Angstrom's family disappearing.

"Poor Miles," Hattie said. "Everybody knew what was going on. The Town Council warned Amos, but you can't tell him anything. He wouldn't leave Miles alone."

293

I know old Amos, all right, McDowell thought. "Miles Angstrom knew the Hart family?"

"Of course."

"Was he seeing Joanna Kerso?"

"Seeing her? You mean dating? Oh, no. Miles—well, people tried—to fix him up, you know. But he never got over what happened to Bonnie. Oh, why doesn't Amos come home? He's going to miss his lunch."

They left her, promising to have Amos call if they found him. In the car Blanchard said, "He went after Angstrom, didn't he?"

All these years, Fowler had been convinced that Angstrom killed his family, and now another woman and child had vanished. "I know what I would do."

"I guess we both do," Blanchard said bitterly.

Walt lounged against a tree looking down at her, sunshine haloed around him. "You're a mess, Jo-Jo. Look at you. Sherri would never let herself go like that."

"Walt?" A croaking from her lips as she tried to say his name. She blinked and he vanished. Where he stood, there was only a pine sapling with a nimbus of light.

What do you expect, Joanna? Never around when you need him.

Steeling herself, she brought her left knee up, pushed, slid her right elbow the few precious inches forward. Pain was a bright snare, catching, twisting.

She is thirteen years old and competing in the Regional Swimming Championship. She fell the day before, a stupid accident, running into the changing room at the Country Club after practice, wet feet on waxed tile. She pulled something in her thigh and banged her elbow. She didn't tell the coach because he would bench her and she has to win this race to have a chance at the Olympics.

She swims but it hurts . . . oh, Jesus, it hurts . . .

She tasted blood and knew she'd bitten her swollen tongue. Can't go on . . . What good is it anyway? Miles would be there. Take her back to that hole in the ground. This time she really would be dead . . . or maybe she wouldn't. Maybe she'd be alive still, buried, too weak to dig her way out again.

But if she stayed here, she'd die anyway. She'd spent her whole life waiting, paralyzed by inertia. Better to try, take her chances. Anyway, she had no choice. She had to get to Lizzie.

"Do you see her?" Lizzie asked as Chief Fowler went down into the cellar.

"Just a minute, honey. It's kind of dark down here."

Lizzie hugged her knees, hoping he would hurry. Everything would be all right now. Chief Fowler would take Mommy to Doctor Bob and arrest Mr. Angstrom. He'd go to jail, maybe to the electric chair. Old Buddy Duffy had told her about the way they killed criminals with electricity cooking their guts out and their hair standing straight up.

They would be safe now . . . but she didn't feel safe. Her neck prickled and she turned to look at the broken window. Nothing was there but she felt cold and shivery and empty inside.

"He's coming," she whispered. She had to warn Chief Fowler, tell him to hurry . . . too late. The front door opened silently and *he* stood there, a finger to his lips, Berry in his other hand. He reached outside and brought in a shovel.

"Did you say something, Lizzie?" Chief Fowler said from the cellar.

Berry dangled helplessly. Mr. Angstrom's hand cupped the little head from the side, holding his jaws shut.

"Keep quiet." Mr. Angstrom mouthed the words. He held Berry up so she could watch the kitten's eyes bulge and his paws twitch.

Lizzie knew what would happen next. She'd seen it all before.

From the cellar, Amos could see the little girl sitting, so pale and still.

He turned back for one last look around the damp little room. He'd hoped—but one miracle was enough, he guessed. More blood on the earthen floor—Joanna's. The bastard wouldn't get away with it this time, couldn't hide behind his phony grief. He had the fucker. But this—Joanna—so damned unnecessary. By God, he'd see to it the blame was put where it belonged, all those pious old farts on the Town Council.

Thing to do now was to get Lizzie out of here. How to tell her about her mother? She was waiting so patiently, staring off into space. Maybe, subconsciously, she already knew.

Moving heavily, Amos began climbing up the steps.

33

Tom followed McDowell into the farm stand, feeling as helpless as the tail of a kite. McDowell was keeping his side of the bargain, Tom couldn't fault him. But it was taking so long and all the while a dark and terrible foreboding expanded in Tom's chest.

Two women picked over cucumbers in one of the sparsely stocked bins, one youthfully middle-aged in tennis whites, the other older, flabby, with raddled orange hair. A teenage boy, lanky and pimply, washed soil from featherytopped carrots. McDowell approached him, asked for Miles Angstrom. They had been to the farmhouse but Angstrom wasn't at home.

"I don't know where he is." The boy wiped his hands on his jeans, took money from the lady in the Goolagong outfit. "I saw his truck leave, musta been about ten o'clock."

"Was he here when Amos Fowler came by?"

"I don't know. I don't think so. Mr. Angstrom's been sick and things have been kinda crazy."

The older woman had sidled over, avidly interested. "I saw Miles at the bank this morning. He still looks terrible but better than yesterday." Her face was flushed and she smelled of peppermint. "I hope he wasn't here when Amos came. Always ragging the poor man. A person doesn't need that when he's sick."

"Mrs. Delsey, are you going to buy that cucumber?" the boy asked.

"I don't know, Timmy. It's got a soft spot." A crafty look. "If you'll sell it for half price—"

"Oh, all right. A nickel."

Tom gripped the edge of the counter, fighting the urge to shout questions. McDowell had warned him to keep his mouth shut.

"How long has Mr. Angstrom been sick?" McDowell asked.

"A while." Timmy looked wary. "Listen, mister, why don't you just come back when he's home?"

"Afraid it can't wait." McDowell flashed his badge. "I'm Sergeant Kevin McDowell, investigating the disappearance of Joanna Kerso."

"The Hart girl," Mrs. Delsey said. "I read about it in the paper. Has something happened to her?"

"We hope not. Now, Timmy—"

Tom recognized that implacable look. Timmy, reluctant, didn't stand a chance. He said that Angstrom was sick on Tuesday. How about Monday? He didn't know about Monday because the stand was closed. Of course he knew Mrs. Kerso. She came here with her little girl.

"Such a pretty little thing," Mrs. Delsey said. "She used to play with the kittens. What happened to that box of kittens, Timmy?"

"I don't know. They were getting pretty big. I guess Mr. Angstrom took them up to the barn."

McDowell questioned him about Fowler. The old man hadn't said anything that morning, just came in, looked around and left. He'd come by twice the day before. The second time he'd gone up to the house. Timmy didn't know whether he'd seen Angstrom or not. Tell the truth, he couldn't remember if Angstrom was there. He'd been in and out.

"I thought he was sick," McDowell said.

"A person can't always sit at home," Mrs. Delsey said. "Even if he doesn't feel well."

McDowell hadn't forgotten Mrs. Delsey. "Did you talk to Mr. Angstrom this morning?" A head shake, no. "What about yesterday?"

"Yesterday? No. He was in line and then he was talking to Hiram—at the bank," she explained.

"You saw him at the bank both days?"

"Yes. Poor Miles. I don't think he should've been out. But I guess it was important. He was trying to take some money out for this investment."

"A lot of money?"

"Ten thousand dollars."

Amos clumped up the steep steps, trying to decide what to say to Lizzie. She sat stone-still, staring. He'd seen that look on shock victims before.

"Lizzie," he said gently as he put his hands on the cabin floor ready to pull himself out.

299

A breeze from the open door touched the back of his neck. He froze, his bowels turning to water. He had shut the door, distinctly remembered it clicking shut. He turned, saw Miles, saw the shovel swinging. It struck him just above the left eye, cutting the skin to the bone, a terrible *thonk* that set off pinwheels of light in his head.

Amos fell . . . down . . . such a long way down. All the air rushed from his lungs as he struck the earthen floor. Blood poured from the cut into his eyes. Must've hurt his arm in the fall, too. Ropes of pain twisting his arm, up his shoulder, across his chest.

Miles came down the ladder with the shovel in his hands, swimming in a red mist. The shotgun . . . upstairs . . . a mistake but that's all it took. One stupid, fatal mistake.

"Murdering bastard," Amos said thickly. "What're you waiting for?"

Miles just stood there, watching. Amos felt the bands tighten around his chest, his heart swelling. A terrible roar and then it burst, drowning him in his own blood.

Joanna measured her life in inches. A gain of six inches for each agonized creep. Do that a thousand times and she'd crawl a mile, easy. But Miles wouldn't have carried her that far, would he? The sixty-four-thousand-dollar question.

Never mind. Don't think about it. Just get ready for the next thrust forward. Twice more, another twelve inches to that birch. Then she'd rest.

She built a dam to hold back the pain. Concrete and stone . . . *move* . . . reinforcing iron . . . *move* . . . The dam collapsed. She closed her eyes riding out the flood.

Can't go on. *Cannotcannotcannot* . . .

All so crazy, impossible. Can't walk. Can barely even drag myself . . .

Should've gone another way, looked for help. Oh, sure, Joanna. Three-hundred-and-sixty-degree circle around that clearing. A lot of directions leading nowhere. Oh, God, why had she always been so good at math?

Pick another goal, another tree. She opened her eyes . . . and saw the cabin. She lay very still. Another hallucination, like the one about Walt. Blink her eyes and it would disappear.

Scarcely daring to breathe, she watched until she was sure the little stone house was real. The path was off to one side but she had a good view of the front of the cabin, the narrow road. The pickup wasn't there. Miles was gone.

Maybe Lizzie is gone, too . . .

No, she's there . . . she has to be there . . .

Just twenty-five feet away, maybe thirty. Move, Joanna. Build the dam . . . stronger this time . . .

The Maple Grove police station was in an uproar when McDowell and Blanchard walked in. Three uniforms on hand, one on the telephone, two more studying maps with Lankersheim. High-detail local maps, McDowell noted. Sitting next to the map-strewn desk was a red-haired man and a boy, a little pale beneath his freckles.

"Chief, we need to talk," McDowell said.

"I don't have the time right now."

"Make time."

Lankersheim glared at him. "All right. Five minutes. In my office."

The computer was off, McDowell noticed as they went

in to wait. He helped himself to a cup of coffee. "Want one?"

Blanchard shook his head, paced back and forth, looking through the glass door at the conference. "This is all a waste of time, McDowell. We ought to be out there, trying to find her."

"What the fuck do you think I'm doing?" The coffee was good. Not like the usual precinct varnish. Pure Colombian, freshly ground, according to the package next to the Mr. Coffee.

"I'm sorry. All I can think about is Claire. How she was gone and time kept slipping away."

If this was an act, it was Academy Award time. Could he have been wrong about Blanchard, after all? Three years. A long time to be certain. Well, Fowler had him beat all to hell. Eleven years since Angstrom's wife and daughter disappeared and the old man had never wavered in his suspicions.

Lankersheim came in saying, "Place is turning into a madhouse. Phone never stops ringing." He sat on the edge of the desk. "I put out an APB on Joanna Kerso. I don't know what else I can do you aren't already doing."

"Tell me about this feud between Fowler and Angstrom."

"Miles? What's he got to do with this?"

"I think Fowler suspects he's responsible for Mrs. Kerso's disappearance."

"Oh, Christ! As if I didn't have enough on my hands. See that cardboard box out there?" He stabbed a finger in the direction of the outer office. "It's got a human skull in it. Boy found it up in the woods someplace. Out of my jurisdiction but the county's short of people, trying to shove the whole thing in my lap."

"Whoever that skull belonged to isn't going to give a flying fuck who investigates," McDowell snapped. "Old Amos left this morning with his shotgun and I don't think he's gone duck hunting."

"I knew one of these days he'd go around the bend." Lankersheim opened the door and yelled, "Stimson, get in here. I'll send a car out to the farm," he said to McDowell.

"He's not there—"

"How long are you two going to stand around here arguing?" Blanchard burst out. "What if Chief Fowler is right? For God's sake, man—"

"*Mister* Fowler is a private citizen," Lankersheim said coldly. "He's been hounding Miles for years without a shred of evidence."

"All the more reason to find your innocent citizen and protect him," McDowell said. "This is your town, Lankersheim. Where else do we look?"

"Well, Miles has a cabin up in the hills but Amos wouldn't go up there."

"Why not?"

"A court injunction. Amos hasn't violated it in the past ten and a half years. I don't think he'll start now. Just a minute," he said, and strode out of the office, bellowing, "Stimson."

"That's where Fowler went," Blanchard said.

"Maybe."

"Maybe? If you read that newspaper article linking me to Joanna, would an injunction have kept you away from my cottage?"

Hell, no, McDowell thought. Even common sense wouldn't keep me away. "Let's find out where that cabin is."

In the outer office Lankersheim was reading a computer printout. Before McDowell could say anything, he held out the paper. "Boy knows approximately where he found that skull, but he was out in the woods, so it's not easy to pinpoint. We checked the records to see who owns property in the area. Take a look."

The computer had listed five names. One of them was Miles Angstrom.

34

Get up, Chief Fowler. Please please get up.

Lizzie could see him lying down there through the open cellar door. He had to be all right. Mr. Angstrom had only hit him once, just like Mommy that first time, and she had been all right.

Mr. Angstrom sat at the kitchen table eating a hamburger. The smell made Lizzie hungry and sick at the same time.

"Sure you don't want one?" he asked. "How about some french fries?"

Lizzie shook her head.

On the floor beside her Berry lay as still as Chief Fowler. His eyes were open and his head was cocked to one side as though he were listening for something—a mouse or one of the bugs he liked to crunch in his sharp white teeth. She stroked his soft fur, remembering the little *snap* before Mr. Angstrom dropped Berry beside her and swung the shovel . . .

Wake up, Chief Fowler.

He'd promised to help them, to help Mommy. Lizzie couldn't see her mother down there. She must be asleep. When people are hurt they sleep a lot.

The front door was still standing open. *Lizzie, if you get a chance, run away. Run into the woods and hide. Promise me.* Lizzie's body felt a long way off, as though it didn't quite belong to her. She knew she couldn't run but it was pleasant to imagine the act: her muscles bunching . . . jumping up. The wild grass whipping against her legs.

Staring out the door, something caught her attention, gradually drew her gaze. On the floor just behind the sofa lay a gun. A big gun with a wooden handle. Did it belong to Mr. Angstrom? Maybe he'd forgot to put it away.

She knew about guns from watching TV, and Buddy Duffy had given her a lesson on how they worked. He and his friends were always playing Rambo in the park and once he'd let her join in. She remembered pointing the ugly plastic gun he called an Oozee, making an *ak-ak* sound and having Buddy shout, "You gotta pull the trigger, stupid!"

If she picked up the gun behind the sofa and pointed it at Mr. Angstrom . . . But it was such a big gun, nothing at all like the toy. It reminded her of a snake lying there. She wasn't sure she could touch it, let alone lift it.

Better to think about running away. About Mommy climbing the ladder and how they would run out the door together.

Oh, Mommy. Hurry and wake up.

THE BOGEYMAN

*   *   *

Miles chewed the last french fry and licked salt from his fingers. The food was cold but tasted delicious. He had been ravenous. He still was. He got up and went to look through the box of food on the counter, tore open a package of Oreos.

When he was finished here, he'd go for a run in the woods. All the way up to Dakin's Point, then back to the pool by the beaver dam. He'd throw off his sweaty clothes and jump into the cool green water, chase a speckled trout bare-handed just like he did when he was a boy.

Why did he ever think he could leave here? The cabin, the woods, the farm . . . home. He looked at Lizzie sitting like a zombie by the cellar. Impossible to imagine he'd ever thought she could take Sarah's place.

That scrawny little body. The limp hair and dull eyes. A willful, spoiled, whiny little brat. He was ready to throw everything away for her. My God. He shuddered as he thought about how close he'd come to disaster.

Well, that was over now. Almost over.

He was going to have to be very careful about Amos. If the old man had told somebody he was coming here . . . no, he wouldn't do that. He'd been breaking the law. The only person he might've mentioned it to was Hattie. So— just in case—there were a lot of curves along the way. Say he had a heart attack, ran his car off the road . . .

Easy, except for getting Amos up from the cellar. But right now he could do anything. Looking into Amos's eyes as he died . . . that power singing in his blood . . . oh, yes, the eyes. That was always the best part.

*   *   *

Lizzie watched him rip open a bag of Fritos and stuff some in his mouth. Once at the zoo she and her father had seen the tigers being fed. Big chunks of meat, the cats ripping it apart and growling. There had been a deep ditch and a high fence between her and the tigers, but there was nothing between her and *him*.

She looked away, out the door. The tall weeds waved in the breeze, sparkling with sunshine. Berry still hadn't moved and even his warm little ears felt cool. Chief Fowler hadn't moved either down there in the cellar.

Berry was dead.

Chief Fowler was dead.

Mommy . . .

Promise me, Lizzie.

Across the room, *he* was pawing through the cardboard box again, his back turned. Slowly she got up . . . ever so slowly. Then, legs pumping, she ran. Out the door, down the road.

"Son of a bitch," *he* roared, and his feet thumped on the wooden floor.

Easy to run on the pavement but it was easy for him, too. He'd catch her, she knew he would. *Run into the woods,* Mommy had said. *Run into the woods and hide.*

She veered off, through the tall grass, to do what Mommy said.

Enough dawdling, Joanna.

She had to get to the cabin before Miles returned. Once inside—her heart leaped as she saw a small figure dart from the cabin. Lizzie! Then a shouted curse and Miles followed, running swiftly down the patchy asphalt.

Forgetting her injuries, Joanna tried to stand. Pain drove

308

her to her knees, engulfed her, and all she could do was watch as Lizzie hesitated, losing precious seconds, then plunged into the weedy yard, heading for the woods, straight toward her.

Miles was only a few seconds behind. Joanna realized he would see her and this time he'd make damn sure she was dead. It didn't matter, nothing did except Lizzie. And now she knew why she'd gone through the horror of getting here. She would be the stumbling block, the distraction that kept Miles busy while Lizzie got away. He would kill her, but she would make sure it took as long as possible.

Lizzie saw her, stopped.

"Run—" The word thick, hoarse. "Run—Lizzie."

What Lizzie saw was a dirtied, bloodied thing. Purpled face, stringy hair, covered with soil and leaves. A grotesque hand reaching out and a horrible croaking sound. Wailing with terror, she turned and ran . . . back toward the cabin, into Miles Angstrom's arms.

Joanna lay in the edge of the woods and wondered why she wasn't weeping. Her chest hurt, the back of her throat knotted, but there was no moisture left to squeeze from her tear ducts. Miles hadn't seen her, hadn't heard her call out. He'd scooped Lizzie up and taken her back to the cabin while Joanna watched helplessly.

Lizzie still cried, a mindless panicked shriek that echoed from the small stone house filling the woods like wounded birds.

Joanna's mind replayed everything she had gone through to get out of that shallow grave and come here, all the agonizing details compressed into a few seconds of actual time. Her only thought had been to help Lizzie.

It's not right. It's goddammit not fair.

Because of her, Lizzie was back in that charnel house. Still alive. But for how long? In that instant when Miles picked Lizzie up, Joanna had seen his face and she knew what Lizzie had seen in her dreams . . . her visions. She'd had a right to wake up screaming.

Joanna began to crawl through the overgrown yard. If he saw her now, it didn't matter. Divert him from Lizzie, that was all she could do, and hope, *pray*, that Lizzie would snap out of her hysteria and get away.

No time to be careful. Her useless leg thumped on the uneven ground. *Jesusohjesus* . . . don't think about it, forget it. Nothing matters. Only Lizzie.

Her fingers brushed stone. The broad, worn step in front of the open cabin door. She reached for the sill, pulling herself up. Breathing in short shallow gasps, she clung there, waiting for her head to stop spinning.

Voices . . . Miles a low rumble and Lizzie's quiet, hopeless whimper. Her head was even with the cabin floor and she could see most of the room. Miles and Lizzie weren't there and she realized they must be in the bedroom.

Last chance, Joanna.

Get him out of there, away from Lizzie. Yes, she had to do that. What she really wanted to do was hurt him, to slow him up. Lizzie was like a terrified litle chipmunk frozen in the road by the sight of a car bearing down on her. She'd need time to snap out of her fear.

Joanna looked around. A rock, a sharp stick . . . near the corner of the house a garden hoe lay on the ground.

310

How far away? Back to measuring in inches. She'd have to crawl over. Crawl back.

From the bedroom she could hear Miles's monotone. Nothing at all from Lizzie.

The poker . . . where was the poker? Forget about hitting him. Maybe if she jabbed him, as hard as she could . . . She inched across the doorsill to look around.

And saw the gun. She sat very still, afraid to breathe. Her feverish mind had produced another mirage. *A shotgun.* Impossible. And yet . . .

She slid across the floor. Quietly now, so quietly. Extended a shaking hand and touched the polished stock. Two barrels. Was it loaded? Oh, God, let it be loaded.

She would have to lift it, cock it, hold it in place. She could never do it, unless . . . She picked up the gun, expecting but still surprised by the weight. The steamer trunk sat on the other side of the front door, the side next to the bedroom.

Slowly she worked her way to it, sitting, sliding her fanny across the floor, the gun in her lap. Reaching the trunk, she propped herself against the wall, laid the gun on top of the trunk, wedged the butt into the cradle of her shoulder. She noticed the cellar door was open, but there was no time to wonder about it.

In the bedroom Miles's voice was rising with a strange and terrible excitement that raised the hair on her arms. Summoning the last of her strength, she pulled back both hammers and said one last prayer. *Oh, God, let him come out of that room alone.*

"Miles." Her voice was strange but surprisingly clear. "Miles, you fucking creep."

He came out. Why shouldn't he? If she wasn't dead, she

311

soon would be. The sight of the gun shocked him as much as it had her. Emotions flicked across his face: surprise, resignation.

And then as Joanna pulled the trigger, she had the strange thought that he was glad to see her.

McDowell drove, following the Maple Grove police car with its flashing lights. Tires howled on every curve of the winding road and the car lurched dangerously. Tom didn't care. All he could think of was that skull in the cardboard box.

Up ahead, the patrol car slowed, turned onto a narrow, rutted road leading into an area wooded with pine and fir. Instead of picking up speed, Stimson hit the brake and pulled over. Lankersheim got out, gesturing toward the woods.

Tom saw the gleam of sunlight on chrome as he and McDowell joined the other two men. A blue Dodge Charger and a pickup. Lankersheim looked grim.

"Amos's car and Miles's truck," he said. "I don't like the looks of this at all. You two better wait here while we check it out."

"The hell I will," Tom said.

"It's official police business," Lankersheim said. "You'll do what you're told."

"Not really your jurisdiction, is it?" McDowell pointed out. "What do you say we stop fucking around and get on with this?"

Lankersheim didn't like it, but he grudgingly agreed to let them come along if Tom stayed in the car. They sat in the back seat as Stimson cut the flashers and crept slowly up the dirt road. Lankersheim peered ahead through the dense trees. A clearing and some kind of building. Lankersheim motioned Stimson to halt and cut the engine.

The two Maple Grove cops got out. McDowell followed. The trio drew their guns and walked cautiously toward the clearing along the edge of the road. Tom gripped the vinyl upholstered front seat, staring at the small house. Still mostly hidden by the trees. Gray stone. Angstrom's cabin, and Joanna was there.

Suddenly he could see every corpse McDowell had dragged him down to the morgue to view after Claire disappeared. Some bloated, mangled; others just that waxy imitation of life. And he remembered his dream . . . Joanna in that long steel drawer . . . Joanna . . .

He stumbled from the car, bile rising in his throat. Ahead, the three men had reached the clearing. They fanned out, ready to circle the cabin. Intent on their job, they didn't notice Tom. When he reached the edge of the woods, Tom stopped. The front door of the cabin was open, he realized. He strained to see inside, eyes burning with the effort, but nothing moved in that dark rectangle.

McDowell and Stimson swiftly approached the cabin from opposite sides. A pause, then McDowell went in through the open door. No gunfire. Just a terrible silence. Tom was already running toward the cabin when McDowell came out, holstering his gun.

The smell hit Tom before he reached the front door, the acrid stench of gunpowder and something else, foul, sickly sweet. McDowell stopped him, grabbing his arms. Stimson and Lankersheim were already inside.

"Get out of my way," Tom said—and then understood that McDowell wasn't barring the way but offering, what? Comfort? Sympathy? "Joanna—is she—alive?"

"Just barely. She's in bad shape, Tom."

"Jesus Christ," Lankersheim said from inside. "Go call in. Get a med-vac in here."

Stimson bolted out looking ashen and ran for the car.

Inside the cabin, Lizzie crouched beside an odd bundle of filthy rags. A body on the other side of the room, the torso torn apart. Blood and gore spattered the walls.

"She nailed the son of a bitch," McDowell said.

She. Joanna? Lizzie sat beside her, smoothing the dirty hair around her mother's gargoyle face.

A white kitten lay on the floor, its head at a peculiar angle. Dead. All the death in the place, how could Joanna possibly be alive? He knelt, touched her cheek.

"Dear God . . . Joanna . . ."

Lizzie looked up at him, recognition coming slowly.

"Mr. Blanchard?"

"Yes, darling." He gathered her up, so sparrow frail he could feel all her bones.

"Mommy promised to save me and she did."

"I know, Lizzie." But at what terrible cost?

McDowell, checking Joanna's pulse, nodded reassurance. "One hell of a lady you've got here, Blanchard."

"Damn right," Tom said.

Kissing the still, bruised face, he told her so, told her he loved her and she was going to make it because he wasn't going to let her go. Not sure that she could hear him but telling her anyway, over and over again, until the helicopter came and the medics took her away.

Epilogue

Three weeks later . . .

McDowell signed in at seven, was just sitting down at his desk when Galvin motioned him into his office. Feeling like a kid hauled in to the principal, McDowell said a polite good morning, then clenched his teeth and waited.

"Looks like you got your shit together," Galvin said grudgingly. "Laying off the booze?"

"Yessir."

He hadn't had a drink in a week except for a couple of beers with dinner.

"Well, get busy, then," Galvin said. "We've got a shit-load of work. Have Twohy fill you in."

Twohy did, warily, like handling a live grenade. Gradually he loosened up. By the end of the day after McDowell had worked steadily, doing more than his share of the paperwork, he was back to normal.

"You know, Mac, getting away really did you a lot of good," he said, taking a break from the typewriter, cracking his knuckles. Outside, rain drummed on the window. Lightning flashed, green, eerie. A summer rainstorm in full force. "Where'd you go anyway?"

"Vermont," McDowell said.

"Oh, yeah? Never figured you for the country, Mac. Do any fishing?"

"Some." But I didn't catch anything. Not yet.

"Wish I could get up there. Spent my vacation fixing up the house. We're having Peg's folks over tonight, kind of a celebration. A whole month and the wallpaper didn't fall off the kitchen." He looked at his watch and back at the stack of reports, said glumly, "If I ever get out of here, that is."

"Why don't you go on. I'll finish up for you."

"Well—are you sure?"

"Positive. Now, get going. The traffic'll be the shits."

After Twohy left, McDowell worked steadily. Gradually the office cleared out. Galvin had gone early, carrying an umbrella. A few of the night shift drifted in, stood around drinking coffee. As soon as he finished Twohy's reports, McDowell went to the file cabinet, pulled the jacket on Claire Blanchard's disappearance and put it in a big manila envelope.

Going to his car, he tucked the envelope under his coat to keep it dry. Twenty-four bars on the way home. He counted them, wanting a drink badly. At home there were two bottles of Amstel in the refrigerator. He drank one right away, savoring the cold malty flavor. Then he opened a can of minestrone soup, scrambled two eggs, had the second Amstel with his meal while an electric percolator burbled.

After dinner he took his coffee over to the Hide a Bed sofa, opened the folder, lit a cigarette. The phone rang.

"Kevin? It's Tom."

Tom Blanchard was still in Vermont, staying with the Harts. He said that Lizzie was better. At her grandmother's insistence, the hospital had let Lizzie visit with Joanna today.

"It helped both of them," Tom said. "Lizzie even wanted to go outside and swing this afternoon."

Considering Joanna's condition when they walked into that blood-spattered cabin, it was a wonder she was alive. She'd lapsed into a coma by the time the med-vac helicopter arrived.

On television patients open their eyes and are immediately back to normal; in reality they drift up through seven stages of coma while their brain slowly reconnects. Joanna was at stage three, Tom said, something like sleepwalking. She hadn't talked about Miles yet.

They'd never know all the details until Joanna recovered, but McDowell and Lankersheim were able to piece together a pretty gruesome picture. Lankersheim was a good cop when he put his mind to it. Amos Fowler had been, too, ahead of them all.

"Kevin, about Claire—have you—did you come up with anything?"

"Not yet," McDowell said. "I'll let you know."

Ruth Hart came on the line to say hello. She reminded him that he'd promised to come for a visit when Joanna was released.

317

His coffee was cold so he went back for a fresh cup. Sipping it, he thought about the days after Joanna and Lizzie were found. Weird the way he'd been drawn into that family circle. Stranger still, Blanchard seemed to want him there. Ruth and Matt insisted he stay at their house; he went to Amos Fowler's funeral.

All the time he sat quietly in waiting rooms with Blanchard, a part of his brain was coldly assessing the man. His concern for Joanna was genuine enough. So what? Murderers were often kind and considerate. He figured Blanchard would weasel out of his promise to talk about Claire. McDowell, the cop, knew the time to hit Blanchard with questions was when he was vulnerable, but fuck it, he was on vacation.

The night before he left for Boston, Blanchard suggested going out for a beer and over a pitcher of Michelob told him everything. The motive—as damaging as McDowell had ever suspected. How had he missed it? No body, no autopsy and, as Twohy had once pointed out, no time.

If he'd found out about the abortion and Claire's affair three years earlier—hell, three weeks earlier—Blanchard would've been in cuffs and Mirandized. Maybe it was all the time they'd spent together, the peculiar bond that had developed. Whatever the reason, he knew if Claire was dead, Tom hadn't killed her.

So where did that leave the case? He opened the file. An hour later he'd read it all—and was back where he started. Nothing there he hadn't remembered three weeks ago in the motel in New Hampshire. No elusive clue waiting between the lines. The things Tom had told him wouldn't help anybody else come up with a solution; they'd just cause the man a hell of a lot more grief.

Carefully he evened the pages and put them back in the jacket, closed the folder. He was probably never going to know what happened to Claire Blanchard. Well, fuck it. He gave it his best shot.

Outside the rain had stopped. He went to open the window, welcoming the fresh clear air. The smell reminded him of the woods in Vermont. Maybe he would take the Harts up on their offer, wrangle an extra day and go up for a long weekend. Might even learn how to catch a fish. Wouldn't that be a kick?

Three months later . . .

Joanna sat in the porch glider watching her father and Tom and Lizzie rake leaves. More leaves fell in a yellow rain, brilliant against a clear blue sky.

"Are you sure you're warm enough, darling?" Ruth sat down beside her, tucking the blanket around her legs. She often found an excuse to touch Joanna as though reassuring herself that her daughter was really there.

"I'm just fine, Mom."

Joanna thought she was, finally, although there would be another operation on her leg, and there were still the dreams that left her shaking and cold, suffocating, the smell of damp earth filling her head.

"He's good with her," Mom said as they watched Tom and Lizzie together.

Joanna thought Lizzie was good for him, too. Tom had had a rough time of it. They all needed each other, but oddly Joanna felt the pressure was off. She was perfectly willing to let things develop at their own pace. One thing she had learned in that grave with the bones of Bonnie and Sarah Angstrom—she could stand on her own two feet, or hobble or crawl, whatever was necessary.

Intoxicated by the winy autumn air, Lizzie gave a shout and jumped into the leaf pile, then ran to the porch. "I just *love* October, Mommy."

Joanna hugged her. Lizzie smelled fresh and crisp as an apple. "I do, too, baby."

Lizzie crawled up between her mother and Gramma, careful not to hurt Mommy's leg. Mommy had the bad dreams now. Lizzie was even able to sleep in her own room with the light off.

Mommy, Mr. Blanchard—they all tried to talk to her about Mr. Angstrom. "He was a sick man," Gramma had said.

"I know."

"But he's dead now. The Bogeyman is dead, darling. You never have to be afraid anymore."

Lizzie didn't say anything because the grown-ups really needed to believe it, all of them except Sergeant McDowell. She thought he knew what she did. That it was only Mr. Angstrom who had died.

The Bogeyman had just moved someplace else for a while.